THE
MYSTERY
OF
ACORN
ACADEMY

Authors Reach
www.authorsreach.co.uk

ISBN: **978-1-8382204-3-3**

FOR PETE, WHO SAILED THE SEAS

Praise for Teresa's debut novel *The Time Crystals*

"A thrilling time travel page-turner"
– Publishers Weekly

CORNISH MYSTERY ADVENTURES:
BOOK ONE

THE MYSTERY OF ACORN ACADEMY

TERESA BASSETT

CHAPTER 1

CALLING a quick goodbye to my friends, I bolted out of the park and cut through the deserted industrial estate. I raced along a back lane and ducked through the gap in our garden fence, snagging my T-shirt on a loose nail. A stitch shot down my side, but there was no way I could stop. I'd promised to be on time, and was already ten minutes late. Dad would be spitting feathers.

Sneaking up to the back door, I prayed I could avoid detection, at least until I'd made myself presentable.

I bumped straight into Dad.

"So there you are." He was standing in the kitchen, his hand on the fridge door. "Look at the state of you, Holly! You're a mess. Which bit of what I said didn't you understand?"

"I—I'm sorry, Dad," I said, struggling to catch my breath. "We were in the park and … I lost track of the time."

Dad sighed. "Go and change right now, and run a comb through your hair, at least. She's waiting in the lounge. I'm just fixing her a drink."

"Waiting? Who is?"

Dad had told me to make sure I was home by four

o'clock sharp. He hadn't said anything about meeting anyone.

"Never mind." Dad raked his fingers through his sparse hair and closed his eyes, as if he wished I didn't exist. "Just do as you're told. Anyone would think you were four, not fourteen."

"Okay, Dad." Avoiding his gaze, I sloped out of the kitchen.

Upstairs in my room, our black-and-white Jack Russell terrier Wilk leapt from the bed and hurled himself towards me, but there was no time to give him more than a quick hug and a kiss on the head. I rifled through my wardrobe, frantically searching for something decent. Whatever I chose, it was bound to be wrong. Dad had always been stern, but since that horrific day a year ago, nothing I did seemed good enough for him, however hard I tried.

I wriggled into a blue cotton dress—rumpled but respectable—and dragged my straggly hair into submission. Uneasy thoughts somersaulted through my head. Dad couldn't have got himself a girlfriend, could he? It seemed unlikely, since Mum had only been gone a few months. But you never knew.

Hurtling down the stairs I remembered something which made me sick to my stomach.

The wine!

How could I have been so stupid? Last week it had seemed like a great idea for my friends and me to have a little taste of Dad's Chardonnay from the nearly full bottle, while he was at work. I knew it was wrong, but

I was angry with him for forgetting my birthday. Besides, I was fourteen, for Heaven's sake. It was high time I tried these things.

We only meant to have a sip, but before I knew it we'd had a glass each and there was only a thumb's width left in the bottle. With Dad due home any minute, I topped it up with tap water and replaced it in the fridge.

I fully intended to ask one of the older boys from school to buy a replacement for me. But, like everything else, it slipped my mind.

As I paused at the bottom of the stairs, tears of frustration stung my eyes. I didn't even enjoy the wine—it made me feel dizzy and sick.

What if Dad offered the watery "wine" to this mysterious guest? I would be dead.

**

I shuffled into the lounge like a prisoner heading for the scaffold.

My worst fears were immediately confirmed. Dad stood in the centre of the room, a full glass of wine in his hand. Worse still, his visitor held a glass, too.

On the sideboard, the bottle stood mocking me. It was the same one, for sure.

"There you are," said Dad, lowering himself onto the sofa. He had on his best cream shirt, and I hadn't seen his eyelids crinkle at the sides like that for ages. "Let me introduce you. Miss Blake, this is my daughter, Holly."

The woman in the armchair kept her gaze fixed on Dad. "Please call me Verena, Mr Champion."

Taking her time, she turned her head and appraised me. In a dress of shimmering grey, with a rope of ash-blonde hair coiled at her neck, she was the picture of elegance and composure. All the same, something about her cool, watchful smile made me think of a spider lurking at the side of its web, sizing up its next victim.

I waited near the door, willing myself to do something, but unable to move. Should I shake her hand? What would Dad expect? This well-groomed woman was all the things I wasn't. As if I didn't feel inadequate enough.

"Don't just stand there, Holly," Dad said, a hard edge to his voice. "Come and sit down."

I crossed to the sofa and sat beside him. I leaned towards the woman and extended my hand a fraction, but she didn't respond. I pulled back, settling instead for a mumbled *hello*.

She raised her wine glass to her lips. I cringed, feeling hot all over. She took a sip and licked her lips, the subtle smile flickering briefly. Then she took a second sip, her steady eyes never leaving my face.

"It's a pleasure to meet you, Holly," she said. "I'm sure we're going to be great friends."

I hope not. Once school started again next week, I would stay out of Dad's way. Good luck to him if he had a new girlfriend. It was nothing to do with me.

Dad raised his own glass of wine. I tried to drag my

gaze away, to pretend I was watching the sunlight play upon the carpet, but it was impossible. Dad took a mouthful and swallowed. A grimace twisted his mouth. He hesitated, then sipped again. His eyes bulged and his face darkened.

I would be in the most awful trouble after Verena Blake had gone, but there was one consolation. I knew he'd be too embarrassed to say anything in front of his guest. I almost smiled at his discomfort.

That was when he dropped his bombshell.

"Verena has travelled over three hundred miles to meet you. She likes to meet all her new students before the start of term. Aren't you lucky to have such a thoughtful headmistress?"

"Wh-what?" Now it was my turn to splutter. Dad had got his own back all right. "What d'you mean, Dad? My head teacher is Mrs Lane. You know it is."

Dad's jaw tightened, and he was showing too many teeth.

"Not any more. You see, Miss Blake here, Verena, has agreed to take you on as a boarder, at Acorn Academy in Cornwall. It's very kind of her. She's already filled her quota for new students this coming year, but she's willing to make an exception in your case."

"Case?" I felt faint.

"I believe you will be very happy with us," said Verena. Her voice had a melody to it, despite her air of authority. "Acorn Academy has achieved great things in the seven years since we opened. Our students have excelled in every subject, and we have a cabinet bursting with awards."

"But—" I looked from one to the other. Harsh words bubbled up, but I didn't dare utter any of them. I liked my school, my home town in the Midlands. They were perfectly ordinary, which suited me just fine. After all that had happened these past months, how could Dad expect me to face somewhere new?

"I can see you're surprised, Holly." Dad was master of the understatement. "However, I know you'll love it at Acorn. There are first class sports facilities, and the school overlooks the sea. You've always wanted to live by the sea."

Dad couldn't have been more wrong. It was Mum who'd wanted that. In fact I hated the sea, after I almost drowned in it once. But I felt too upset to challenge him.

"Sea?" I sounded stupid to my own ears. Couldn't I speak in words of more than one syllable? In my mind's eye, I saw my friends, the girls I had seen only this afternoon. It was thanks to them I had survived these long months and found a way to enjoy life again, or at least tolerate it. Now Dad planned to banish me to the other end of the country. How could he be so cruel? *How dare he organise all this behind my back?*

I blinked away a tear. If I cried, my humiliation would be complete.

Dad smiled. "Well, Verena, my daughter is too happy to speak right now. But rest assured, she'll be on the train as arranged, next Saturday afternoon. Have you forgotten to say something, Holly?"

I stared down at my lap, refusing to meet her eyes. I didn't want to thank her. I wanted to run to my room and howl. But I was in enough trouble already. Dad would be even angrier if I forgot my manners.

"Thank you," I mumbled.

Verena picked up her glass and finished her drink. Her Mona Lisa smile suggested she knew perfectly well I was to blame for the wine which had been turned to water. If she did, though, she clearly had no intention of saying so.

She rose to her feet and extended a white-gloved hand. I had never seen anyone wear white gloves before. I didn't know they existed outside the pages of romantic novels.

"Well, Holly. I look forward to welcoming you next week. I'm sure you will be very happy with us."

My own hand was hot and sticky, bound to make her glove grubby, but I held it out anyway and tried not to tremble. Her fingers fluttered over mine like a moth's wings.

Dad was all honeyed smiles as we accompanied Verena to the door and watched her climb into her white sports car. He waved as the car slid out of our driveway, but Verena Blake didn't look back.

When he turned to me, his smile vanished like a flame dunked in water.

"Right, Holly Champion. What the hell did you do to my wine?"

CHAPTER 2

DAD kept his distance all week. I expected to be grounded at least, but other than a quick telling off and a lecture on the evils of alcohol, he didn't even punish me for stealing his wine. He said I could do what I liked with my last few days of freedom. As if I were being sent to prison, rather than to a new school.

Whenever our paths crossed, he scuttled out of the way—scared, perhaps, that I'd try to talk him out of it. Not so long ago, I would have confronted him. Yelled at him for arranging this without discussing it with me. Maybe even refused to go. But things were different now. I could tell from the grim set of his face that his mind was made up, and that pleading with him would do no good.

For the first time since she'd left us, I considered calling Mum, but she lived miles away, in France, and we hadn't spoken properly in weeks. Besides, what could she do? Dad's stubbornness was legendary. If she tried to talk him out of it, it would only end in a bitter row, and I knew what that would cost her. Even getting rid of a pushy salesman could bring on one of Mum's migraines.

Quite possibly, Dad had already told her about Acorn Academy. Quite possibly, she agreed with the plan.

***

As I threw the last bits and pieces into my backpack on Saturday morning, Wilk watched me from his usual spot at the bottom of my bed. His front paws were crossed, and there was an anxious look in his brown eyes.

"I know," I told him. "I don't want to go either." I went and sat beside him for a moment, stroking his ears, and he leaned in close, cocking his head to one side. My gaze roamed the *good luck* cards my friends had sent, together with their parting gift, a bear I'd named Horace.

I would miss everyone so much. I'd even miss my teachers, especially Miss Rowse, who had been so encouraging about my paintings. She'd told me I might make something of myself, if only I'd buckle down and stop larking about, and not fly at everything like the proverbial bull at a gate.

There was movement outside my room, and I looked up to find Dad standing in the doorway, an envelope in his hand.

"Here's some money for you." A faint flush rose to his pale face, as if even talking to me embarrassed him. "It should tide you over for a few weeks, until you get back for half-term. I'll send some more if you run out."

Mumbling a quiet *thanks*, I got up and carried on packing. I wished I could tell him what to do with his money, but, unfortunately, I had next to no funds of my own.

He stepped inside the room and placed the envelope on my bedside table. I noticed, too late, that I'd forgotten to hide the second gift from my friends, a cherry lipstick Dad would certainly disapprove of. Mercifully, he ignored it.

"It'll be hard at first," he said, pushing his glasses up his nose. "But it's no life for a girl your age, stuck in this house with just me for company."

Well, this was new. He was trying to be nice, but it rang horribly false. Anger bubbled inside me, but I didn't want to give him the satisfaction of shouting, which would only confirm his bad opinion of me.

"All my friends are here," I said, coolly.

"Right. You mean those ragamuffins from school you hang around with? The ones I saw smoking in the park last week? They're a bad influence. You'll make much better friends at Acorn." He glared at the faded pullover I was trying to ram into my backpack. "Don't take that old thing, Holly. It's falling to bits."

I sighed, dragged the pullover out again. "Okay. *Whatever.*" I added the last word deliberately, because I knew how he hated what he called teen talk.

Dad just stood there, a faraway look on his face. As I finished my packing, I watched him from the corner of my eye, thinking how much he must dislike me, to send his only child away.

I knew I'd never match up to Mum, in his estimation, but I wasn't that bad, was I? My friends seemed to like me, despite my habit of speaking first and thinking afterwards. As for looks, well, my hair was always tangled, but it was a nice shade of brown, the colour of dried ferns, Mum always said, and my eyes were the light blue of her favourite Holly Blue butterfly, after which I was named. *Merry eyes,* she called them, before the merriment stopped.

I yanked the straps of my bag, trying to force it shut. Who was I kidding? I knew the real reason Dad hated me, and I couldn't blame him, either.

"You're going to love it at Acorn," he said. "Verena will look after you. I mean, I wasn't sure about the idea at first. But now that I've met her …"

This was as much as he'd told me about Verena. Up until now, he'd clammed right up whenever she was mentioned, and refused to answer even my most basic questions. Perhaps this was a good time to have one last go.

"How did you hear about Acorn Academy, Dad? You never mentioned the place before. I can't even find it on the Internet."

A dreamlike expression crossed his face. He looked over my shoulder, towards the window, and stood there, still as stone. Several seconds passed.

"Dad? What is it?" A flicker of worry tugged at me.

Dad shook himself, as though coming out of a trance. "Hurry up, Holly. The train leaves in an hour."

***

Dad stood on the platform, Wilk in his arms. Of the two, it was Wilk who showed the most emotion, his terrier face scrunched up and confused. As the train pulled away, he barked and struggled, trying to jump out of Dad's grip and come after me. I waved at Wilk, reserving a cold stare for Dad. I wasn't even tearful—I felt too angry. Dad tried his best to smile, an expression which didn't suit him. For a moment, I wondered if I hated him.

The train was packed and stuffy. I found myself squashed next to a bulky man who sniffed and coughed continually, and took up half my seat as well as his own. I pulled out my sketch pad, thinking drawing might take my mind off things, but the sight of Wilk, staring out from the sketch I'd made of him the night before, made me too miserable to continue. There was no room to move my elbow anyway. I gave up and gazed out of the window instead.

I knew I should forget the past and make a new start. However, despite the beauty of the English countryside rolling by, all I could think of was Verena Blake's cool, steady gaze, and the moth-like flutter of her hands over mine. Why did even the thought of her make me jittery?

***

The train remained crowded, and at Bristol, people had to stand in the aisles. An elderly woman with a blue rinse and bacon breath leaned in close and scowled.

"Um, would you like to sit here?" I mumbled.

"No *thank* you," she warbled, clearly annoyed at the implication she was old and frail. I turned away, thinking even the simplest interactions seemed beyond me these days, potential minefields others took in their stride. Over the woman's shoulder, a girl seated nearby flashed me a sympathetic smile. I smiled back hesitantly.

She looked about my age, plump, with perfect skin, full lips and black, glossy hair curling round her shoulders. She leaned forward to someone sitting opposite her, and a boy peered around the edge of his seat. He had similar black hair, but was more solemn-looking. Were they boyfriend and girlfriend?

Their cheerful chatter, punctuated by the girl's laughter, made me wish I was sitting with them, instead of next to Coughing Man. When the carriage thinned out, the boy got up and fetched a guitar case from the luggage area, and at last I caught a proper glimpse of him. He wore black jeans and a purple tour T-shirt from one of my favourite bands, and was tall and long-limbed, with a loping, graceful walk. As he glanced in my direction, I realised I'd been staring, and flicked my gaze away.

The boy stowed the guitar case at his feet.

"Oh *Adam*," said the girl, rolling her eyes. "Why didn't you leave it where it was? It was perfectly safe."

He whispered a reply. The girl's next words, which I barely caught, gave me a jolt.

"No one at Acorn will be interested in your cat-wailing, anyway."

I froze. Had she really said Acorn?

This time I heard the boy's reply. "The correct term is *caterwauling*."

She made a face and grinned. "Well you said it, not me."

"Oh ha ha."

"Actually, I think you play okay, when you put your mind to it."

There was more murmuring, followed by a mock-shocked "Adam!"

By now I was bristling with curiosity, and couldn't quite believe my luck. If I'd heard correctly, this was my chance to find out more about the school and, more importantly, to start making friends.

I had to speak to them, even if they found me a bit pushy. Mustering my courage, I got up, squeezed past Coughing Man and moved towards them. As I approached, they looked up. Then my foot caught on the end of the boy's guitar case, and I went crashing into their table.

"Oh goodness, are you all right?" The plump girl leapt to her feet and helped me straighten up. "That's my stupid brother for you. Put it back where it was, Adam, or we'll get thrown off the train."

Lowering his eyes, the boy wiggled his guitar a fraction, so that it no longer stuck out. The girl moved some bags and shifted to the window seat.

"You're sure you're all right?" she asked, pulling me down beside her.

My cheeks were glowing from embarrassment, and my foot throbbed. Now I would arrive at Acorn limping as well as with Coughing Man's flu. I wished I'd stayed in my seat.

"I'm Jess," she continued. "That beanpole there is Adam. He thinks he's going to be the next big thing." She winked at me. "Can't bear to be parted from his darling guitar. I swear if he had to rescue me or his guitar from a burning building, that thing would win hands down."

"Guitars don't argue," he said sweetly. "They do what you tell them, not like sisters."

So he was her brother, not her boyfriend. Sneaking another glance, I noted his brown, intelligent eyes and athletic build.

"I love music," I said. "I've always fancied singing in a band."

He eyed me thoughtfully. "I couldn't have a girl in my band. Too distracting."

"Oh, right," I murmured. I definitely should have stayed in my seat.

Jess tutted. "Adam, you can be so rude." She turned to me. "He thinks he's being funny. He doesn't even have a band. Just ignore him, er …"

"Holly. Holly Champion."

"Where are you headed? We're on our way to Lamledra, on the Cornish coast. We're enrolled at a school near there."

I smiled. "Acorn Academy, by any chance?"

***

15

By the time we crossed the Tamar Bridge into Cornwall, we were chatting like old friends. Or rather, Jess and I were chatting and Adam was gazing out of the window, apparently much more fascinated with the view than with us. I told Jess all about my meeting with Verena the week before, including my scrape with the wine, which made her squeal with laughter, and even brought the trace of a smile to Adam's face.

"That's so cool!" Jess ripped open a chocolate bar and broke off the top. "Like some?"

I must be one of the few people in the world without a sweet tooth, but the cheese sandwich I'd brought was long gone, and besides, I didn't want to seem unfriendly. I took the strip of chocolate and bit off half.

"Thanks. Did Miss Blake come and meet you, too?" I asked, recalling something Dad had said about her meeting all her new students beforehand.

Jess shook her head. "Oh no, we haven't met her."

"That's odd," I said, disappointed we couldn't compare notes. "I wonder why she travelled all that way to meet me, when she didn't meet you."

Jess shrugged. "No idea. I'll tell you something, though—my arm ached from all the forms we had to fill in. She wanted to know everything. Height, weight, clothes sizes. We even had to have a medical."

"Huh? I never did anything like that." Dad might have filled some forms in, of course, behind my back. He wouldn't necessarily have told me. "Isn't stuff like that confidential?"

"Dunno. I didn't mind. I suppose she needed our sizes for uniforms and stuff. And they'd need to know about allergies and things, wouldn't they?"

"Yeah, suppose so. How did your parents find out about the school?"

Jess lowered her eyes. "Our parents—"

"We're travelling down from Scotland," interrupted Adam. He lowered his voice, almost to a growl. "We've escaped."

"Oh, I love Scotland," I said, remembering the camping trips I'd had with Mum and Dad when I was younger, in happier times. "Your family lives up there?"

Jess opened her mouth to speak, then blinked a few times and closed it again, a sad look on her face.

"Doesn't matter," I said quickly.

Adam grabbed his guitar and stood up. "Look sharp, you two. We're here."

CHAPTER 3

THE deserted platform glistened with drizzle. We took up position outside a forlorn-looking waiting room, and Adam plonked a woolly hat over his rain-misted hair. It was striped black and yellow, making him look like a bumblebee, and he glowered at me, as though daring me to laugh. I pressed my lips firmly shut and forced my gaze onto a clump of ferns on the railway track.

"Where is everyone?" Jess asked. "We can't be the only new students, surely."

Just as we were beginning to get worried, a middle-aged woman with a sour expression appeared from behind a notice board.

"Here you are! Come on, we've been waiting for you."

She marched out of the station. Grabbing our bags, we followed at an almost-trot. A smart blue minibus stood by the kerb, emblazoned with the school coat of arms. The logo showed two lambs kneeling either side of a shield, overlooked by a golden lion. At the bottom, the scrolled writing read *Gloria in Oboedientia*.

Jess's nostrils flared. "I think that means *Glory in*

Obedience, doesn't it? What fun Acorn sounds."

Adam said nothing, but his mouth twitched.

The woman looked us up and down. She was small and thin, with a weasely face and a big mole on the bridge of her nose, like a third eye. Not exactly the best look, but Mum had always said I should never judge people by appearance.

"I'm Mrs Craddock," she announced grandly. "The gentleman you see in the minibus is Mr Craddock." A bear-like man with white hair and eyebrows revved the engine. "We are Acorn's managers, second-in-command to Miss Blake herself. Now put your things in the back."

Last in line, I struggled with the straps of my backpack, which had welded themselves to my shoulders.

"Hurry up, child," said Mrs Craddock, making no attempt to help. "If there's one thing our principal hates, it's dawdling."

Jess scowled at her and stepped back to help me. "Can't stand little Hitlers," she said with a half-wink.

***

We left the small town behind and ascended the wooded hillside. Sheep huddled in sodden, windswept fields, glimpsed through the branches of enormous trees.

"It's certainly different from Kings Hollow," I said, gazing in awe at the trees' twisted shapes, which reminded me of dancing ladies.

"Looks awfully quiet," said Jess. "Hardly a house in miles."

Adam sat alone in the seat in front of Jess and me, turned sideways to accommodate his long legs. So far, every attempt I'd made to include him in the conversation had failed.

"My mum grew up in the country," I said, trying to catch his eye, "but I've only ever lived in town."

Ignoring me, he looked out of the window. What was it with him? He was the best-looking boy I'd seen in ages, but—just my luck—I had the distinct impression he wasn't interested in me.

The lanes grew dark and narrow, the trees arching above us as though linking arms. Finally, at the end of a muddy track, the view opened out, and a fantastic mansion was revealed.

Set back from the cliff, the silver-grey building stood amid lush woodland and lawns, fronted by a cobbled courtyard.

"Wow!" I said. "I certainly shan't be short of things to draw and paint." I exchanged a glance with Jess, who looked equally impressed with the view.

"You like art? I wish I could do something clever like that."

The bus turned in at the gate, drove along the driveway and pulled into a parking space near Verena Blake's sports car. I climbed out onto the gravel and took a deep lungful of the fresh, tangy air. The drizzle had stopped, and birds sang all around.

Despite myself, I felt a stirring of excitement. Maybe things would work out for me here after all. Maybe it really was the brilliant opportunity Dad said it was, one I could grab, for once, instead of throwing away. For a second I pictured myself coming top in exams, Mum and Dad smiling at the awards ceremony, together again. Me grinning, a confident, happy-go-lucky girl, someone who wasn't afraid to enjoy life. The girl I used to be.

Tearing my gaze away from the Academy itself, I looked beyond the lawns to the sea. There was something enchanting about it, I had to admit, the water steely blue, lit by shafts of evening sunlight. As I watched, a shape formed in the haze, out towards the horizon.

"Look," I said to Jess, repressing a childish urge to jump up and down. "There's a little island out there."

"Yeah … so there is." Jess turned back to the school building and squinted up against the sunlight. "Holly, never mind that. Look upstairs. The windows have got bars on them."

"You're right," I said with a nervous laugh. "I wonder why."

Mrs Craddock appeared at my shoulder. "The bars are to stop you running away," she said, cackling in a way quite at odds with her airs-and-graces.

"Mrs Craddock will have her little joke," said a voice.

We all jumped, including Mrs Craddock. Behind us, flanked by a small group of students, stood Verena

Blake.

My stomach contracted. Verena looked as cool and poised as I remembered, her gossamer hair wound into a knot at the back of her head. She wore a silky dress similar to the one she'd worn before, only this one was pale lilac, matching her eyes. When she moved, it shimmered like a dragonfly's wings.

"Everyone asks about the bars," she said. "Truth is, this building is over three hundred years old. After the Tresawle family sold it, it served for several years as a psychiatric hospital."

The students around her eyed us solemnly before returning their gaze to Verena.

"Welcome to Acorn Academy," she said. "I'm sure you will have a productive and useful life within our walls." She gestured to a tall girl, dressed in a smart grey skirt and pullover. "Carole is in her final year with us. She'll show Jess and Holly to their rooms and act as their mentor while they settle in."

Verena turned to the boy beside her, who was short and sandy-haired—and the only student who smiled. "This is Peter, our other new student. He's been here for a few days. Peter, take Adam to the boys' wing."

"Sure," he said, moving to Adam's side.

Jess and Adam looked startled, as though the thought of being parted had knocked the stuffing out of them. I sneaked my phone out of my pocket, intending to rattle off a quick message to tell Dad I'd arrived safely, as he'd made me promise.

Verena homed in on me. "Ah, Holly dear, thank

you for reminding me. If you'd like to hand over your phones, tablets and similar gadgets, please."

I stood rooted to the spot, the offending mobile clasped in my hand.

"At Acorn, we don't encourage access to the endless distractions of modern life," Verena explained. "We consider it unhealthy for the mind. Your devices will be returned to you at weekends. There's a payphone in the lobby, and in addition I will be ringing your homes myself, to inform your relatives of your safe arrival."

My mouth dropped open. I was too shocked to speak. Verena held out her hand for my phone, her eyes steady and unblinking, strangely flat, as though they didn't reflect the light. "If you have any other gadgets in your luggage, laptops and the like, please leave them with me, or give them to Carole later." She waited.

Frustration welled up in me, but I had little choice. Looking equally shocked, Adam and Jess withdrew their own phones from their hiding places. As he handed his over, Adam stared at me, as though it was all my fault. In a way, I suppose it was.

***

As we passed beneath the granite portico and entered Acorn, I felt like I had slipped back in time. Carole led us past several bookcases through an elegantly-furnished lounge, then stepped onto an imposing oak staircase to the rear. The place looked fit for royalty.

"The bedrooms are up here," she said. "Girls in the

west wing, boys in the east."

"Too bad about the phones," I whispered to Jess. "What a cheek!"

Carole glanced over her shoulder. "You'll soon see how much more you can achieve without the constant chit-chat and trivial demands of others. Acorn students often realise they don't want their phones back at all."

Jess rolled her eyes, clearly finding that as hard to believe as I did.

"Do you have any other devices?" Carole asked. "If so, you must hand them over."

Jess and I both murmured a no. *If I did, I certainly wouldn't give them to you.*

At the top of the stairs, we headed left past a life-sized statue of a medieval knight in armour, then a soldier on horseback, his sword raised in triumph. The hallway was silent, the only sound the tick of a grandfather clock. I had an impression of stillness, as though the house had remained unchanged through many long years.

"Where is everyone?" I asked Carole, lowering my voice.

"What do you mean, everyone?"

"Students? Teachers?"

"You'll meet us all tomorrow, when you'll be shown round properly. We have two full-time teachers, apart from Miss Blake. Their names are Mr Foreman and Miss Mallett."

I raised my brows. "Two teachers for a whole school?"

"There aren't many of us," said Carole.

"How many altogether?" asked Jess.

Carole hesitated. "With you two, Adam and Peter, that brings us up to thirty-five."

"Thirty-five?" I said. "In a great big building like this?"

"Yes. How many were you expecting?"

From what Dad had said, I'd imagined more like a hundred. Did he know anything at all about the school he'd picked for his only daughter? He hadn't even hinted at how much he was paying to send me here, although I knew it couldn't be a fortune. He had a decent job, as an engineer, but his salary had to cover everything now that Mum had left. There wouldn't be much to spare for posh schools, however much he wanted to be rid of me.

Carole stopped and opened a wood-panelled door. "This is your room, Holly."

My eyes were on stalks. The room was the grandest I'd ever seen, spotlessly clean with gleaming wooden floorboards and old-fashioned sash windows, and even its own little bathroom cubicle. A Japanese-style screen blocked off a fireplace. Two school uniforms, grey with navy trim, bearing Acorn's coat of arms, lay neatly packaged upon the bed.

Crossing the threshold, I wrinkled my nose. "Ugh! What's that smell? Did someone die in here or what?"

"Holly!" Behind me, Jess giggled and put a hand over her mouth.

Carole's face creased into a frown. "It's a little

25

musty, that's all. It's been empty since …"

"Since what?" I asked.

Carole blinked away the frown, her face once more deadpan. "It's been empty for a while. Meet me in an hour in the dining room. Jess, come with me. Your room is next door."

With a quick glance back at me, Jess followed Carole along the corridor.

Dumping my bags on the floor, I went straight to the barred window. Students were striding across the courtyard below, at the centre of which was an ancient-looking stone well. Steps led down to the lawns, beyond which I had a stunning view of the sea, including the intriguing island, which I hoped we might one day be allowed to visit.

I grasped the window and pushed, but it was jammed firmly shut. No wonder it was so stuffy in here.

As I turned away, I spotted a trio of people on the lawn edge, near the cliffs. Straining my eyes, I made out Verena and Mr Craddock. With them was a large woman with bright blonde hair and a crimson face, who was waving her arms around. It looked like she was shouting, but I couldn't hear anything from this distance. Mr Craddock grabbed her wrist and she pushed him away, her mouth open.

Verena remained unruffled. She said something, and whatever it was, her words had a striking effect. All the fight seemed to go out of the woman, her shoulders slumping as though she'd been punched. With a grim smile, Mr Craddock led her away.

***

The dining hall, like the rest of Tresawle House, looked as though it hadn't changed in centuries, with oil paintings lining the walls and graceful chandeliers sparkling in the light. I gazed in awe at a gilt-edged oval painting taking up most of the ceiling, which showed an array of angels in what looked like a heavenly Garden of Eden.

Acorn's students sat eating quietly at wooden tables, gazing into space as though contemplating some deep problem. Jess squinted round, no doubt searching for Adam, but as yet, he wasn't there.

Carole pointed to a sheet of paper pinned to the wall. "That's the rota for helping in the kitchen. All students do their share."

"Uh, okay." I didn't mind the idea. I'd spent many happy rainy afternoons in the kitchen with Mum, helping her make scones or potato salad.

I glanced through a hatch into the kitchen, where Mrs Craddock, assisted by Peter, stood ladling custard over slabs of yellow sponge.

"Good job I like fish," I whispered to Jess, as the distinctive smell wafted towards us from the warming cabinet.

"Oh no!" Jess bounced to a halt, muttering under her breath. "There'd better be something else."

A panicky look crossed her face as she scanned the

meals laid out beneath the glass counter. Most of them consisted of a fish fillet with mashed potatoes and peas, plus half a tomato plonked in the middle like a big red nose.

"You're holding us up," said Carole, tapping her foot. She pointed to one of the plates, which had a slightly smaller fish than the others. "That one's yours, Jess. What are you waiting for?"

Jess gave a high-pitched laugh. "Er, that's for me?"

"Of course. The label has your name on it."

Carole lifted up the glass front. "Some of us have allergies, so our meals are tailor-made for our requirements."

Jess covered her mouth with her hand. "I'm really sorry, but I can't stand fish. Even the smell of it makes me sick. Is there something else I can have?"

Carole widened her eyes, showing the most emotion I'd seen in her face until now. "What do you mean? Haddock is good for the brain. All our meals are specially designed for the utmost nutrition and balance. Miss Blake doesn't approve of faddy eating. Be sure to eat it all. Nothing must be wasted."

Jess hovered by the cabinet, chewing her lip and blinking. Carole selected her own plate and took a seat at the nearest table.

"Bad luck, Jess," I whispered as I located mine. "You can have my mash if you like. I'll swap you for the fish, okay?"

Jess grinned. "Thanks so much, Holly. I'd be sick, I know I would."

***

At ten o'clock, I fell at last upon my bed. I was used to being alone, and didn't mind that, but apart from the odd sleepover, I'd never stayed away from home before, not without my family. As my gaze fell upon my new teddy bear, Horace, the faces of my old friends grinned up at me from a photo printed on his T-shirt. A lump stuck in my throat. At least they'd all know where I'd gone, unlike Wilk, who would wonder why I'd left him.

I wouldn't expect Dad to spare me a thought, but, like I did most nights, I tried to imagine what Mum might be doing right now. Heading home from a fancy French restaurant with her new boyfriend, perhaps? Would she even know I was here?

I was bone tired, but sleep wouldn't come. My head spun with the events of the day, with hopes and fears about what lay ahead. I thought for a moment about the woman with blonde hair, the one I'd seen through the window, wondering why she was so upset, but too many other questions were vying for my attention.

The mansion seemed eerily silent, and moonlight through the window bars cast jagged shadows across the room. My empty backpack looked like a corpse, punched out of shape, its head part-severed at the neck.

Turning to the wall, my hand fell on a series of indentations in the plaster, like furrows gouged out by tiny fingers. In such an elegant, well-kept room, the marks seemed out of place. Maybe the previous occupant hadn't slept well either, and had scratched the wall during nightmares.

After I'd drifted into a groggy doze, something jolted me awake. Creaking outside my room. I stopped breathing, listening hard, but heard nothing more.

The temperature had dropped by now. I was shivering and my feet had frozen to blocks of ice. Hoping there might be extra blankets in the wardrobe, I switched on my lamp and hopped out of bed. Through the barred window, the courtyard was wreathed in darkness, the sea glimmering faintly just beyond.

As I scurried across the room, my eyes fell on a square shape on the floorboards, just inside my door.

It was an envelope. I grabbed it and tore it open. Inside was a single sheet of paper.

There were only two lines of writing.

All is not as it seems.
Ask about Lydia.

CHAPTER 4

I met Carole and Jess outside my room the next morning.

Carole crossed her arms and appraised my crisp, cream shirt, grey sweatshirt and matching pleated skirt. "You look acceptable—but tired. There are bags under your eyes."

She sounded more like a teacher than a student, but she was right. After finding that weird note, I couldn't stop going over it in my mind, and hadn't slept at all. Should I mention it to anyone? If so, who?

"I wish I had your figure," said Jess, who had chosen the alternative option of trousers. "Clothes never look good on me. I'd die if they made me wear that hideous skirt—er, I mean, it doesn't look hideous on you, of course." She flushed beetroot red.

Carole strode towards the staircase. "Miss Blake will address us after breakfast, and then we'll show you around our house and grounds. By the way, I heard footsteps on the landing last night."

Jess started, her eyes wide. "Footsteps?"

"It wasn't us," I said, immediately on the defensive. Then it struck me: whoever Carole had heard, more than likely he or she was the person who'd left that note.

"Miss Blake doesn't approve of meetings in rooms after lights-out at ten," Carole said. "That includes girls in other girls' rooms, as well as the obvious boy-girl scenario."

"Does Miss Blake approve of anything?" I asked. It was a feeble attempt at a joke, but Carole's face showed no flicker of a smile.

"Miss Blake approves of many things," she said. "Good behaviour, principles, moderation. *Gloria in Oboedientia*, that's our motto. It's a shame more people in the world don't follow it."

Jess stifled a giggle, but Carole didn't seem to notice. Descending the staircase, I examined the lifelike paintings lining the wall. Some showed hunting scenes or country landscapes, but the majority were portraits, dour-looking lords and ladies with identical haughty frowns.

"Are these the people who used to live here?" I asked.

"Mostly, yes." Carole smoothed her immaculate bob. "The Tresawle family. They owned the building from when it was built, in seventeen-seventeen, in the reign of Queen Anne. But the last owner, Godfrey—him," she said, pointing to a red-faced man with jowly sideburns, "he was a womaniser and an alcoholic. He gambled away the family fortune and lost the estate in the nineteen hundreds. That was when Tresawle House was turned into a hospital."

Despite the changes of use over the years, and the

loss in fortune, the elegant furniture and fittings appeared unchanged since the seventeen hundreds. I paused by a portrait of a stern lady dressed in a long purple gown, posing by a grand piano.

"That's Violet Tresawle," said Carole. "Godfrey's daughter and sole heir. Her father spent her inheritance and she could do nothing but watch, powerless to prevent it. It sent her mad, so the story goes. They say she vowed to haunt the place, until the fortune comes back into the family."

Jess made a face. "Ewww, I hate ghosts."

I laughed. "Oh Jess, you sound as if you've met heaps of them."

I didn't believe in ghosts myself. All the same, something about Violet's cold, intense stare made me shudder, and when I moved on, her eyes seemed to follow me.

As we reached the dining hall, Carole said something which took my breath away.

"You know, Jess, I used to be your size."

I glared at Carole. If Adam had been with us, maybe Jess would have stood up to her. Instead, she said meekly, "Gosh, really? But you're lovely and slim now. How did you do it?"

Carole shrugged. "I have some diet sheets. I'll copy them for you."

"Surely it's up to Jess," I said. "She looks fine as she is to me."

Jess gave me a grateful smile.

"Excess weight will put a strain on her heart," said

Carole as she chose a box of cereal from the selection on offer. "Miss Blake requires us all to be in the peak of health."

As Carole moved off I whispered in Jess's ear. "Carole's a right charmer, isn't she?"

Jess shrugged. "Don't worry, I'm used to it. It's a shame about all this prison camp stuff though. What's so bad about meeting up in our rooms?"

"Search me," I said. "Why don't we get together anyway? They won't know."

"Good idea! Pop into my room after ten. I'll get Adam to join us."

***

Emerging into bright sunshine, we found the entire school congregated at picnic benches. All eyes were on Verena Blake, who stood in shadow against the backdrop of the mansion.

She waited while we found a seat opposite Carole and another girl. Jess waved at Adam, two tables away, but he was deep in whispered conversation with the other new student, Peter, and didn't look our way.

At first Verena's speech was as I'd expected. She reiterated how incredible Acorn was, listing triumphs in sports and sciences, including awards for excellence from various foreign dignitaries—nothing she hadn't suggested before, though I couldn't help feeling impressed that Acorn had done so well, considering how few students there were.

I drifted off, wondering once again whether I

should mention to Jess the strange note I'd received. *All is not as it seems. Ask about Lydia.*

Who was Lydia?

With a start, I realised Verena had paused. Her Mona Lisa smile had vanished, and she was gazing directly at me, lips pressed together. I sat up straight and widened my eyes, doing my best to appear attentive.

She cleared her throat and went on. "Here at Acorn we boast students from around the world, as well as from the United Kingdom. Yet despite their varied backgrounds, all have one thing in common. After an unpromising start in life, they have overcome their difficulties and moved on to become model citizens, achieving great things. Just like our humble namesake, the Acorn, when it becomes the mighty oak."

She gestured to the table nearest her. "Faruzi, would you?"

A boy of around fifteen stood up and gazed ahead, his dark eyes solemn.

"I am Faruzi. My family lives in Kenya, and is very prosperous, but I let them down. I had no interest in my studies and wasted the money they spent on me. Now, after a year at Acorn Academy, my parents are proud to call me their son. When I leave, I will be taking my rightful place in the family business."

Verena nodded and smiled as the boy sat down. Jess raised an eyebrow at me. It was admirable, what Faruzi said, of course, but something about the matter-of-fact way he said it made me uncomfortable.

Verena nodded at a slender girl with red hair.

"My name is Marysia," she said, rising to her feet. "I am from Poland. I was working in the UK illegally, in a restaurant. Two years ago, someone reported me and I would have been sent back to Oświęcim, but Miss Blake intervened and provided me with a home and a future."

Like Faruzi, she told her story simply and without emotion. Two more students followed: Pavak from India, who had turned to crime in order to survive after the death of his parents, and Amy from Palm Beach in America, who had been out-of-control and spoilt rotten until she came into Acorn's care.

Though fascinated, I started to squirm. Were they all going to share their stories? If so, would new students be expected to do the same? My mouth went dry and my hands clenched into fists. I would honestly rather die than tell these strangers what had happened to me over the past year.

As Verena's steady gaze fell on me, I tried to shrink into myself, praying she wouldn't call my name. To my intense relief, she looked away.

"I hope you will buckle down and work hard," she said, nodding towards Peter and Adam. "If you do, you will have an unparalleled life here with us. But I must emphasise our school motto. *Gloria in Oboedientia.* Remember that, and all will be well."

As she swept away towards the school, a movement near the windows caught my eye. A man holding a rag was staring in my direction, stony-faced. With his straggly white hair and ruddy complexion he looked out of place somehow, reminding me of a Viking I'd seen in a history programme on TV. It seemed to me he should be invading somewhere in a longboat, rather than cleaning windows. As my eyes met his, he looked startled and turned back to his task.

I leaned towards Carole. "Who's that?"

She swivelled her head, but the man had gone.

"He was cleaning the windows," I explained.

Carole frowned. "Oh, that'll be George Kellow. He helps out with the gardening and other jobs. He's Canadian."

I got up to admire the island, which was clearly visible today amid a calm, sparkling sea. Perhaps a mile away, it brought to mind a turtle, with a chequered green shell and a flat outcrop of rock for its head.

"Does anyone live on the island? Does it have a name?"

Carole followed my gaze. For a moment, she looked disorientated, her stare glassy, and I thought she wasn't going to answer.

"It's privately owned," she said at last. "A nature reserve."

"Cool." I peered across, wondering what kind of wildlife might live out there, on the rocks or in the sea nearby. Seabirds and seals, for sure. Maybe even dolphins. I opened my mouth to ask Carole, but when I turned I found myself alone. Almost as one, the students had risen to their feet and were making their way indoors.

CHAPTER 5

THE tour of the mansion was brief, taking in only the downstairs rooms, many of which we'd already seen by now. Verena Blake had disappeared, and Jess, Adam, Peter and I were shown around by sporty Miss Mallett, the nicest person we'd met so far, even if she did have the face of a horse chewing a toffee. She pointed out two elegant rooms on either side of the building, where we would be taught, boys in one and girls in the other, regardless of our ages, which varied from twelve to sixteen.

She finished talking, and I became aware of Adam standing at my shoulder. I glanced around, hoping he'd say something, but his eyes flickered only briefly over mine before he moved away. Irritated, I hung back.

As we waited for Mr Foreman to take over from Miss Mallett, I stopped next to Carole by a glass-fronted cabinet near the staircase. This must be the one Verena had described as bursting with awards, and she hadn't exaggerated. There were trophies, statuettes and engraved shields, each one accompanied by a little plaque bearing names and dates.

"Ooh, look at that," I said, pointing out a bronze figurine of a tribesman holding a spear and shield, complete with a beautifully woven and bejewelled head-dress.

"A present from an education minister in Africa," said Carole. "The golden globe next to it is for winning the regional tennis championships, two years ago."

"What happened last year, then?" I asked, a vain attempt at making Carole laugh.

Carole's face remained blank. "What do you mean?"

"You didn't win any prizes last year?" I explained, embarrassed that my joke had fallen flat—and grimly aware that Adam was within hearing. "I, um, thought Acorn won everything."

"We no longer compete in local sports. We prefer in-house competitions."

"Oh, that's a shame." I'd been looking forward to meeting up with other schools, whose students might be more fun, more like those from my old school. But Acorn Academy, it seemed, preferred to keep itself to itself.

Mr Foreman, a fussy little man who wafted aftershave, showed us round the grounds, mostly lawns and clipped hedges, but which also included a neat vegetable garden and a coop with brown and white hens.

At the end of the tour he clapped his hands and smiled. "Th-that's it, everyone. You may have the rest of the day off. R-rest and explore, and prepare yourselves for the hard work to come."

I turned to Jess, glad to have some free time, then looked around for Adam. I thought he'd be sure to join us, but he was already with Peter, striding off towards Tresawle House. I didn't know whether to be disappointed or relieved.

Jess and I strolled along the cliff edge, ignored by the other students, who patrolled the lawns in small groups or played tennis on the courts near the wood.

"Would you rather be with Adam?" I asked.

She shrugged. "I'll see him later. I don't want to crowd him. Besides, they've probably gone to the boys' common room. We're not even allowed in there." We had already been given a pamphlet listing Acorn's various rules, although no mention was made of the punishments for disobeying them.

Jess peered at me. "Carole was right about those bags under your eyes. Didn't you sleep well?"

"I didn't, to be honest."

"Something wrong?"

We had reached the stone steps leading down to Tresawle Cove, which also belonged to the Academy.

"Pretty cool to have our own private beach," I said, ignoring her question. "Shall we go down?"

"You're kidding! There must be a *thousand* steps."

"Come on. It looks lovely."

Jess looked as if she'd rather cut off her leg, but all the same she smiled and followed me. "All right. But only if you tell me what's up."

"Okay."

She moved carefully, stopping half-way to catch her breath. I jumped away from the steps and clambered the last ten metres down the mussel-clad rocks.

"You're a show-off," Jess complained. "A right little mountain goat."

"Thanks!"

I hopped onto the sand and waited for her. We sat together on a nearby rock.

"Out with it, then," she said.

With a sigh, I pulled the crumpled paper from my pocket and handed it to her. "I didn't want to worry you."

She unfolded the note and squinted. "*All is not as it seems. Ask about Lydia*. Who's Lydia?"

"No idea."

"How did you get it?"

"Someone pushed it underneath my door last night."

"Hmm." She frowned. "A bit spooky. Someone having a joke, d'you reckon?"

"Maybe, but why?"

We watched the sea for a moment, listening to the soothing lap of the waves upon the shingle.

"Perhaps we should show it to Adam," Jess suggested. "He likes mysteries."

"Oh no! I mean, I'd rather you didn't."

We turned at the sound of sand scrunching underfoot. Six students were striding in our direction, their expressions serious, as if on a route march. Carole was centre front, flanked by Amy and Marysia, with three other girls behind. They were dressed in identical sports kit of black shorts and white polo shirt, not a hair out of place.

I raised my hand in greeting, but they marched past without so much as a glance. Stopping by the rocks near the shore-line, they threw down their small backpacks and changed into swimsuits, matching green ones with a diagonal stripe. As Jess and I watched with our mouths open, they strode calmly into the surf and launched themselves into the sea.

"Oh my Lord," squealed Jess. "It must be freezing! They didn't even hesitate."

"I hope we don't have to do that," I said, shivering at the mere prospect. "I'm terrified of the sea."

"Are you? Why?"

"I nearly drowned, when I was little. Fell out of my parents' dinghy. I've never been in the water since. I can't even wash my hair in the shower."

I watched in mingled disbelief and admiration as they swam to and fro in the icy sea. After a full ten minutes they filed out of the water and got dressed. Without a word to each other, they shouldered their backpacks and jogged back up the beach.

As they passed I caught Carole's eye and smiled. "That was amazing. Didn't you get cold?"

The group stopped as one and looked at me.

"We swim once a day," said Carole. "You should come with us. It refreshes one for the work ahead."

"Um, no, that's okay," I spluttered, wishing I'd kept my mouth shut.

The girls jogged on.

"Carole, wait," I called after her.

"Yes?" she said, turning her head.

"Do you know who Lydia is?"

The same vague—or maybe furtive—look I'd noticed before crossed her features. "Lydia… Lydia is no longer here."

So Lydia was a real person, at least.

"You mean she's a former student?"

Carole's eyes looked distant, as though she were watching something over my shoulder.

"Lydia left before the end of the school year." She hesitated, as if about to say something else, then frowned, as though she'd forgotten what.

"What happened?" prompted Jess.

"She left," Carole repeated. Before we could ask more, she turned and jogged away.

***

Shortly before lights-out, as I prepared my uniform for the next day, there was a knock at my door.

"Come on in," I called in an excited whisper. Jess must have decided to visit me, instead of the other way round, as we'd arranged. We'd gone our separate ways after our walk on the beach, and I was looking forward to catching up with her.

The door was already opening. But it wasn't Jess. It was Mrs Craddock, approaching with a mug of something dark and steaming. Behind her in the hallway I spotted a trolley loaded with similar mugs, all bearing the Acorn coat of arms.

"What's that?" I asked, unnerved by her sudden intrusion.

"Your bedtime cocoa," said Mrs Craddock. "Acorn's speciality. Miss Blake can be very strict, but she believes in rewarding good behaviour. Virtue is its own reward, in my opinion, but as long as you're good, you can expect your cocoa most nights." Placing the mug by my bed, she watched intently with her three eyes—her two proper ones and the matching mole.

"Thanks," I said.

"Drink it while it's hot."

I gazed into the thick goo, the smell making me queasy. Not wanting to make a fuss, I picked up the mug and took a little sip. As I expected, it was sickly sweet, sticking to the roof of my mouth.

"Well?" she asked.

"Um, nice."

Mrs Craddock tutted. "Is that all you've got to say? One hundred percent cocoa beans, that is, enriched with herbs and spices to tone the mind. *Mens sana in corpore sano*, as Miss Blake says. A healthy mind in a healthy body, that means."

"I know," I fibbed. "What herbs are they?" Mum had always been trying to teach me about herbs and flowers. For the first time, I wished I'd paid more attention.

Ignoring my question, she turned to leave.

"Oh, Mrs Craddock," I called after her. "I can't get

my window open. It's stuck."

She halted in the doorway. "I'll let Mr Craddock know."

"Okay, thanks."

She shut my door. I listened as she proceeded down the corridor, her trolley rattling and squeaking.

I wrinkled my nose at the cocoa and sighed. It was a shame to waste it, but apart from not liking the taste, chocolate made me feel jittery. Why couldn't we just fetch a cup if we wanted it? I was beginning to suspect we weren't allowed to think for ourselves about anything.

In my bathroom cubicle, I poured the cocoa down the sink. When the hallway fell silent, I slipped out into the corridor and tapped on Jess's door.

"Come in," she said in a loud whisper.

Jess's room was a mirror image of my own, except hers smelt a lot nicer, her open window letting in the scent of the sea. Jess was propped up in bed wearing zebra-print pyjamas. They must have a thing about stripes in her family, I thought, remembering Adam's bumblebee hat.

"This cocoa is lush," she said, taking a sip. "Almost makes up for that ghastly fish yesterday. Hand-delivered to our door, too, that's a nice touch."

"I suppose so, but that Craddock woman gives me the creeps. I didn't like the way she came bursting in. Have you got a key for your room?"

"I don't think any of us have. The doors have locks, but no keys. So we'd better keep our voices down." She patted the bed. "Come and sit here. Have you found out any more about the mysterious Lydia?"

"No," I admitted, flopping beside her. "I asked some of the boys about her after dinner, but they were just as vague as Carole."

"What d'you think of them, the boys? Everybody I've met so far seems a bit, well, not exactly friendly? Is that unfair?"

"No, you're right. They don't say much."

Jess sighed. "What's wrong with them? It's like no one's interested in us."

I shook my head. "I don't know."

Jess was right—but it was more than that. Something about their vacant stares. Like something was missing.

Jess drained her mug and put it down beside her lamp. "Poor Lydia. She doesn't seem to have made much of an impression on anyone. It doesn't make sense, in a school this small. Maybe you should ask Miss Blake about her?"

I made a face. "Oh, I don't know." The less I had to do with Verena the better, as far as I was concerned.

Jess grabbed my arm. "Hey, did you hear that? A noise?"

I grinned. "The ghost of Violet Tresawle, I expect, on her way to bed."

"Oh no, do you really think so?"

"Of course not. There's no such thing as ghosts."

Jess licked her lips nervously, clearly not reassured. "Adam not coming?" I asked.

She sighed. "No, his room's miles away, on the other side of the house. He didn't want to risk getting us into trouble."

"Oh." Once again, I felt relieved and deflated at the same time.

Leaning forward, Jess pulled open her bedside drawer. "I've got something for you. Here."

Opening my palm, she dropped a small object into it. A little bracelet, made of blue beads interspersed with purple stones.

I stared at her. "A present?"

"It's a hobby of mine," she said with a smile.

"You made it? Wow, it's lovely."

In the dim light from her lamp, her eyes sparkled more brightly than the gems. "Yeah. The stones are amethysts, my favourite."

"But I haven't got anything for you," I said.

"I make lots of things for friends. I don't want anything in return."

"Okay. Thanks!" I slipped it on my wrist and stretched out my arm, admiring how the amethysts caught the light. One of them had bands of white through it.

"I'm glad I met you, Holly," she said. "We must stick together."

I beamed. "I'd like that."

"And Adam."

"Adam? Oh, I don't know. I'm not sure your brother likes me."

Jess raised her eyebrows. "What? 'Course he does.

He's his own worst enemy, that's all. Horribly shy with people he doesn't know—especially girls—and everything he says comes out the wrong way. Don't take any notice of that moody look of his. It means he likes you. In fact, I sort of hoped …"

As her words tailed away, I felt myself smiling. Could she be right? Was it only shyness that made him so awkward around me?

"Hoped what?" I prompted.

She looked away. "Well, what I mean is, we could both do with a friend. It's been quite a year."

I could have said the same thing to her. I waited for more, but she fell silent.

"I wish I had a brother," I said.

"Yeah, we've always been close. I'm very protective of him."

"You sound more like an older sister than a younger." Jess had already told me that Adam was fifteen, a year older than her.

She grinned. "I suppose I do. He was seriously ill for weeks, when he was six. It was awful. He was in so much pain, I used to sing to him, to take his mind off it. When he got well enough, he'd join in, and we'd make up songs together." All at once, she squeezed her eyes shut, and her face crumpled.

"Our parents died," she said.

"Oh!" I looked away, shocked.

"They were scientists, on their way to Norway for a conference. It was a small plane, owned by their company. Seems the pilot got disorientated in the fog.

Eleven people died, including them. That was eight months ago, and since then we've been pushed from pillar to post. Nobody knew what to do with us. We've only got an old great-uncle up in Scotland, and he isn't really interested."

I tried to think of something comforting to say, but my mind was blank. I raised my hand, then let it fall to my side. My gaze fell on a photo in a silver frame, showing two adults and two kids sitting in a boat, all with glossy black hair and huge smiles.

"That must be your family?"

She nodded as she wiped away a tear. "Yes. When we were little. I know I should be grateful to Uncle Tam for sending us here. He's not that well-off, and you can't blame a seventy-year-old academic for not wanting two teens around. Don't tell Adam I told you all this. He wants to keep it quiet. He hates people feeling sorry for us."

"I won't say anything. You know, in some ways it's similar for me." As soon as the words were out, I regretted them. It wasn't similar at all.

"Oh, Holly!" cried Jess. "I thought your parents were both alive."

"Sorry, I didn't mean … They are. But something happened, well, I did something. Something stupid, and the result was, my parents split up. They said it wasn't because of—of—the accident. But I know better."

"Oh no, what happened?"

A loud rap sounded at the door. Before either of us

had time to react, the door opened and Verena Blake swept in. She stood in front of us, arms folded over a dressing gown of blue silk, her hair in a braid to one side.

She appraised us coolly. "Didn't Carole explain about fraternising after lights-out?"

Jess stared, a frightened fawn.

"It's my fault," I said. "It was my idea."

As Verena's gaze ran down me, I felt a familiar sensation. As though a moth had fluttered over me, or a spider's web had brushed my face. I had a horrible suspicion she was enjoying herself, even triumphant, as though it was no less than she'd expected.

"As you're new, I shall be lenient. Let me think. Some extra time without your infernal phones should do it. You can have them back in a fortnight, rather than at the weekend."

"What?" I objected. "But I'll need to ring my dad."

"I've already told you. There's a payphone in the lobby. And since this disobedience was your idea, Holly, not to mention your rudeness, a further punishment would be appropriate for you. You will be on cleaning duty until the weekend, responsible for the girls' wing."

It wasn't a good start to my Acorn career. Dad was right about me. Nothing ever went smoothly, however hard I tried. Like he was fond of saying, if I were a stick of Blackpool rock, I'd have *trouble* written right through me.

Shame-faced and silent, I followed Verena out of

Jess's room and into my own. I sloped across to my bed, while Verena stood in the doorway, shadowy and still. She watched me for a moment, unblinking. The dull expression in her eyes made my skin tingle. Then she seemed to snap out of it, and gave a tight little smile.

"See Mrs Craddock before breakfast. She'll show you what to do."

She pulled the door shut behind her.

CHAPTER 6

THE next few days were the most exhausting of my entire life. Lessons were relentless—exercises and essays mostly, which we worked on alone, helped by textbooks or strictly supervised access to the Internet. We were expected to work constantly and concentrate hard, and homework was always set for the next day. There was also a strict regime of sport. Running or tennis outside, and volleyball or gymnastics in an old barn which had been converted into a first-class sports hall.

On top of all that, thanks to my own stupidity, there was cleaning duty to fit in. My tasks were to collect laundry and ensure the girls' rooms were clean, after they'd gone down for breakfast. On the plus side, Jess insisted on helping—said she felt guilty I'd been given an extra punishment—and there wasn't a lot to do. By the time we arrived, beds were made, sinks were cleaned, clothes tidied away. I hoped I might find something to help me solve the puzzle of Lydia, but drew a complete blank. The rooms were as neat and orderly as unused hotel rooms.

I couldn't wait for the weekend, when I hoped to enjoy a welcome rest. On Friday afternoon, however, my plans for a lazy Saturday were squashed.

"You'll be g-going to Tredethy tomorrow morning," Mr Mallett told us during the final lesson. "Walking along the cliff path."

"So much for my rest," I muttered.

"Miss Blake will be leading you herself," Mr Mallett went on.

Great. Better and better. I tried to catch Jess's eye, but she'd been told to study with Carole and Marysia, a couple of desks along, and I couldn't see her face.

The lesson finished early, giving us an hour to ourselves. I slipped to the lobby to try to call Dad, almost—but not quite—looking forward to speaking to him. Just as on previous times I'd tried, though, I couldn't get through. I wouldn't be getting my phone back at the weekend, so, for the first time ever, I decided to write him a letter.

I sat on a bench overlooking the sea, which was choppy, the turtle-shaped island enveloped in a silver haze. I scribbled a few lines, general stuff about Acorn, but then I started to think about home, the way Dad had sent me away. My pen ground to a halt, almost tearing the paper, and I sat gazing at the ocean. Turning the page, I began a sketch of Tresawle House instead.

Drawing always calmed me, and within moments I had drifted into a familiar, absorbed state, one where nothing else seemed to matter, where I could almost imagine myself content.

"*Ho-lly!*"

Jess was puffing across the grass, Adam at her side, guitar slung over his shoulder. I quickly hid my drawing beneath the half-finished letter.

"There you are." Jess looked pale and exhausted, her eyes a little bloodshot. "We've been looking for you everywhere. Adam wants to show us something. Want to come?"

I hesitated. I'd seen little of Adam all week. Whenever our paths crossed, I'd smiled and slowed my steps, but Adam had rushed on as though he had much more important things to do. He obviously didn't like me, and it was stupid to waste time hoping he'd change his mind.

On the other hand, Jess was the only friend I had at Acorn, and it was clear she and Adam came as a package.

"Sure." I glanced at Adam coolly, then flicked my gaze away. Two could play at being aloof.

Jess looked down at my envelope. "Writing home?"

"Yeah. Letter to my dad. I'm not desperate to keep in touch, but I want to see if there's any news from Mum."

"I think that payphone's out of order," Jess said. "But don't worry. You and I may not be allowed our mobiles, but Adam will get his back tomorrow morning. We can borrow it, can't we, Ad?"

"Of course," he said, surprising me.

Jess grabbed her brother's arm and set off, chattering breathlessly, as though she hadn't seen him in years. I followed slowly, watching the guitar swing across Adam's back, wondering if I'd ever hear him play the damned thing.

"That's the way to the village, isn't it?" Jess stopped at the edge of the lawns, where the cliff path headed west towards Tredethy. "Where we're going tomorrow? I'll bet it's miles. I don't know how I'm going to make it. I just want to sleep for a week."

"You'll be fine," said Adam, patting her arm. "I'll be there too. The whole school's going." He turned and ducked between the gorse bushes. We followed him along a woodland track which snaked between coppery gold and emerald trees. It ended at a rusty iron gate, which nearly fell off its hinges as we pushed through.

"Well? What d'you think?" asked Adam.

Jess screwed up her face, peering about at the deserted churchyard. "You brought us all that way for this?"

Adam shuffled from foot to foot. "Um, I think it's interesting. A lot of these old houses had private chapels."

The place did have a wistful charm, with its small granite chapel and half-overgrown graves. I even recognised a fig tree, one of the few things I'd learned from Mum.

"At least it's hidden away," I said, reaching up to pull a fig from the tree. "Back at school, I feel like eyes are on me all the time."

Jess glared at her brother. "Well I think it's spooky. Thanks for giving me the creeps."

"You're welcome." With a shrug, Adam strolled

along the path. "You know, some of these graves are really old. I expect the patients are buried here, from when Tresawle House was a psychiatric hospital." He twisted his mouth to one side, as though stifling a grin.

Jess poked her fingers in her ears. "Tra la la, I can't heeaaar you!"

Adam leaned his guitar against the chapel wall and flopped onto a wooden bench. I waited for him to budge up so that Jess and I could sit together, but he didn't, so we squeezed in either side of him. I pulled my fig apart and sucked out the gooey flesh.

"Are you sure you can eat that?" asked Jess, peering around Adam. "It looks gross, if you don't mind me saying."

"It's a fig. My mum loves them. Try one." I fetched a couple more from the tree and gave one to her.

Jess took a tentative bite and smiled. "Hmm, not bad."

"Adam?" I asked, holding one out to him.

"Ugh, no thanks," he said with a grimace.

Silence fell as my irritation grew. Then, just as I reached the point of giving up on him as a lost cause, he turned to me and smiled. A wide, heart-melting grin, one which set butterflies flapping in my stomach.

"How are things with you, then?" he asked.

For a second I was too surprised to do more than gape.

"Fine," I spluttered at last. Mesmerised by the velvety brown of his eyes, I couldn't think of a single thing to add.

"You like Acorn?" he prompted.

"Well, um, it's a bit quiet. My old school was big and rowdy. Acorn feels like a morgue. No one talks to us. Or to each other, come to that."

"Oh? Have you got computers in your common room? Can you get online?"

"I wish! The height of our entertainment is board games and table tennis, but the other girls just do homework, mostly."

"They're nice enough, though," said Jess evenly.

"Huh?" I said, turning to her. "What about those comments Carole made about your weight? If you ask me, they're all a bit weird. The way they trail round after Verena, or should I say *Miss Blake,* as if she's some goddess or something. I can't stand her myself."

"Can't stand her?" Jess echoed. "Why not? I think she's amazing. She's strict, but she's head teacher. She's got to be. What did you expect?"

I gawped at Jess, taken aback. I'd been certain she'd agree with me.

Embarrassed, I tried to explain. "It's just ... don't you think it's odd, the way everyone falls over themselves to please her?"

"I guess that's what's known as hard-working," said Jess, without a trace of a smile.

I stood up and gazed at the sea, uneasy. Something was wrong at Acorn, I could feel it. Why couldn't anyone else? Turning back, I found them both staring at me with identical frowns.

"I think it's great here," said Jess. "Why are you

getting worked up?"

"Oh, I don't know," I said, shaking my head. "Just ignore me."

Adam cleared his throat. "Holly does have a point, Jess. Has anyone mentioned a hobby to you? They don't seem to have any. They just work. No one's interested in music. We're not even studying it. And that's all I want to do, when I leave."

"That's another thing that seems off," I said. "History, maths and English, geography, sciences … no arts at all. Not even a foreign language."

"Our mum loved languages," said Jess. "When she was alive she used to—oh." She covered her mouth with her hand.

Adam's face darkened. "You've told Holly, then?"

"Me and my big mouth. Sorry."

Adam's cheek twitched, as though he was grinding his teeth.

Jess put her hand on his arm. "I'm sorry I said anything, but Holly's our friend. She's had it tough, too, this past year."

"Oh?" Adam locked eyes with me, then his gaze swivelled down my front. "Um, Holly, you've got fig juice on your shirt."

"Oh no!" I brushed at myself furiously.

"Shhh!" Jess put up a hand, arching her brows towards the far side of the churchyard.

A man was slinking between the graves. We watched in silence as he went from stone to stone, reading the names, before moving on.

"What's he up to?" Jess mouthed.

Something about him looked familiar. Then it clicked. "I know him. It's the Viking."

"Huh?" asked Adam.

"He's not really a Viking," I whispered. "He's from Canada. Helps out at the school."

Still not seeing us, he crouched before one of the granite headstones. He gazed so intently, he looked quite comical, as if he were in love with it.

Jess started to giggle, covering her mouth in a hopeless attempt to stop. The man—George Kellow—looked up.

I expected him to say something, to acknowledge us, at least. Instead, he straightened up and strode off, his mouth set. We waited until he had vanished.

"Why was he looking at us like that?" asked Adam. "Aren't we supposed to be here?"

"There's another mystery for Holly, and she hasn't even solved the riddle of Lydia yet." Jess clapped her hand over her mouth again. "Oops. Sorry, Holly."

"Who's Lydia?" Adam asked.

With a sigh, I pulled the note from my pocket and thrust it at him. As he scanned it, his brow knotted.

"*All is not as it seems. Ask about Lydia.* What's that supposed to mean? Where did it come from?"

"Someone pushed it under my door, the night we arrived."

"Could mean anything—or nothing."

"I think someone was playing a joke," said Jess.

"The answer's obvious. You should ask Verena.

You'll be seeing her tomorrow."

Thanks Adam. Great idea. Jess had suggested exactly the same thing, but approaching Verena was the last thing I wanted to do.

Adam leapt up, clearly pleased with himself. "Anyway, shall we go and check out those graves? See what the Viking was staring at?"

"Sure," I said crossly.

We meandered through the churchyard, Jess on tiptoes. "I don't want to step on the graves," she explained. "My gran reckoned it was bad luck."

The tombstones looked perfectly ordinary, giving people's names, birth dates and death dates, plus mottoes like *Requiescat in Pace.*

"Violet Coombes," I read, stopping by the grave Kellow had seemed to study the most.

"Another Violet!" said Jess. "Like the ghost."

"Ghost?" Adam grinned.

"Just something Carole said, about Acorn Academy being haunted by the last daughter of the Tresawle family."

"Well, that'll spice things up a bit," said Adam, "but I don't see any connection. This woman was Violet Coombes, not Tresawle. Violet's a common enough name."

I studied the grave. "She died six months ago, aged forty-five. Not much of an age, is it? Why was George so interested? Could she be related to him?"

"I don't intend living till I'm old," said Adam. "I want to get my magnum opus written, become world famous, then go out in a blaze of glory."

"Great." Jess poked his shoulder. "Typically selfish, that is. What about me?"

"You'll be married with three kids by then."

"*Ha, ha.* Funny."

"I'll be the doting uncle, dropping in between world tours, bearing exotic gifts."

Instead of laughing, as I expected, a blank look crossed Jess's face. She took a few steps towards the next grave, and stood gazing into space, one hand on a Celtic cross.

"Jess, what is it?" I asked her. "Is something wrong?" Goosebumps prickled the back of my neck.

"I'm a bit tired, that's all. I think I'll get back. I've got heaps of homework to do. And we've got to be up early tomorrow for that trip to the village."

"It's time for dinner, anyway," said Adam. "We'll come with you. Won't we?" He looked at me, eyebrows raised.

"Cool," I said.

We walked back to Tresawle House, Jess moving slowly, as though she had backache. I left them at the foot of the staircase and dashed off to rinse my fig-stained shirt.

Adam called after me. "Holly, um, would you mind meeting up with me for a minute or two? After dinner?"

I was so taken aback, I could only nod.

"On the beach?" he suggested.

"Fine."

CHAPTER 7

DARKNESS had fallen by the time I slipped outside and hurried across the cobbled courtyard. The lawns and paths lay in shadow, lit only by an occasional old-fashioned streetlamp. As I approached the stone steps, I spotted a group of four boys headed in my direction. They strode along quietly, glancing round, looking for all the world like policemen on patrol. The list of rules I'd been given didn't exactly forbid one-to-one meetings in the school grounds, only in rooms. Nevertheless, instinct told me Verena would be unlikely to approve.

I didn't think the boys had seen me, but to be on the safe side, I darted behind a tree. My heart raced as they got closer. If they passed my hiding place they would see me, for sure. Luckily, before they reached me, they turned aside and veered towards the gym. Breathing a sigh, I ducked onto the steps and made my way down to the beach.

At first there was no sign of Adam. Then, against the backdrop of the lapping waves, I became aware of a quiet, sweet melody. Someone was strumming a guitar and singing—Adam, it had to be. I glanced nervously up the cliffs towards Acorn, anxious someone would hear, but decided there was no way the soft music would carry so far.

I slowed my steps, mesmerised by the haunting quality of Adam's voice and the soothing harmonies of the guitar. He was like the Pied Piper, I thought wryly, luring me along the beach.

I found him between two rocks, the guitar braced across one thigh. As I got near, I listened carefully to make out the words.

The season turns
A candle burns
The book slams shut

Noticing me, he stopped playing and flashed a smile.

"Hey, don't stop," I said. "What was that?"

"Oh, just something I'm working on. Only noodling."

I had no idea what he meant, but I smiled back and found a place to sit further along the rock. His fingers, gripping a small object I couldn't quite see, hovered uncertainly over the strings.

"Go on," I said. "Play some more."

After a pause, he strummed a few notes and sang along softly. I listened, trailing my fingers in a rock pool.

It came like a stillness
A frost creeping over a meadow

Occasionally I caught him glancing at me, then looking quickly away. For a weird moment I had the crazy notion that Jess was right, that he liked me after all. Was that why he'd invited me here, to get to know me better? Ask me out, even? I thought about it for a second, then shook my head and told myself not to be so daft. There must be some other reason why he wanted to see me.

The music faded and he stared away into the distance.

"What's that little thing you're using to pluck the strings?" I asked, unable to think of anything better to break the silence.

"It's called a plectrum. Saves wear and tear on the fingers."

"Oh." Silence fell once more.

"You're good," I told him.

He grinned. "You really think so? Soon as I start earning money, I'm buying myself a Gibson Les Paul. That's my favourite guitar."

"I see why you're so keen to study music."

His eyes gleamed as he told me all about it—that he'd been teaching himself since infant school, and writing his own songs for the past three years.

He stopped talking and an awkward silence fell. I began to think he was never going to tell me why he'd asked to meet me.

"Want to walk a bit?" I suggested.

"Sure."

He slung his guitar over his shoulder and we headed along the beach. We strolled quietly in the moonlight, caught up in our own thoughts.

"Come on then, what's up?" I asked at last.

He gave a big sigh. "I'm worried about Jess."

It wasn't what I'd expected, but it made perfect sense. Her odd behaviour in the graveyard earlier had worried me too.

"She was awfully tired today," I said, "but she swears it's nothing more. I guess it's understandable. I've never worked so hard in my life as I have this week."

He nodded. "Yeah, that's true. I made her promise to get an early night, forget about the homework. But … I don't know. There's something a bit different about her. Have you noticed?"

He came to a halt and looked at me. Now I thought about it, Jess wasn't quite the warm, bubbly girl I'd met on the train.

"She seems tense," I said.

"Exactly. Look, would you do me a big favour?"

"Um, okay."

"Keep an eye on her for me? She's all I've got."

"No problem," I said.

"Thanks."

"I'm sorry about your parents."

"I know," he said. He lapsed once more into silence. The waves breaking on the shore had a hypnotic effect, like his music. I didn't intend to stay long—all the more likelihood of being missed—but I couldn't seem to move.

"Try not to worry about Jess," I said. "If she has something on her mind, I'll dig it out of her. It isn't good to bottle stuff up." A counsellor had told me that.

Outlined against the shingle, Adam brushed the hair from his eyes.

"You really believe that?" he asked.

"Of course. Why?"

"No reason … Well, Jess said you'd had a tough time too."

"Right." I'd meant what I said about bottling things up. Yet wasn't that exactly what I'd done myself, these past months?

He looked at me, eyes narrowed. "I'm rubbish at all the chat stuff, but Jess tells me I'm a good listener. Only if you want to talk, obviously."

I felt odd, not quite myself. I didn't know Adam very well, wasn't sure he even liked me. All the same, as memories of the past year surfaced, it seemed like I'd burst if I didn't let them out.

We walked slowly along the shore. I fixed my gaze in the middle distance, but saw nothing there except my memories, which mocked me like conjured-up devils.

"The thing that happened," I said, shivering. "It wasn't something I did intentionally. But I did do it."

He nodded. "Okay."

"It was a normal day. Or it started normally, but by the end of it my life was smashed to bits. I was walking home from school." I paused, remembering the feeling of lightness, the birdsong, the jangling chimes of an ice cream van trundling by, a winking clown's face on its side. I felt like I was talking about someone else. In a way I was. That girl in my mind's eye lived in a distant, golden land, one I'd never see again.

"I was minutes from home."

"What happened?" Adam slowed his steps.

"I saw a dog on the other side of the road. No one was with him. I worried he might get run down or put in the dog pound." I paused, took a breath. "The dog saw me, and I thought for one horrible second he was going to run across the road. I dashed out to stop him—and—and—I don't remember the actual accident. It's all a blank. A car came round the corner. All I remember is the driver's face."

I saw him again now. Huge eyes bulging in panic. A red mouth frozen in a ghastly grin. A face I saw every morning when I woke up, and every evening as I drifted off to sleep.

We came to a stop by the rocks.

"Holly? You okay?"

"I survived. But the driver didn't. He died."

"Oh."

"Yeah." I looked towards the dark shape of Turtle Island on the horizon. "It's hard to explain how unreal it was. They told me what happened after I woke up in hospital. Apparently the driver *was* going too fast—because he was a doctor on call, on his way to see a patient. When he swerved to try and miss me, his car mounted the pavement and smashed into the side of a house."

I paused, waiting for Adam to say something—anything.

After a while, he cleared his throat and said, "What

about the people inside the house? Was anyone else hurt?"

I shook my head. "No, thank God. I don't know about the patient, the one the doctor was going to see."

We weaved slowly between the rocks, circling back the way we'd come.

"It was an accident," Adam said eventually. "Not intentional."

"I know. You can put it how you like. I didn't mean it, but it *was* my fault. If I'd thought about what I was doing, that doctor would still be alive. Because of me he's dead. I've got to face that."

The familiar ache washed over me. I couldn't expect Adam to understand. One of my friends said she didn't see why I was so cut-up over it. It wasn't as though I knew the man, after all. She was trying to help, I knew, but I found myself avoiding her. No one around me understood how it felt, to cause someone's death.

Startled, I realised something must have changed. For the first time, I'd been able to talk about it—and to a virtual stranger.

"What happened to the dog?" Adam asked.

He was the first person to ask that. "We ended up adopting him. We love him to bits, even Dad. It wasn't Wilk's fault."

"And your mum and dad split up?"

"They couldn't handle what had happened, kept arguing about it. Things hadn't been rosy for some time, if I'm honest."

"How d'you mean, argued?"

"Well, Dad's reaction was to blame me. Said I should have paid more attention, seen the car and stayed where I was. He's told me hundreds of times not to daydream. Mum was more on my side, said the doctor shouldn't have been going so fast, that kind of thing. But … bad things make Mum ill. She gets migraines. Can't even speak properly, says it's like her brain's on fire. In the end she sort of flipped. Went off with someone."

"What? Your dad blamed you and your mum just *left*?"

Something rustled nearby. I scanned the moonlit shore.

"There's a man," I whispered, horrified. "By those rocks." Without thinking, I grabbed Adam's arm.

"Is someone there?" Adam called out, his voice firm.

The shadow took shape and came towards us. Peering into the gloom, I recognised George Kellow.

"Him again," I muttered, turning aside. "I don't believe it."

Kellow looked windswept and scruffy.

"Hi. Nice evening," he said, his Canadian accent clear in his words. "You're new, aren't you? I'm George. I live in Tredethy, do a bit of work at Acorn. Like to stretch my legs after supper."

He sounded distinctly uncomfortable. He was lying, I felt sure. Had he been hiding, listening to us?

"You shouldn't be on the beach this late," he continued. "It's dangerous out here in the dark. You could get into trouble."

I felt sick, convinced he'd heard my story. As though awakening from a dream, I was overcome with regrets. It was bad enough I'd told Adam. Bad enough I'd told him first, instead of Jess. Now this stranger knew as well. I had to get away from him, from both of them. I ran towards the steps.

Adam started after me. "Holly, wait."

I rushed along the beach and took the steps two at a time. At the top I paused and looked down. Adam had stopped by the rocks, and George Kellow was striding away along the beach.

CHAPTER 8

UNABLE to sleep, I watched the shadows creep across the ceiling, thrown by the moonlight through the bars at my window. Worry about Jess mingled with bitterness that Kellow might have overheard my story. What had possessed me to tell Adam, anyway? Would Jess be upset I'd told him first? Adam might not reveal my secret, but they were so close, there was every chance she'd guess he knew.

I didn't have cleaning duty today, but when the time came to get up, I promptly fell asleep. Fifteen minutes later, I awoke feeling groggy and exhausted. I yawned as I dragged on my jeans and jacket, ready for the trip to Tredethy. By the time I stepped into the hallway, there was still no sign of Jess. A sense of foreboding ran through me.

"Jess?" I tapped on her door. "Coming for breakfast?"

No answer. I rapped again, louder this time.

"Jess? We'll be late." I turned the handle and slipped inside the room.

Jess was fast asleep, her brow furrowed, one arm thrown above her head.

I gave her a shake. "Wake up!"

She jolted awake and stared about, her eyes unfocused. "No," she cried. "Don't!"

"Hey, it's only me," I said, resting a hand on her wrist.

Jess's eyes went glassy, as though the life had drained out of them. I thought for one horrible moment she'd fainted. Then she peered at me and squinted.

"Holly? What are you doing here?"

"You overslept. Was it a nightmare?"

She shook her head. "I *saw* her. Violet Tresawle. She was coming for me."

"In your nightmare, you mean, yeah?"

"I—I—" She put her fist to her lips, chewed her knuckle.

"We've got this trip at ten, remember, to the village?" I forced a smile, trying not to let her see how worried I was. "Are you all right?"

Jess shook herself and sat up, puffing out her cheeks. She was paler than ever, and a mist of sweat stood out on her forehead.

"I'm fine," she said.

"You don't look it. What you said about Violet Tresawle …"

"It was only a dream." Her leaden voice had an edge to it, a hardness I didn't recognise. Maybe this was what Adam had meant.

"I really think you should stay in bed. Shall I ask Verena to get you a doctor? Or send Adam up?"

"Don't you dare!" Jess heaved herself out of bed and began gathering her clothes. "I can't wait to get out of school, even if it's only for a day. Feels like we've been cooped up here for years. Like nowhere else exists."

"But the walk …"

Jess's eyes flashed. "Just because I'm fat, Holly Champion, doesn't mean I can't walk anywhere. Miss Blake is right, walking is good for our health. You go and have breakfast. I don't want any. Besides, I've got an assignment to finish. I'll meet you outside at ten. Stop looking at me like that. I'm fine."

***

After forcing down a quick bite in the dining hall, I headed for the sunlit courtyard, glancing about for Adam. I'd have to tell him about Jess's behaviour. If anyone could talk her into seeing a doctor, he could.

Students were gathered quietly by the stone well, but Adam wasn't with them. Then, at last, he came strolling out of Tresawle House, Jess at his side. She looked nervy, and her normally curly hair lay flat against her head. Adam whispered something in her ear and she smiled, at least.

Verena Blake hadn't struck me as much of an outdoors type, with her trademark silky dresses and elegant shoes, but this morning she strode across the courtyard looking every inch the rambler, dressed in sturdy walking boots, jeans and a weatherproof jacket. Mrs Craddock trotted beside her, carrying two baskets.

"I trust you're looking forward to our trip," said Verena. "Mrs Craddock will issue your packed lunches, and we'll be off."

Mrs Craddock, smirking as usual, handed round the packages. As I took mine, I heard Adam's voice.

"Miss Blake, I thought our phones were to be returned to us today. It's Saturday."

"Very astute, Adam, indeed it is. But there's been some storm damage on the cliffs, and the footpath is perilously close to the edge in places, with sheer drops of over a hundred metres. We need to pay attention, not waste time fiddling with phones."

Adam muttered something, but the wind snatched his words away.

As Mrs Craddock retreated inside Tresawle House, Verena strode towards the cliff path. The students marched in pairs behind her, with Adam, Jess and me bringing up the rear.

"She's making excuses," Adam grumbled. "She doesn't want to give them back, I reckon."

Jess shrugged. "I don't need mine. Miss Blake is right. They're too distracting."

Adam's eyes sought mine, but, remembering last night on the beach, I couldn't meet his gaze.

"Feeling better, Jess?" I asked.

"I was fine before. Why are you making such a fuss?"

Adam looked puzzled, but didn't say anything. I clearly wasn't going to get a chance to talk to him alone, so I dawdled a little, trailing behind. Adam glanced over his shoulder and hesitated, waiting for me to catch up. I walked slower, unsure myself why I found it so hard to face him. He hadn't forced me to tell him my secret, after all.

The autumn day was fresh, the walk exhilarating, but the beauty of the wide, sweeping bay and hazy island was lost on me. As I went over things in my mind, my thoughts kept returning to Lydia. Who on earth was she? I'd drawn a blank with everyone I'd asked. I couldn't shake the feeling that, whoever she was, she held the key to unravelling the odd things I'd noticed at Acorn, and that Jess's behaviour was connected, too.

I hated to admit it, but Jess and Adam were right. I should approach Verena about Lydia. Much as she intimidated me, she was the school principal, and the obvious person to ask. Whatever her reaction, it would tell me something.

I couldn't do it now. She forged ahead with Faruzi and two other boys. They flanked her like security guards, slowing down where the path strayed close to the cliff edge or holding back windswept branches which almost blocked the way.

Maybe I'd get a better chance later. I almost hoped I wouldn't.

The students came to a halt. Beyond them, a flight of steps led down to a little harbour.

Verena smiled. "We're almost there. Good work, everyone. You will have an hour to explore, then we'll meet on the quay for lunch."

I didn't want to look around on my own, and the prospect of hooking up with Carole was far from exciting. It was feeble of me to keep avoiding Adam and Jess. With a little trot, I caught them up on the bridge, where a turbulent river gushed into the sea. Adam turned and grinned, clearly relieved.

We explored Tredethy together, sauntering along the narrow, winding roads with their old granite cottages. Out of season, there was little traffic, and even fewer tourists. Everywhere I looked I saw scenes which, under happier circumstances, I would have loved to paint. Boats bobbing in the harbour. A small boy leading a moorland pony along a track. Jade green clifftop fields which looked so impossibly steep, it seemed a miracle the sheep didn't roll into the sea.

Adam and I stopped to admire a smuggler's cottage dating back to the fourteen hundreds, according to the plaque, but Jess showed no interest, trudging on past us up the hill.

"What's going on?" Adam hissed. "Have you and Jess fallen out or something?"

"Of course not." Looking up, I nearly bumped into her. She'd stopped outside the village shop and was peering through the window at the Cornish pasties laid out in neat rows, steam rising from their golden crusts.

"They smell lush," I said as the enticing aroma reached me.

Jess gave a bleak smile. "We've got packed lunches, remember? They'll be better for us."

As I spotted the post box outside, I cursed as I

remembered the letter to my dad, which lay unfinished in my room.

The hour was nearly up, so we made our way back towards the quayside. At the bottom of the hill, Verena stood alone near the fishing boats. This was my chance.

The pungent odour of rotting fish made me queasy. Before my nerve failed, I sprinted ahead, determined to corner her before the others arrived. My footsteps clattered, but she didn't look round. I followed her gaze back along the coast, to where the little turtle-shaped island had shrunk to a tiny speck.

"Can people go there?" I asked. "The island, I mean? I'd love to see it."

She turned icy lilac eyes on me. "It's a nature reserve. Visitors aren't allowed."

"Oh, right." I glanced about nervously. Jess and Adam stood chatting by the river's edge, and behind them, Carole and red-haired Marysia were striding towards us.

"Miss Blake," I began. "I wanted to ask you something. Did a girl called Lydia study at Acorn?"

Verena remained completely still, though her knuckles moved a fraction where she gripped the handrail.

"Who spoke of her to you?"

"I overheard someone mention her," I said, thinking quickly. "I, um, saw her name on one of the trophies and wondered who she was."

Verena pressed her lips together as she searched my face. Maybe one reason would have been more convincing than two.

"We did have a student named Lydia, true," she said. "But I certainly don't remember her winning any trophies."

"Oh. Well, perhaps I'm mistaken. What happened to her? Did she get a job?"

Verena frowned, looking pained. "Lydia left before her school career ended. She was a great disappointment to me. To us all. Don't speak of her again."

She turned and strode off. I looked round to find the other students waiting silently nearby. They followed Verena to the side of the beach, where some benches stood on a concrete plinth near the rocks. One by one, the students took a seat. There wasn't enough room for all of us, so Adam, Jess and I sat on a low wall running alongside.

Our packed lunches were all the same. Egg mayonnaise sandwiches, made with eggs from Acorn's own hens, plus an apple from the orchard.

While the rest of us set upon our lunches, Jess sat quietly, not moving.

"Eat up, Jess," said Adam. "Aren't you hungry? I'm starving."

Jess pulled her sandwich out of its paper bag, held it up by one corner and stared.

"The eggs are from real chickens, remember," I said, devouring mine.

Adam grinned. "Makes you wonder what false chickens are."

I smiled, but Jess ignored him. Gripping the sandwich, she took a careful bite and chewed, then stopped and gazed at it again.

"Jess?" Behind her back, Adam shot me a worried look.

Carole's strident tones reached us from the nearest bench. "How is your diet going, Jess? Were the notes I gave you useful?"

Jess's eyelashes fluttered. Her mouth dropped open, but no words came out.

I whipped my head around and glowered at Carole. "Leave her alone."

Carole returned to her sandwich, face blank. Jess's breathing grew wheezy as she leaned forwards. Her skin looked clammy, as though she felt feverish.

"Jessie? What's up?" asked Adam, an edge of panic in his voice.

Slowly, Jess laid the sandwich flat on her hand. Then, visibly shaking, she peeled back one corner.

She screamed and sprang to her feet, dropping the sandwich in the sand.

"The maggots! Oh no, can you see them? There're hundreds. I could feel them wriggling through the bread."

I looked at the sandwich, then at Adam. There were no maggots. It seemed perfectly ordinary.

"But Jessie—" began Adam.

"Stop watching me." Jess stared at a nearby rock, which was roundish, with jagged ridges and swirling grooves. "Oh God, look at its face, its horrible tooth."

She stared about at other rocks. "They're all laughing. Make them stop. Make them stop!"

Clasping her hands over her ears, she sank to the ground and moaned. I leapt up from the wall and fell to my knees beside her.

"Miss Blake! Come quickly," I yelled over my shoulder.

"Get an ambulance," cried Adam, his face white. "There's something wrong with my sister."

Verena crossed to us and knelt in the sand. While Jess twisted her head left and right, Verena took her wrist, feeling for her pulse. Then, her face giving nothing away, she pulled out her phone and paced over the sand, towards the shore.

"Right now," I heard her say. "On the quayside."

Adam and I stayed with Jess. Her groans quietened to a whimper as she closed her eyes, her mouth slack.

"Oh God, she's bleeding." Adam pulled out a tissue and dabbed at drops of blood trickling from her nose.

Slowly, Jess opened her eyes. They had a swollen look, the pupils dilated and the whites tinged red.

"Can you hear me?" Adam cried. "Answer me!"

She tried to raise a hand, but it fluttered like a wounded bird. Her eyes bulged as she cried out. It seemed to me she couldn't see us. Like she saw something else, something that horrified her.

As the seconds stretched into endless minutes, the whimpers faded until Jess was so still and ghastly pale, I felt certain she was dying. Adam watched in silence.

I squeezed her hand, feeling sick. "Hang on in there,

Jess," I whispered. "The ambulance is coming. It'll be here any second."

The sound of a heavy vehicle backing into the road beside the quay made me dizzy with relief. But it wasn't an ambulance. It was the school minibus.

Adam and I exchanged a glance.

"Where the hell's the ambulance?" he asked.

Verena waved the minibus into the nearest gap. Mr Craddock sat behind the wheel, his wife bolt upright beside him.

"Jess has collapsed," Verena informed them as they stepped out onto the sandy kerb. Steering them aside, she stood with them a moment, quietly giving instructions. Mrs Craddock nodded briefly, her gaze darting.

She and her husband set to work smoothly, crossing the sand and lifting Jess into a collapsible wheelchair, then bundling her across the beach and up a pull-out ramp into the back of the minibus.

Adam dashed after them. "I'm coming too. She'll need me when we get to the hospital."

I caught him up, hoping Verena would let me go as well.

Mr Craddock barred our way with his meaty hand. "You can see her later. You'll only be in the way."

"But—" said Adam.

"Come on, Ken," screeched Mrs Craddock. "Hurry up."

Shoving Adam and me out of the way, Mr Craddock slammed the doors. Within seconds, the bus had vanished up the hill.

Too shocked to talk, Adam and I stood on the quayside. His face was gaunt, drained of colour. The other students hadn't even moved. They remained on the benches, solemn and still.

Verena Blake clapped her hands. "Pack up your things."

"Are they taking Jess to the hospital?" I asked. "Didn't you call 999?"

She glared. "Are you questioning my judgement, Holly?"

"She needs a doctor!" I cried. "Not *them.*"

"Holly's right," said Adam. "Why couldn't we go with her?"

Two red spots appeared on Verena's cheekbones as she stared at us, stony-faced. "Jess needs rest and quiet. Since you both see fit to question me … Mr and Mrs Craddock are trained paramedics. Though I refuse to see why I should explain myself to you."

Adam edged closer to me, his fists clenching. Verena sounded confident, but how could she possibly know what Jess needed?

"Get ready for the walk back," said Verena. "I won't ask you again."

"You expect us to walk back?" I blurted out. "After this?"

She exchanged a look with Carole. Carole nodded.

"I don't like your tone, Holly Champion," said Verena. "You'll come to my office at seventeen hundred hours. Meanwhile, I have matters to attend to. Carole, lead the group home."

"Of course." Carole's voice was flat.

"I will give you an update on Jess's condition later," Verena added. "Hysterics will not aid her recovery."

She turned and marched up the street.

CHAPTER 9

I walked with Adam in silence along the cliff path. He swiped at his cheek, as though flicking away unwanted tears. Up ahead, the rest of the group marched like soldiers, two abreast.

"The hospital will know what to do," I said, quickening my stride. The words sounded stupid to my own ears. I hoped and prayed the doctors could help Jess—but how could anyone know for sure?

"Verena must be going straight there," I added. "Maybe she's called a taxi." I looked across the sparkling bay, trying not to let him see how worried I was.

"Why wouldn't they let us go with her?" he asked. "We should be by her side."

I searched for something comforting to say, but all I could think of was the terror in Jess's eyes, the pallor of her face. I should have told him about Jess's nightmare. I should have insisted on getting help for her in the morning. Something had clearly been wrong. Was this going to be another regret I'd wear forever like a second skin?

"Has anything like this happened before?" I asked.

He shook his head. "Never. Jess has always been healthy, unlike me."

He stopped walking as Amy, Carole and Marysia blocked our way. They stood staring at us, arms crossed, expressions stern.

"You should not have talked to Miss Blake like that," said Carole. "Miss Blake knows what she's doing."

"Oh, get lost," said Adam.

Carole blinked.

"We're worried sick about Jess," I snapped. "Aren't you?"

Carole's eyes widened, but otherwise she appeared quite calm. "Miss Blake will not tolerate disrespect." As one, the three turned and continued on their way.

"What on earth's the matter with them?" said Adam. "They're like bloody robots." He didn't even try to keep his voice down.

"I *know*," I whispered. "It's what I've been trying to say. I can't put my finger on it, but it's all wrong, the way they are."

Adam's cheek twitched as he ground his teeth. "We should have listened to you."

Our arms brushed as we kept pace on the narrow path.

"Let's get back as quick as we can," I said. "Find out which hospital Jess is in."

***

85

We hurried through the lobby and along the hallway to Verena's office. I pressed the buzzer two or three times, but there was no answer.

Adam gave the door a frustrated kick. I looked at my watch. Barely an hour had passed since we'd left Verena on the quayside. I couldn't think straight.

"She'll be with Jess at the hospital," I said. "We'll have to look out for her."

He slumped against the wall. "I'm going to see if I can get hold of my uncle in Scotland. On the payphone, if it's working. See you later ... and thanks." He locked eyes with me an instant.

I wasn't sure what he was thanking me for, but I forced a smile. "She'll be okay. I'll go and check if the Craddocks are back. They'll know what's happening. I'll come and find you if I get anywhere."

As I headed off, Adam called my name.

"Holly, don't worry about last night. What you told me. I don't think that man Kellow could've heard much. That's why you ran off, isn't it? You thought he'd heard? I came after you, but figured you preferred to be alone."

I nodded. I didn't trust George Kellow, but this was no time to discuss it. What difference did it make if he'd heard, anyway?

"It doesn't matter," I said. "Nothing matters except Jess."

***

Most of the students had vanished to their rooms—catching up on their homework, no doubt—and Tresawle House was eerily quiet. First I tried Mrs Craddock's upstairs office, which was along the hallway from my room. No answer. I headed downstairs towards the kitchen, where she spent a lot of her time.

As I rounded the banister, I bumped straight into her. A box she was carrying crashed to the floor.

"Watch where you're going, you clumsy girl." She bent down and began scrabbling for the tiny cartons and sachets which had spilled out of the box.

I bit back an angry retort, determined to stay polite—she'd tell me nothing otherwise. "Sorry, let me help." I bent down, grabbed a handful of sugar sachets and piled them in the box amongst packets of teabags and jars of coffee and cocoa.

"Leave it," she snapped. "We don't want your mucky paws all over our supplies." She stopped for a moment and fanned herself with one hand. "Lordy, you gave me such a fright. Sneaking about like that."

"Any news about Jess? Which hospital did you take her to?"

A furtive expression came into her eyes. Slowly and methodically, she picked up her box and tucked it under one arm.

I stood firm, blocking her way. "Why won't you tell me? Could you or Mr Craddock take us to see her, Adam and me? Please?"

"You'll have to ask Miss Blake." As she pushed past,

I noticed the logo on the box. A gigantic eye, the pupil of which was a black and white map of the world. It gave me the creeps.

"Was she speaking?" I persevered, desperate for news.

Mrs Craddock stopped and turned. "They're keeping her in overnight for observation. She fainted, that's all. You young people, so melodramatic." She marched off.

***

Adam sat alone on my favourite bench, staring out to sea. It was only four o'clock, but the sun was already sinking towards the horizon.

I called to him, anxious to put him out of his misery. "Hey, Mrs Craddock said Jess fainted, that's all."

His eyes narrowed. "She said that?"

"Yes. And they're keeping her in for observation." I flopped beside him on the bench.

"But she's okay?"

I nodded. Mrs Craddock hadn't said she was okay, not exactly, but she *had* insisted it was just a faint. Why didn't I feel more relieved?

"Did you get hold of your uncle?" I asked.

"I tried to, but that payphone just rang and rang. Must still be out of order. Mind you, Uncle's not often home. Spends most of his time at the university."

His eyes looked moist and distant. It struck me how

different things would be for him if his parents were still alive.

"I guess Verena will contact him there if she can't reach him at home." It was the most reassuring thing I could think of, though I wasn't sure I believed it.

"I doubt he'll come down. He's quite frail, and he won't want the hassle, I know that much. Listen, do you have any money?"

"A bit. Not heaps, though. Why?"

"I thought we could get a taxi," he said with a sigh, "but I haven't got much either."

I doubted we'd have enough, even if we knew where to go. "You're welcome to what I've got. But Verena will take you when she gets back, won't she? Surely."

He thought for a moment. "Yeah. I guess."

"I've got to see Verena at five, remember? She won't want to miss telling me off." My stomach churned at the thought. "If she hasn't turned up before then, come with me to her office. We'll find out what's going on and make a plan. She'll have to give us our phones back at least—and the number of the hospital."

A trace of hope lit his eyes. "Okay."

***

At five to five, we arrived together outside Verena's office. Although neither of us had seen her come back, a firm voice answered my knock.

"Come in."

We exchanged glances. Adam looked as nervous as

I felt. Finally, we would get some answers.

The office was smaller than I expected, stiflingly warm, with a flowery scent I didn't much like. Not a fresh, cheerful one like my mum wore, but a heavy perfume which reminded me of funerals. The décor was the same as in the rest of the house, with oil paintings and tapestries lining the walls. One of the paintings, near the sash window, showed a haughty-looking child in a purple velvet dress, clutching a porcelain doll. I wondered if she might be Violet Tresawle, painted in her youth.

Verena sat at her antique wooden desk, filling in a chart. She had changed into a pale suit, which glimmered in the dim light. My eyes were drawn to a gold brooch at the lapel, in the shape of a scorpion, with black gemstones along the abdomen and pincers, and tiny red rubies for eyes. Trust her to have a scorpion for a brooch.

She looked up expectantly, her brows perfect arches. "Adam, why are *you* here? I wasn't expecting you. Didn't I make myself clear?"

"Where's my sister?" he demanded.

Verena smiled and spread her palms towards us. "Jess is fine. She'll be home tomorrow."

The fist around my heart began to loosen. Adam exhaled slowly.

"Can I see her?" he asked.

Verena leaned back in her chair. "Jess needs rest and quiet. The doctors have advised against any visits. She'll be back with us soon."

Adam opened his mouth, then shut it, obviously sensing it would do no good to plead.

"Could we have the phone number of the hospital, then?" I asked. "So we can ring and see how she's getting on?"

Pursing her lips, Verena consulted a notebook and scribbled down a number. She gave it to Adam, pointedly ignoring my outstretched hand.

"I'll need my phone," he said. "The one in the lobby's out of order."

She walked to the nearby cupboard, unlocked it and withdrew Adam's phone from its bag.

"May I have mine?" I asked, as she handed it to him. "I'd like to talk to Jess, too."

"Hmm, I don't think so, Holly." She held my gaze. "Your punishment for disobeying my rule about fraternisation. Don't you remember?"

"Come on, let's go." Adam half winked at me as he headed for the door, and I realised it didn't matter, he'd already promised to let me borrow his.

"Not you, Holly," said Verena sweetly. "Have you forgotten I summoned you here?"

Adam shot me a sympathetic glance. After he'd gone, Verena gestured to a chair. I sat down, bracing myself for the worst. She remained silent, staring at me.

Perspiration broke out on my forehead, and I could feel heat rising up my neck. Trying not to fidget, I gazed out of the window, where George Kellow was busy bagging up hedge trimmings.

She steepled her hands beneath her chin, her mouth

twisted in a thin smile. "How are you finding things here? Are you happy?"

Her air of concern didn't fool me for one minute, but it wouldn't help to antagonise her, so I smiled and said, "Yes, thanks."

She picked up a sheet of paper and waved it in front of me. As I tried to make out the writing, she withdrew it and placed it in a drawer. "The reports from Miss Mallett, from Mr Foreman, are not particularly good. Inattention. Thoughtlessness. Lack of respect. I'll need to let your father know, if things don't improve." She waited for my reaction, her steady eyes boring into mine.

"I'll try harder, Miss Blake," I said. I'd been doing fine, or so I thought, but there seemed little point in saying so. When she said nothing, I added, "I noticed there's no music or art on the timetable. Will we be studying them later on?"

She licked her lips. "We hold the view that arts encourage the cult of the self. They incline one to self-absorption and selfishness, and we don't have room for that at Acorn. Here we pull together for the good of all."

For the good of you, I thought.

"As a punishment for your disrespect, you will be on kitchen duty for the coming week," she said. "Starting tomorrow."

I stifled a sigh. I'd only just finished cleaning duty. Still, as punishments went, it could be worse.

"As well as cleaning duty," she continued.

"Oh. Okay," I said, desperate to get out of the stuffy office.

She slid on a pair of glasses and looked down at the papers in front of her. "All right, you may go."

I made for the door, trying not to run. As I turned the handle, she called, "One last thing. I don't want you fraternising with Adam. I suspect he's the reason you're not concentrating hard enough on your studies. It was understandable for the three of you to spend time together when Jess was here, but now she's not …"

"You said she's coming back tomorrow."

She paused, shut her eyes briefly. "If I find you alone with that boy, I'll be writing to your father. I shall also suggest that you stay with us throughout the half term holiday. If you want to be allowed home, don't disobey me."

***

After lights-out, I paced the floor of my room. It seemed that everyone I'd ever cared about—Mum, Wilk, my friends, Jess, and even Adam—was being taken from me. I was existing on the edge of life, like an astronaut I'd seen in a film, trapped in space on the end of a cable, praying it wouldn't snap.

I looked at the heap of exercise books cluttering my desk. Though homework was the last thing on my mind, I'd have to tackle it tomorrow. The threat of being denied my half term holiday had done its job. I hadn't realised until now how much I longed for home.

It wasn't so much that I wanted to see Dad, though I missed Wilk and my old friends, of course. No, there was something more. Maybe it was just the thing with the phones, and my money running out. Whatever it was, day by day, my feeling of being trapped deepened.

Despite the chill outside, it was even stuffier in my room than in Verena's office. I'd mentioned the stuck window to both the Craddocks by this time, and also to Carole, but still no one had come to fix it. Fanning my face, I sat in darkness in the window seat, pulling my knees up beneath my chin.

The courtyard below lay in misty shadow. Beyond the cliff edge, slivers of moonlight sparkled on the ocean. A boat was heading out to sea, a little cabin cruiser perhaps, taking lucky people to some exotic destination. I wished I were with them.

As I clambered out of the window seat, I bashed my foot against the radiator. There was a resounding clang, but also another sound. A muted plop, as though something had fallen to the floor.

For one horrible moment, I imagined a bird had become trapped in the room and died. Then I realised how unlikely that was, in a room where the window wouldn't even open. I dropped to my knees and peered beneath the radiator.

It was too dark in the narrow space to see anything. Then I remembered. Hanging from the zipper of my backpack was a little keyring with a torch on the end. Dad had given it to me some time ago, a promotional knick-knack from one of his clients. I retrieved my bag from the top of the wardrobe. Yes, it was still there, a tiny thing in the shape of a trumpet. I twisted it from the zipper.

I switched it on and shone it down the back of the radiator. Yes. There was definitely something there. A small object, wedged between the radiator and the wall.

Kneeling, I groped for it in the gap. My fingertips brushed spiders' webs, but I couldn't quite grab it. Reaching even further, I at last managed to dislodge it and pull it out. I climbed back into the window seat to examine what I'd found.

It was a slim book, grimy with dust. The cover bore a sticker saying *Keep Out*. Just inside were the initials L. G.

CHAPTER 10

I spent Sunday morning trying—and failing—to engineer a moment alone with Adam, so that I could show him what I'd found. I'd barely slept, tossing and turning while a mixture of worry and excitement churned inside me.

There might be no link between Lydia's disappearance and what had happened to Jess, but this was my first real progress in solving the mystery. A quick flick through was all it took to convince me that the little book was Lydia's, and I couldn't wait to discuss it with Adam and see what he thought.

I spotted him shortly before lunch, as I rushed towards the kitchen for my first stint helping Mrs Craddock. He stood alone by Acorn's awards cabinet, absorbed in the display. The droop of his shoulders and general air of gloom were clear signs he'd had no news of Jess.

As I opened my mouth, Faruzi and Amy appeared, as if from nowhere, halfway between us. They didn't say anything, but from their steady glances, I felt sure they knew I wasn't supposed to be alone with Adam. I sensed another thing too—that they wouldn't hesitate to tell Verena, if I broke the rule.

Reluctantly, I sped past. Adam turned and saw me, and a tense, panicky look flitted across his face. I felt sure he'd call out, but, saying nothing, he returned his attention to the cabinet. With a sinking heart, I realised he'd been given the same warning as I had, and that he wasn't prepared to go against it.

I continued towards the kitchen, my eyes blurry. Part of me thought it was ridiculous. I could speak to anyone I wanted to, and so could Adam. Verena Blake was a head teacher, that was all. What was the worst she could do? Another part of me, a bigger part, didn't want to risk finding out.

Kitchen duty was straightforward enough. Mrs Craddock didn't utter a word, other than to issue surly instructions, which suited me just fine. As I washed dishes and prepared carrots and potatoes for the evening meal, I seethed with annoyance that Adam had given in so easily.

Mrs Craddock set a cheese and tomato sandwich beside me. "When you've eaten that, go through to the dining hall and collect the plates."

"Sure." I kept my voice perky. I wasn't giving her the satisfaction of seeing how miserable I was.

Ten or so students were still having lunch in the dining hall, including Adam, who sat alone at the far end of the room, picking at some pasta.

I weaved between the tables, listening out for anything of interest, but the conversations going on around me seemed more subdued than ever.

Need to work harder on my geography.

We could take turns to test each other on the periodic table.

Moderation and restraint. Those are the key words for being a good citizen.

I sighed. There was nothing wrong with students taking their studies seriously, I got that. But couldn't they give it a rest now and then? It was the weekend, for goodness' sake. No one laughed, no one so much as commented on a film or a book, unless it was a documentary or a textbook.

Even Peter was at it, the student who'd started at Acorn alongside Adam, Jess and me. Head lowered and hands in his lap, he sat quietly next to Faruzi. They were discussing what a great teacher Verena was, though in fact I had yet to see her take one class.

As I got nearer to Adam, a chill ran through me. The students had stopped murmuring and, faces blank, had turned in our direction. Adam glanced at me briefly, then looked away. I was too upset to even say *hi*. Instead, fighting back tears, I grabbed his plate, almost knocking it to the floor. All around me, the students resumed their conversations.

As I made to pass Adam's table, however, I felt his hand brush the pocket of my apron. When I looked down, a corner of paper peeped above the nylon edge. Hiding my surprise, I wriggled quickly to make it slip out of view.

***

Half an hour later, back in my room, I unfolded the note.

Meet me on the beach, behind the rocks, left-hand side. Eight o'clock.

***

Time had never passed so slowly. All afternoon, as I worked on a geography assignment in the library, I kept glancing out at the courtyard, hoping to see Jess arrive, but there was no sign of her. Later, I endured another stint in the kitchen, helping Mrs Craddock clear up after dinner. At last, at ten to eight, I slipped up to my room. I fetched the little journal from its hiding place behind the radiator and squeezed it into my jacket pocket. Grabbing my keyring torch, I headed downstairs.

I rushed past the portrait of Violet Tresawle, taking the steps two at a time. I felt lightheaded and fluttery, both about seeing Adam and hearing what he had to say.

Few students were around, but as I passed Verena's office, the door opened and she materialised in front of me. I stopped dead.

"Hello, Holly. How are you enjoying your kitchen duty?" Her tone was light, and she was as calm and immaculate as ever.

"It's fun," I said, trying to sound cheerful. That might annoy her a little, at least. Her gaze travelled down over my jacket. I pulled my hand out of my pocket, where it had been resting on the journal. I had a horrible feeling Verena might guess what was there, although I knew there was no way she could.

"I really enjoy cooking," I added.

"How fortuitous for you. We shall have to double up your duties there. Other students will be delighted to have you cover for them, I'm sure."

Don't rise to the bait. "I haven't seen Jess anywhere," I said coolly. "What time is she due back?"

Verena retreated into her office. "Come inside a moment."

Puzzled, I followed her, leaving the door open behind me. She stood with one hand on her desk.

"Shut the door," she commanded.

My unease growing, I did as she asked, standing just inside the room. The office was stifling as usual. Verena remained silent, her gaze on a Chinese rug at her feet.

"What's wrong?" I asked.

Verena didn't reply.

"It's Jess, isn't it," I said, more a statement than a question. "She isn't coming back today."

"No. The doctors have decided to keep her in for another night, just to be on the safe side."

"But she's okay, right? Can Adam and I—um, I mean, can I see her?" I stopped short, annoyed with myself for mentioning his name.

"Seeing you would be disruptive," said Verena.

I opened my mouth, then shut it again. If I spoke without thinking, as I did all too often, I'd be sure to make matters worse.

Verena continued, "I've been to check on her myself, this morning."

"You have? How was she?"

"The doctors have decided she needs to be alone."

"Oh. Right." Tears pricked my eyes. Poor Jess. She'd be so unhappy, separated from her brother like this.

"Did she give you any message for me ... or anyone else?"

"No. She did not."

Dismissed from her office, I paused in the lobby, pretending to scan the notice board. When no one was in sight, I hurried out of the front entrance. Keeping to the shadows by the walls, I crept along the sides of the building, bolted across the lawn and ducked onto the steps leading to the beach. A light rain was falling, making the stone slippery, but I didn't dare use my torch, not yet, so I gripped the rail, barely able to see my feet. At the bottom, I had a moment of panic. What had Adam meant by left-hand side? Left as you approached, or left if you stood with your back to the sea? I was hopeless with directions.

Undecided, I peered into the moonlit darkness. Left as you approached, surely. I shook my head, irritated. Anxiety was making me complicate things.

To my relief, I spotted Adam's tall figure among the rocks. His collar was up against the wind, his face a pale oval. When he saw me, he pressed a finger to his lips, turned, and hurried away along the beach. Silently, I trotted after him.

After a good five minutes, he stopped outside a ramshackle shed, close to a low cave at the base of the cliff. He opened the door and I followed him inside.

"Phew," he said, pulling the door shut behind us. "What a horrible, horrible day."

"You're not kidding. D'you think it's safe to talk?" I glanced around. "What is this place?"

His teeth flashed in a smile, lit by the dim light trickling through the murky windows. "It's an old boathouse. Look."

He gestured to where an oblong shape lurked in the shadows. I switched on my torch and saw a small rowing boat, wreathed in cobwebs. It must have been a hundred years old, the peeling blue paint giving it the look of a faded map. I squinted to read the name inscribed in fancy script on the side.

"Her name's *Louise*," said Adam as we crossed for a closer look. "Nice, isn't she? Dad used to take us rowing at weekends."

I remembered the photo at Jess's bedside, the family with glossy dark hair and identical smiles. Absent-mindedly, he ran his hands along the boat, brushing away the cobwebs.

He screamed, leapt backwards and waved his arm frantically in the air.

"Something landed on me!" he yelled, his eyes round and staring.

Shining my torch, I spotted a gigantic spider with thick black legs scuttling along his sleeve.

"It's still there," he cried. "Do something, Holly!"

I stifled a grin. "Don't panic. Keep still."

Adam stopped hopping while I located the culprit, cupped it in my hands and let it free outside the boathouse door. Adam watched, eyes wide, until the spider was safely out of sight.

"Um, thanks," he said, letting out a breath.

"No problem. They're more scared of us than we are of them, that's what my mum always says. Or rather *said*." A sense of loss rolled over me as I pictured Mum's face. It seemed such a long time since I'd seen her. "Oh, Adam, what're we going to do?"

"Well, after Verena told me we were banned from spending time alone, I immediately went off looking for a private place where we could meet. That's if you want to. I mean, it's still a risk. We'll be missed if we stay here for long."

I grinned. I'd been wrong about Adam. He wasn't giving in without a fight, after all.

"It's a good place," I agreed. "I doubt anyone comes here. But what the hell is Verena playing at, telling us not to talk to each other? Who does she think she is?"

"Dunno."

I clenched my fists. "She's inhuman—it's like something's missing. She told me about Jess, by the way. They're keeping her in for another night, right?"

Adam ran a hand through his hair. It was lank and untidy, as though he hadn't slept in days. He nodded a fraction and tilted his chin towards the ceiling, which was dripping with condensation.

"She said there were 'complications', but not to worry."

If we were talking about anyone other than Verena Blake, I'd have told him he could trust her to do what was best. What I felt was exactly the opposite.

"She didn't mention any complications to me," I told him. "She's not taking you to visit, either?"

He paced the boathouse floor, his voice rising. "No. Says there's no point, the doctors wouldn't let me see her. But why does Jess need to be alone if there's nothing really wrong?"

I tried to think of something comforting to say, but drew a blank. I felt torn between trying to put Adam's mind at rest and confronting my own fear.

"How about the hospital? Did you get hold of them?"

He shook his head. "I tried the number Verena gave me, but it just rings and rings. She still won't tell me where Jess is, just ignores me when I ask."

I didn't like the sound of that, not one bit. "You'll have to keep trying. It must be the right number. Even Verena wouldn't lie about that. Why would she?" I turned aside so he couldn't see my face. I was beginning to think her capable of anything.

"Anyway," I added. "Take a look at this." I pulled the journal from my pocket.

"What is it?" He took a step towards me.

"I found it. Last night, hidden behind my radiator. It's a diary. I can't be sure, but I think it's Lydia's."

"Really? Hang on." Adam fetched a couple of crates

and placed them side by side so we could sit. He rested the book on his lap and I shone my torch while he opened the journal.

"What makes you think it's hers?" His foot was tapping, making the book jiggle up and down.

I pointed. "Those initials, for a start. L. G."

"That's a bit lame. L. G. could be anyone."

I remembered the marks on the wall beside my bed, like the gouge marks of little fingers. "I reckon she used to have my room."

He shrugged. "Okay. I'm not convinced, but let's assume you're right."

"Let's do that. Keep your foot still, Adam."

"Sorry. Nervous habit. Have you read it yet?"

"I had a quick flick through, last night, but it's hard-going. Her handwriting's terrible, even worse than mine. I can't make out all the words. But listen to this bit."

I found a page near the start. "*I'm so grateful to Miss Blake. It's so good of her to take me in. Who would have believed I'd be at a school like Acorn? I've never had a chance like this, and I plan to make the most of it.* You see? Lydia loved it here. So why did Verena tell me she was a disappointment?"

"Hmm."

"Hmm what?"

"Well, all Acorn students love it here. You *might* have noticed?"

"As far as I can tell, the only thing they love is Verena."

"Not sure about *love*," he said. "It's more like some sort of blind hero-worship."

I sighed. "You're not wrong. By the way, have you seen much of Peter?"

"Why?"

"Nothing definite. I saw him at lunchtime, when I was on kitchen duty. He seemed, I don't know, serious. You don't think …"

"You're worried something will happen to him, too?"

I shrugged. "Well … Even before she got ill, Jess changed. You saw it yourself. She started to become more like the others. Nothing's happened to us, so far. But what about Peter?"

"I haven't seen much of him lately. He's been working all the time. D'you think I should talk to him?"

"No. He might tell Verena we're suspicious."

"Yeah, okay. I'll keep an eye on him, then."

We glanced through a few more pages, reading parts at random. The early entries were dated around a year before, and most of them concerned everyday things, reminders about homework and comments about bands and celebrities.

"That's odd in itself," I said. "The other students never mention famous people or anything, do they? It's like they're not interested."

Adam shrugged. "Good for them. Neither am I. Celebrities are over-rated."

"Except for musicians," I said sweetly.

"That goes without saying. Look, this is interesting. *Three a.m. Still don't feel too good.*"

We both went to turn the page at once. I pulled back quickly as our hands touched.

Adam cleared his throat, then read out the entry. "*Don't feel good today. I was dizzy and tired, and couldn't get to my lessons. When Mrs Craddock brought up my lunch, I was sick. But the scary thing was, when she bent over me, she changed. It was like in a horror film. Half her face looked like a devil's face, with one normal eye plus a horrible staring one. Her tongue was poking out, all black and sticky, like it had been cut in half.*"

He turned away, his eyes downcast. I remembered Jess's nightmare, the morning she was taken ill. Her terror on the beach, as though she could see something we couldn't.

"Everyone says Lydia left Acorn of her own accord," I said.

"You don't fool me, Holly. You think whatever happened to Lydia, the same thing happened to Jess." He looked me directly in the eyes. "I know you do. Oh God."

I hated hearing the pain in his voice. That was exactly what I did think.

Holding the torch in one hand, I turned a few more pages. "Look, here's a mention of Carole. *Carole Bishop is going to help with my citizenship homework. Miss Blake wasn't happy with my test result.*"

"So Carole definitely knew her, then," I said, remembering how vague she'd been when I questioned her.

"You're sure it's the same Carole? I hardly know anyone's surname round here."

"I've seen it on the noticeboard. It's definitely her. Which makes it all the more puzzling that she couldn't, or wouldn't, tell us much about Lydia."

"Listen to this," said Adam. "*I went to see Miss Blake but she wasn't there, and Mrs Craddock sent me away. I want to go to the village to speak to Auntie Jeannie, but I don't feel well enough to go.*"

I looked at him. "Lydia's got an auntie in the village? I guess she means in Tredethy?"

"What's it say at the end?" Adam flicked through the pages. About three-quarters through the journal, we found the final entry.

I don't feel well today. If anything, it's worse than yesterday. I wish they'd let me see a doctor, a proper one, but they keep telling me nothing's wrong. I wish there was someone who cared.

After that, the pages were blank.

We sat for a while in silence. The final entry, followed by the blank pages, was the most ominous thing of all. I was more convinced than ever that something was wrong at Acorn, that Jess was in danger.

Adam lifted his gaze to mine. "What do we do, Holl?"

I didn't hesitate. "We find Aunt Jeannie."

CHAPTER 11

ON my way down to breakfast the next morning, I paused at the top of the staircase as voices reached me from the floor below. Adam and Verena stood by the banister, partly turned away. Verena seemed to be frowning at Adam, her face stern, while Adam stared down at his feet. I backed out of view, straining to hear their words, my chest tightening as I imagined the worst.

"I'm sorry, Adam. I'll be sure to tell you any news, as soon as I hear anything."

I shut my eyes for a moment. It was bad, for sure. But it sounded like Jess was alive, at least.

Adam looked up at her, his gaze defiant. "Why can't I—"

"I'm not telling you again." She strode off towards her office.

I waited until she'd gone. Adam's arms hung limply by his side, and he looked more tired than ever, his face scrunched up, eyes half closed. With a small cough, I stepped out of the shadows and walked down the stairs.

When he saw me, he glanced around and touched a finger to his lips. In silent agreement, we fled along the corridor, away from the dining hall, into a small, empty room. He pulled the door quietly shut.

"She's not coming back today," he told me, a tremble in his voice.

Nor tomorrow, nor the next day. "And they won't let you see her, right?"

He shrugged.

"So you'll come to Tredethy with me, try to track down Aunt Jeannie?"

Adam frowned. "I don't know. Maybe we should stay here, in case Jess gets back. I'd hate her to come back and find me missing."

I sighed, trying not to roll my eyes. "And if she doesn't, we've lost another day, dragging our feet when we could be finding out what's going on."

He thought for a moment. "We'd have to get to the village without anyone seeing us. And this place is like Big Brother. You know, eyes and ears everywhere."

"Thanks, I do know what Big Brother means."

"Okay, okay. I guess we could walk to Tredethy along the cliff path, tonight, but it would be dangerous in the dark, and if we go along the beach instead, we could get cut off by the tide. If we go during the day, there's a bigger risk we'll get caught."

"If, if, if! Nobody said it would be easy." I'd been thinking about it all night. I crept to the door and glanced through the small window. No one was around, the hallway outside deserted.

Back at Adam's side I whispered, "I've got a plan."

He peered at me. "Well?"

"The Viking—you know, George Kellow, the handyman."

"What about him?"

"I don't trust him, so I've been keeping tabs on him. His hours are a bit random, but when he's in, he normally leaves when it starts to get dark. He's got that decrepit old van. Seen it?"

"What's your point? Spit it out."

"The point is, he lives in Tredethy. He told us, that night on the beach."

Adam stared. "You can't mean … He'd never agree to take us."

"Don't be an idiot. I know that. But we could hide in the van. He parks it round the side of the school, out of view of the classrooms and Verena's office. We'd be in the village in minutes, surely. It would cut the amount of time we're gone, and better still, no one would see us leave. We can walk back here along the road. It'll be dark by then. I doubt anyone will spot us." I smiled, proud of myself.

Adam's eyes glimmered with a trace of hope, then he shook his head and sighed. "Holly, you're crazy."

"What?" I opened my mouth to argue. Then, remembering he was my only ally, I took a deep breath and pressed my lips together.

Adam glanced around the room, avoiding my eyes. "Oh, I don't know. I agree, everything seems wrong. But it's too unreal. Look at it another way. Maybe Lydia had a vivid imagination, and tended to get ill a lot. Some people do. The other students don't remember her because they never got to know her well. And this thing with Jess—well, it's a coincidence. In a day or two, she'll be back with us, right as rain."

I couldn't believe what I was hearing. He must be kidding himself, trying not to think the worst. "But last night—"

An icy feeling stole through me. I stopped talking and searched his eyes, terrified they'd be vague and glassy, like those of the other students.

He blinked. His eyes had bags under them, but other than that, they were the same soft brown. Weren't they?

"Why are you looking at me like that?" he asked.

"No reason."

He folded his arms. "You've got one of those faces, Holly. You can't hide things. Tell me."

"It's just … You sounded like them."

A smile pulled at his lips. "Don't be daft. And here I was thinking you found me so irresistible, you couldn't stop looking at me."

"As if!" My cheeks were going red. "Adam, it's not a joke. You're talking as though you trust Verena."

"You're wrong. But she's the head teacher of a respected school. I'm only trying to see it from all sides. Could it be that we've let our imaginations run away with us? Just a bit?"

I glared, hands on hips. "I can't believe you sometimes. What about the students, the weird way they behave? How much more proof d'you need? We've got to solve this, Adam. What on earth's the matter with you?" My voice was rising higher.

Maybe Adam had decided to trust Verena because he couldn't face the alternative, but instead of sympathy, all I felt was outrage. I looked away, struggling to stay calm. "Well, if we find Aunt Jeannie, we'll know, won't we? Lydia might even be with her, and we can laugh about *my* silly suspicions."

"Shhh! They'll hear us." He looked towards the door, his mouth set in a stubborn line.

I shrugged. "Well, I'm going anyway. I'm not scared. I'll go on my own."

"Suit yourself."

"Fine!"

***

I thought the day would never end. We had double history with Mr Foreman in the morning, who kept nervously repeating what he'd already told us, then yet another citizenship lesson in the afternoon with horse-faced Miss Mallett, who set us to work listing the prime ministers of England for the past two million years.

Sitting quietly at the back, I gazed out of the window, praying that a taxi might pull up, or an ambulance, and that Jess would climb out of it. I knew it wasn't going to happen.

Was Adam right? Could I be imagining things? I glanced around the room, thinking about the classes at my old school. People giggling and chatting, girls whispering about boys, and vice versa.

Here, the only sound was the ticking of the antique clock in the corner. Miss Mallett sat bolt upright at her desk, sipping quietly from an Acorn mug, and the other students worked alone, dull-eyed, showing no interest in one another. They were all so polite, well-behaved and respectful, it was hard to tell them apart.

No, I was right to be worried. But would I really have the nerve to stow away in the Viking's van?

He didn't work at Acorn every day, and I almost hoped he wouldn't appear, which would give me a cast-iron reason for chickening out. Then, at three o'clock, I spotted him beyond the courtyard, repairing the fence that divided the lawns from the cliff path.

Maybe my plan was stupid, like Adam seemed to think, but I'd never forgive myself if I didn't at least try. I would go today, before my courage drained away.

At four o'clock, as we trooped out of the lesson, I remembered an annoying snag. Kitchen duty!

I'd been so wrapped up in my worries, I'd completely forgotten I was due to help Mrs Craddock in an hour. No way could I get to the village and back before then.

There was no time to think it through. Uttering a dramatic sigh, I slid to the floor. "Ooh, help me, someone."

Further along the corridor, Carole glanced over her shoulder. Her face puckered into a frown as she retraced her steps.

"What is wrong?"

"I felt a bit dizzy." Sitting up, I noticed everyone

else had carried on walking. If I'd really been ill, no one would have cared.

Carole hesitated, then turned away. "I'll fetch Miss Blake."

"No, wait. I'm fine, Carole. I'm just *so* tired." I gave a huge yawn, stretching my arms. "Maybe I'm coming down with something. Could you do me a big favour? Cover my kitchen duty so I can have a rest? I'll do the same for you, whenever you like. Promise."

I made a show of struggling to stand up, and Carole took my arm and helped me to my feet. Letting one leg go limp, I leaned back against the wall and fanned myself.

Carole stood watching me. "You don't look tired."

"Well, I am. And I feel faint."

As she peered at me, I flinched from her glassy gaze. The neat bob framing her face was so perfect, I felt a weird urge to stretch out a hand and mess it up.

"You look pale," she admitted.

I sighed again and huffed. "Will you help or not?"

Her face expressionless, she turned and walked away. "All right, I'll see to it."

***

Up in my room, I threw on jeans and a hoodie, then sat in the window seat, watching through the iron bars. I'd been too nervous to eat much at lunchtime, and now I was starving. An hour passed, maybe more. I was desperate to move, but didn't dare leave my spot. Inky clouds crept across the sky. It looked like it might rain.

The Viking took no notice. Instead, absorbed in his work, he progressed slowly along the fence, showing no sign of leaving. Just my luck he was so dedicated! My stomach felt hollow, yet there was no way I could risk going down to grab something. I'd be sure to miss him leave.

When it started to get dark, I could stand it no longer. I slipped downstairs and crept across the courtyard, praying I wouldn't bump into Carole or Mrs Craddock. I glanced into the distance, to where the Viking had been. Yes, he was still working, but the fence looked good as new. After hammering in a nail, he began gathering his tools together. It was now or never.

While he faced the sea, I sidled past him and around the corner, keeping close to the wall of Tresawle House. I passed a classroom window and stopped by the back of Kellow's scruffy van. It was parked close to the walls, out of anyone's view. If I hurried, I could slip inside without being seen. Provided it wasn't locked, of course.

Praying it wasn't, I turned the handle and pulled.

The door opened onto a dark interior, stinking of grease and petrol. What if the Viking saw me when he threw in his tools? As my eyes adjusted, I made out a large shape, like a grubby tarpaulin, towards the back.

Hopping up over the tow bar, I scrambled inside. I pulled the door shut behind me and crawled towards the tarpaulin, wincing as discarded cans and sharp objects bit into my knees.

I grabbed the tarpaulin.

"Hey!" said a familiar voice.

My heart almost stopped. Someone was already in the van, right in front of me.

"Adam? Is that you?"

"Who d'you think it is?" said the voice.

I could just about see him, a pale moon-shape peering at me from beneath the tarpaulin.

Relief washed over me. "You changed your mind."

"Seems I did. Shh! He's coming."

Footsteps approached the back of the van. Then, to my horror, I heard voices. Kellow had someone with him. I knew who it was, too. I would know those silky tones anywhere.

A second before the back door opened, I wriggled beneath the tarpaulin and pulled it up over our heads. Tools and other DIY stuff dug into me, not to mention Adam's knees, but there was no time to make myself more comfortable. Adam's head was so close I could feel his breath on my cheek. A hint of spearmint mingled with the smell of grime.

"You've taken care of everything?" asked Verena, outside.

"Yep." Something large thudded into the van, landing near Adam. I felt him twitch, but he didn't cry out.

"Come and see me tomorrow morning. I want you to clear the basement for more storage space."

"Sure, no probs, Miss Blake. See ya."

Verena stalked away over the gravel. I held my breath, waiting for Kellow to close the door. Instead, there was an endless pause, and I imagined his eyes lingering on the space where we lay. My skin prickled and it took every ounce of willpower I possessed to stay still. I shut my eyes, as if that would somehow stop him seeing me. After what seemed like ages, he slammed the door and strode around to the driver's side.

He got into the front seat and started the engine. The van left Acorn Academy behind and rattled along country roads, the lurching making me nauseous. As he drove, Kellow sang along at full volume to a Bon Jovi song blasting from the radio.

After a few minutes, he slowed and turned off the road. I heard the gears crunch into reverse, followed by a beep as the van edged backwards. So far, so good. As long as Kellow didn't need anything from his van, we'd done it.

Our luck was in. The driver's door opened and closed. The Viking's footsteps receded. Seconds passed, then another door banged, some way distant. I waited a moment, then threw off the tarpaulin and shook the dust from my hair.

"Phew," I said, letting out a breath of stale air.

"Okay?" Adam's teeth shone in a grin.

As I tried to get up, my hand sank into something damp and squidgy, a teabag perhaps, or a half-eaten sandwich, there was no way of telling in the gloom.

"Ugggh!"

"Quiet!" Adam groped for the inside handle,

released the catch and eased the door open. It banged against a hard surface. I cringed as the noise reverberated.

Adam cursed. "We're parked right up against a wall."

I waited while, breathing heavily, he squeezed himself through the narrow gap. Only then did it cross my mind that we might find ourselves trapped inside a garage. As I poked my head outside, sharp, icy rain told me otherwise.

I wriggled between the half-open door and the wall of a house. We slipped along the drive, joined the road and stopped for a moment on the granite bridge. Wind howled through the trees and rain lashed my face, slicing the air in every direction.

"We're by the quay," I said, peering through the darkness towards the beach where Jess had been taken ill. Glancing back the way we'd come, I noticed that the Viking's place was the end cottage of a row of three, near the river. As I watched, a light came on in the upstairs window.

Adam set off up the hill. "C'mon. Better hurry."

"Hey, you're limping." I raced to catch him up.

"Yeah, not sure what he threw at me, a hammer I think, but it landed right on my effing knee. I don't know what was worse, that or his singing."

"Ouch … So what made you change your mind?"

"It's that phone number," he muttered, barely audible against the roar of the river. "The one Verena gave me for the hospital."

"You still can't get anyone to pick up? That doesn't make sense."

"Exactly. So I looked up the numbers of all the local hospitals, and the number she gave me doesn't match any of them."

"She deliberately gave you a wrong number?" I couldn't quite believe it, even of Verena.

"She must have. What other explanation is there?"

I stomped along the road, my footsteps quickening with anger. "What a *bitch*!"

"It gets worse. I phoned every hospital I found, right up as far as Devon. None of them have heard of Jess. *She's just not there.*"

CHAPTER 12

As we struggled up the rain-soaked road, I remained silent, shocked by Adam's words. So Verena had lied about the hospital. But why? And if Jess wasn't at any hospital, where the hell was she?

"Did you ring anyone else?" I asked, thinking he might have tried his uncle in Scotland, or even the police.

"My phone went flat. I've left it plugged in. I plan to, though, soon as I get back."

"Good." *About time.*

"Where shall we start?" He flashed me a smile. "I hope you've got another cunning plan, Holl."

"I have, as it happens. Let's try the shop, the one we saw last time. Maybe someone in there will know who Aunt Jeannie is, and where she lives."

"Good thinking. Um, I'm sorry, by the way. You've been right all along."

"Oh well. I so wish I wasn't."

***

The shop was bright and welcoming after the wind and

rain outside, with several customers milling around. I scanned them nervously, anxious I might see someone who recognised us, one of Acorn's part-time staff perhaps.

"Aren't you hungry?" I whispered as my stomach rumbled again. Adam shook his head, making for the counter. There was no sign of the delicious-smelling Cornish pasties I'd seen before, so with no time to lose, I grabbed the first things that came to hand. Peanuts, plus a packet of noodles I might be able to make up later with some hot water from the kitchen.

No one was waiting at the till, but as I fished in my pocket for some change, a queue formed miraculously behind me.

The man behind the counter was tall and broad-shouldered, with a curling black beard and a ruddy face. "That'll be one pound ninety-nine, please, Miss," he said, his voice laced with a Midlands accent.

I handed him some coins. "Thanks. By the way, I wonder if you can help. We're looking for a—a friend. Her name's Jeannie." I was uncomfortably aware of several sets of eyes boring into my back. "Sorry to hold everyone up," I mumbled, glancing round.

The shopkeeper frowned, his gaze flitting past me towards the waiting customers. "Can you give me a surname?"

"Um, no," I admitted.

"Hmm. I've been here a year or two. Know most people. But, no. Don't think so. Now, if you'll excuse me…"

I tried to think of something else to ask, but a double-chinned woman slammed a range of chocolate bars onto the counter, elbowing me out of the way. Adam and I trooped towards the exit.

As the door swished open, the shopkeeper called after us. "Wait, I've just thought of someone. There's a woman who comes in from time to time. Lives on the caravan site, about a mile up the hill. I think her name's Jeannie."

"How do we find it?" asked Adam.

"Take the first left off the main road out of Tredethy. It's mostly holiday places there."

The woman with the chins began bending his ear, and he turned back to his task.

***

"This must be it," Adam said fifteen minutes later, stopping next to a shadowed lane. We gazed up at the little sign hanging from a tree bough, which creaked to and fro in the wind. "Sunnyview Park."

"Nice sense of irony," I said, shivering as the rain dripped down my neck and slid beneath my shirt. It seemed a desolate place. Throughout our walk up the unlit, single-track road, sandwiched between two hedgerows, not a single vehicle had passed.

Adam waited a moment, as though no keener than me to enter the tunnel-like lane. "She may not be here, if it's a holiday place. Or she might be the wrong Jeannie, anyway."

"Let's get on with it," I said. "We're going to be sooo late back."

Adam shrugged, as if he no longer cared what trouble we got into.

We tiptoed carefully across a slippery cattle grid and were immersed in a darkness so complete it felt like we were descending below ground. The lane was flanked by dense hedges, trees arching overhead. There was a smell of decaying leaves, and little rustlings as animals scooted past. Spider webs brushed my face, and I yelped as a tiny shape flew past my ear, a bat, maybe.

"You can hold on to me if you like," Adam said. "Not that I'm … I can't see a thing myself."

I took his arm, grateful for the extra balance on the slippery track. I was glad he couldn't hear my heart, which began thumping against my rib cage.

The lane petered out and we turned right, through a gateway. Scattered lamps revealed a field lined with caravans. Most were in darkness, with lights in only two or three. An owl hooted.

"How on earth will we find her?" I whispered.

Before he could reply, a woman emerged from a nearby shower block. She wore blue overalls and carried a mop and bucket.

"Excuse me," I called.

She looked startled. "Yes?"

"We're looking for Jeannie. Which caravan is she in? We're, um, relatives of hers."

The woman squinted. "Relatives? That's nice. She doesn't get many visitors." After a pause, she pointed to a grey oblong on its own in a far corner of the field. "She's in that one."

"Thanks." We set off across the field, our footsteps squelching in wet grass.

"We've found her, then," I whispered. "Sounds like she lives here all year round."

"Don't get too excited. I agree Jeannie's not a common name, but it's not rare, either. Like I said, she might be someone else altogether."

"Spoilsport."

Unlike many of the other caravans, the grey one had no garden ornaments or cheery curtains at the windows. A dim light came from inside, suggesting she was at home. The hairs rose on the back of my neck. Any moment now, we might find out what had happened to Lydia.

"Here goes, then." I reached for the bell.

The door opened a crack and a slice of round face peered out at us. "Who are you?"

Even standing back from the door, the fumes on her breath almost knocked me over.

"We're friends of Lydia's," I told her.

She stared at us, motionless, then opened the door wide and swept us inside. Adam raised his eyebrows at me. We clearly had the right woman. What was more, as light revealed the rest of her haggard face, I had the weirdest sensation I already knew her from somewhere.

"Sit down." She gestured towards the built-in sofa beneath the bay windows.

While we took our seats, she lumbered over to an

armchair, waving a cigarette in nicotine-stained fingers. The stuffy room reeked of cat litter, smoke and damp washing. At Jeannie's side, on a small table, was a nearly empty vodka bottle next to a plate of bread crusts and congealed brown sauce.

She took a puff from her cigarette and blew smoke in our direction. "You're from that school, are you? Acorn."

I wondered how she knew. "Yes. We started this term."

Adam shot me a look. *Damn.* I'd forgotten that, if we really were friends of Lydia's, we would have started before then.

Luckily, Jeannie didn't seem to notice. Instead, she jerked forward, eyes gleaming. "You've got news? Something to help me find her?"

Adam and I glanced at one another. Up until now I'd held out some hope Lydia would turn up alive and well, working in a nearby town or studying at some college. Now I knew that wasn't going to happen.

Jeannie pulled a ragged tissue from her pocket, wiped her brow and blew her nose. She looked about to burst into tears.

"They don't tell me anything up there," she said. "Won't accept any responsibility. Said Lydia wasn't fitting in very well and had gone off the rails. She'd been caught drinking and *frat-er-nising* with boys. They told the papers she'd been seen on the cliffs, walking alone."

A black cat with matted fur jumped on Adam's knee

and dug its claws into his jeans.

"That's Biggsy," Jeannie said with a nod. "Play nice, Biggs."

Adam smiled feebly. "Did Lydia get ill?"

Jeannie looked puzzled. "Ill? Dunno anything about that. She just vanished. Right before Christmas it was. Ruined Christmas for me, it did."

"Was there an investigation?" I asked.

She looked at me like I was an idiot. "Of course there was an investigation, but they didn't find anything. That snooty madam up there—Verena Blake—told everyone it was Lydia's choice. Said she'd gone off upcountry with some boy or other from the village. But it can't be true, 'cos there's no one else missing from around here, no one she could have gone off with."

"Have you got a photo of her?" asked Adam.

She eyed him suspiciously. "I thought you were friends of hers. Why d'you need a photo?"

Adam and I just sat there. As Jeannie continued to stare, I suddenly realised where I knew her from. She was the blonde woman I'd seen from my bedroom window, the first day I'd arrived at Acorn. The one Mr Craddock had led away. So that's what she'd been doing there—searching for Lydia.

"Well?" Jeannie asked.

I sighed. "All right. We're not friends, exactly. But we heard about Lydia's disappearance. We wanted to help."

"Oh." Her eyes narrowed to slits, as though she

didn't believe us. Why would strangers want to help? Then she shrugged. "Well, doesn't matter. P'raps you'll have more success than me." She lapsed into silence, staring off into the distance.

"So," said Adam. "Do you have a photo, then?"

"No," she said sadly. "Hang on, wait! I do have one." She stood carefully, putting out a hand to steady herself, and crossed to a nearby drawer. After some rummaging, she pulled out a crumpled scrap of newspaper.

"That's her." She handed me the clipping and I held it out so Adam could see. The black cat had curled up on his lap and was purring away like a rusty engine.

The photo showed a round-faced girl with long fair hair and a sweet smile. Below it was a newspaper report about the disappearance of thirteen-year-old schoolgirl Lydia Goddard. From the way it was written, the police clearly thought she had gone away of her own accord.

"It says all her stuff was missing from her room," I said. "Surely that backs up the idea that she went somewhere?"

"Maybe," Jeannie said, reaching for another cigarette from the little table beside her.

"It explains why the police think that way," said Adam.

Jeannie pursed her lips.

Adam's eyes widened as he read on. "Hey, what? It says there was a letter. From a boyfriend."

Jeannie shrugged. "Yeah, the police found it. I've got a copy. Would you like to see?"

"Thanks, that'd be great." Adam let out a quiet whistle. It seemed more and more likely Lydia had gone off with a boyfriend.

Jeannie returned to the same drawer, withdrew a second piece of paper and handed it to Adam. The short paragraph was neatly-written, the handwriting bold and angular.

Dear Lydia,

It won't be long before we're together again. You know what we arranged. Bring all your stuff. I'll be waiting for you. Tom

I didn't know what to say. As Jeannie busied herself pouring the remains of the vodka into her glass, Adam leaned in close and hissed in my ear.

"We're wasting our time. Mystery solved."

"Shh, she'll hear you."

Adam turned to Jeannie. "They're still looking for her then, the police?"

Jeannie dropped back into her chair. A second cat, short-haired with mackerel markings, jumped onto her lap and began licking one paw. She gave the cat an absent-minded stroke.

"I dunno. They don't tell me much. I did say I wasn't happy about it, but to be honest with you, I've never been one for getting too involved with that lot. Had a few run-ins with them in my time."

"But you're her auntie," I said. "The police would have to involve you, wouldn't they?"

"Aw, no, not her real auntie," Jeannie corrected. "She just called me that. I was her mum's friend, that's all, before her mum took poorly and died."

My eyes welled. Poor Lydia had no one she could really call her own, not even Aunt Jeannie. Then I reminded myself. Lydia did have someone—Tom, whoever he was.

Jeannie's eyes were barely visible in the puffy folds of her face. "I've followed it in the papers, as you can see. The police kept looking for a time, I know that. But, well, Verena Blake had them twisted round her little finger. She convinced them there was nothing to be done, no way of finding her, said it was Lydia's own doing, no reflection on the school that should have been looking after her." She leaned forward and took a large swig from her glass, squeezing the poor mackerel cat almost flat.

"Did you see much of her, before she vanished?" Adam asked.

Jeannie's eyes darted from side to side. "I didn't like to interfere. Lydia was busy with her own life. I went up a couple of times, took her some o' those puzzle magazines. She loved doing crosswords and suchlike." Jeannie was quiet for a moment, gazing through the window into the darkness. "She had it hard when her mum died. I'd have had her to live with me, honest I would, but … Well, Jase wasn't too keen."

Her gaze shifted to a gold-framed photo on a nearby shelf, crammed in among ornaments of cutesy cats wearing gaudy dresses. It showed her arm-in-arm with a skinny man with a drooping moustache, against the backdrop of a fair.

"He's cleared off now," she continued. "So perhaps I could've. But anyway, look around. 'Tisn't really suitable for a kid, is it? I can barely look after myself."

I glanced around at the damp-stained walls, the bottles edging the cluttered sink. It was hard to disagree.

She lapsed into silence, her eyes drifting shut as her head slipped towards her chest. Adam cleared his throat loudly.

Jeannie jolted, her eyes springing open. "Where was I?"

"Lydia had nowhere to live," I said.

"Yeah, poor little mite. I thought it was a Godsend when Miss Blake stepped in and took her into Acorn. You've heard talk, I suppose. Was it the sherbet, then, that sent her off the rails?"

"Sherbet?" Adam asked.

"You know, sherbet. The sauce. The smiling assassin." She tilted her glass.

"Oh," he said with a nod. He made another attempt to dislodge the cat which had taken such a shine to him. Biggsy arched his back, digging in his claws, then plonked himself down again. Knowing when he was beaten, Adam gave the cat a stroke.

"Just my theory," said Jeannie. "I did visit her, up at Acorn, not long before she vanished, but they only let me see her for five minutes. She didn't seem herself—all glassy-eyed and vague. Gave me the creeps, it did. Like there was no one inside." She tapped her head, then picked her way to her feet. "Well, you'd better be off."

Adam leapt up, sending Biggsy off with a miaow. Swaying a little, Jeannie showed us to the door.

"We used to hang round together, her mother and me," she murmured, words slurring. "She liked a tipple too, see. S'hard to stay out of its evil clutches, if you're born to it, like we both were. I hated me own dad for throwing away his life. Now look at me. It's all bread and potatoes."

"Bread and potatoes?" I asked.

"Yeah. You grind the grain, boil the potatoes, before you can digest 'em. That's how drinking is. Processing life, like, to make it bearable. Poor Lyddie was the same, I expect, like her mum. Had a bit too much of what wasn't good for her. Nice kid, too. Clever, in her way, with her poetry and her books. But not much common sense."

We stepped out into the rain. "Thank you for talking to us," I said, as though we were reporters or something. "If we do get any news, we'll be sure to let you know."

Jeannie didn't seem to hear, lost in her own thoughts. "There's no way she's upcountry somewhere, living it up with some lad. She was only thirteen, and young for her age, too. She fell off that cliff, I reckon, and was washed out to sea. Lydia's dead, I'm sure of it."

***

We made our way downhill, moving as fast as we could

in the dark. The rain had eased a little, but I was soaked through by now and shivered with every gust of wind.

"We can take the road by the Viking's cottage," said Adam, raindrops glistening on his face. "Looked to me like it follows the coast, parallel with the cliff path."

"Let's hope so, or we'll be completely lost." My head was fizzing. We'd found some answers, but they had thrown up a heap more questions.

"So what d'you reckon, then?" I asked.

"Seems clear-cut," Adam said with a shrug. "So clear-cut, I don't understand why Jeannie's so sure something different happened to Lydia. She met someone and went off with him. End of story."

"What, you believe that?" *How could he be so naïve?*

"You're not convinced, Miss Marple?"

"No, of course not. Who would she go with? She was only thirteen. And you heard Jeannie. No one else around here disappeared."

"Might not have been a boy from the village. She could have met him on a trip, a sports event or something."

I thought back, remembering the conversation I'd had with Verena on the quayside, before Jess was taken ill. "I agree, it might help to explain why Verena was so disappointed in Lydia. But … Oh, I don't know."

"You read the report in the paper. You saw the letter from whatshisname. *Tom.*"

I stopped. "Yes! That's it. The letter."

"What about it?"

"Didn't you find it a bit strange?"

"How so? I realise people don't often write letters to each other nowadays, but when you consider Verena's rules about phones—"

"It's more than that," I said. "Lydia's only thirteen, and she's arranged to elope with a boy. Wasn't that note kind of lame? *You know what we arranged. Bring all your stuff?*"

"Hmm. You'd expect the full Romeo and Juliet? *Mine heart will bleed until my lips alight on your rosebud lips,* that kind of thing?"

"Exactly. Hey, you've got hidden talents," I told him.

"Gee, thanks. But maybe Tom's not romantic. Just because Lydia liked poetry and all that, doesn't mean Tom did."

"No. Guess not."

"I see your point, though. If we were eloping, I wouldn't tell you to bring your stuff. I'd credit you with the sense to bring whatever you wanted."

There was an awkward silence while I imagined the crazy scenario of Adam and me eloping.

"That's right," I agreed. "Why tell her to bring her stuff?"

"It's the kind of note the police would need. To convince them she'd left of her own free will."

"Yeah," I said, speeding up, "and anyone can pack someone's suitcase and pretend they've gone. Come to that, why would Lydia leave the note behind anyway? Wouldn't she take it with her, or throw it away?"

We strode along for a while in silence.

"She doesn't mention any Tom in her diary," I said. "Lydia loved poetry and literature. If she was in love, don't you think she'd write about it?"

"Not if she wanted to keep it secret."

The glow from a streetlamp enveloped us as we reached the bridge near the Viking's cottage. His van stood outlined against the grey pallor of the night sky.

I grabbed Adam's jacket and pointed. "We'd better be careful. The last thing we want is to run into him."

I shrank back as a figure stepped into our path. *Speak of the devil.*

George Kellow peered into our faces. "Holly and Adam, isn't it? Shouldn't you be in school?"

CHAPTER 13

ADAM and I froze. One thing was for sure: we were in trouble. After a brief hesitation, we both spoke at once.

"We needed to get out," I said.

"We're on an errand," said Adam.

Since we were out of school uniform and it was dark, I was surprised the Viking had recognised us, even knowing us by name. Backlit by a pool of light from his cottage, he stood with his arms folded, as though he could see right through us.

"You'd better come with me," he said.

Adam and I sat squeezed into the front of his van, so close our knees were jammed together. The Viking drove in silence, while I combed my mind for something to explain why we were in the village.

Finally he said, "It's not my business, but you shouldn't be roaming around on your own like that in the dark."

I looked at Adam, but his anxious frown told me he hadn't come up with a proper excuse, either.

"How did you know we were here?" I asked. Had he been on the look-out for us? It would explain the way he'd been lurking in the shadows.

He kept his gaze on the road ahead. "Miss Blake rang me. Your absence was noted, shall we say. She asked me to help find you. What's your game, then? Secret date, eh?" His voice remained level.

Neither of us replied. Glancing aside, I noticed Adam's cheeks were as red as mine must be.

"Have you worked at Acorn long?" Adam asked.

"Nah, only started six weeks ago." He tossed his white hair back from his weather-beaten face.

"We heard there was a girl named Lydia at the school," Adam said. "Have you heard anything about her?"

I drew in a breath, shocked that he'd just come out and asked Kellow like that—someone I felt sure we couldn't trust.

The Viking's hands kept the wheel steady, but it seemed to me they tensed a little. "Why? What have *you* heard?"

I nudged my knee against Adam's, warning him to be careful.

"We heard she vanished," he said. "That she went away with a boyfriend."

"I heard a rumour," said Kellow, "but I don't know the details. Any news about your sister, Adam? Madam Craddock told me she was taken ill."

"No." He stared into his lap. "She's supposed to be coming home any day now."

Kellow turned the van into the gravel drive and pulled over beside Tresawle House. He'd rung ahead to let Verena know we were on our way, and my throat tightened as I spotted the welcoming committee.

Verena stood beneath the portico with her arms crossed, flanked by the Craddocks and Carole. All were staring at us, their faces blank.

The Viking turned off the engine and wound down his window. Adam and I got out of the van and trudged towards the group. I moved as slowly as I could, playing for time.

"Thank you, George," called Verena, a faint smile on her face. "It was kind of you to run our little escapees home."

"No harm done." He glanced in our direction. "All's well that ends well, eh?"

An irrational feeling ran through me, like I didn't want him to leave. Something about Verena's smile chilled me more than the icy rain seeping through my clothes. But Kellow had already re-started the engine.

"See ya tomorrow, then," he called as the van disappeared into the darkness. As one, Adam and I turned to Verena.

The faint smile had vanished, her mouth a thin, twisted line. "This is intolerable. I cannot have my students roaming at will in the countryside. Not to mention the tiny fact that you have been banned from spending time together."

Adam stood in front of her and folded his arms. "Where's Jess?"

"Is that what you've been doing? Looking for Jessica?"

"She's not at any hospital. I've rung them all.

Where's my sister?" His face was pale, his eyes dark and glittering, and he looked for all the world as if he'd like to thump her. I wouldn't have blamed him.

Mrs Craddock glared. "You should show more respect."

At a nod from Verena, Mr Craddock stepped to Adam's side, while Carole leaned forward and grasped my arm. I tried to shake her off, but her grip was firm, her fingers digging into me.

"Escort them to their rooms," Verena said.

"Why won't you take me to see her?" insisted Adam, his voice cracking. "She needs me! She won't understand why I'm not there."

"That's enough," said Verena. "The doctors know what she needs, not you. Come to my office tomorrow morning, both of you. Adam at eight o'clock, Holly at half past."

Inside Tresawle House, Verena waited by the banister while we climbed the staircase. As we passed the portrait of Violet Tresawle, I couldn't help glancing at it. Her eyes seemed even more scornful than usual.

***

I lay in bed, my mind spinning with a hundred horrible possibilities. At three o'clock, still wide awake, I got up and pulled Lydia's journal from my pocket, hoping it might take my mind off tomorrow's interview with Verena. I took it to the window seat and flicked through it by the light of my little torch, hoping to find something new that would help me track Lydia down. Every so often I glanced through the bars, checking no one was outside.

The diary contained lots of doodles I hadn't paid much attention to before, mostly cats and birds, and severe-looking faces with giant eyes. There was also a poem, towards the end.

I assumed she'd copied it out of a book, but when I looked again, I noticed something odd. While most of the entries in the journal were marred by Lydia's awful handwriting, the verse was incredibly neat, with flowery lettering, the words carefully spaced to make a perfect square. For the first time, I read the poem to the end.

V

If by chance you read my script
With a wave I will say hi
Win or lose my heart will skip
With the joy of beating time
On the earth I spend my years
Water runs through wood and sea
Crying ever happy tears
Smothering where others be
One who misses other fame
One who spoils another call
Even shocking all who came
Where the dove met V Tresawle

I wrinkled my brow and read it through twice more, but I couldn't make head or tail of it, and my brain ached from the effort. However, the mention of Violet Tresawle persuaded me Lydia had written the verse herself. First chance I got, I'd show it to Adam.

***

I considered trying to bump into him as he made his way to Verena's office at eight, or waiting for him outside the door, to catch him on his way out. But I suspected that would only land us in more trouble. Unable to face cleaning duty, let alone breakfast, I waited in my room, emerging only five minutes before the dreaded interview was due to take place.

I stood for a moment on the shadowed landing, thinking how quiet it was, as though no one lived here. Halfway down the stairs, I stopped again in front of Violet Tresawle's portrait. I'd never actually looked at it in detail before. It always made me too nervous, and I'd skipped past as quickly as I could.

She stood by a piano, proud and haughty in her violet gown. From the paintings behind her and some of the furniture, I recognised the room as the lounge at the foot of the stairs.

My gaze was drawn to the window on her right, at the back of the room. Partially-drawn curtains fluttered in a breeze, and though it was dark outside, shadows were visible. Layers in the mist appeared to show a ghostly figure peering in. The silhouette of a long-haired girl, perhaps, one arm half-raised.

A line from Lydia's verse came back to me: *With a*

wave I will say hi. Could this be where the dove met V Tresawle?

I shook my head and continued on my way. I was being daft, my imagination working overtime again. The rhyme didn't make any sense. Doves don't meet people. Lydia's poetry was tying my brain in knots.

No voices came from Verena's study, so I could only assume Adam had been and gone. Taking a breath, I knocked on the door and was buzzed inside.

Verena sat perfectly still behind her desk. "Sit there." She gestured to an antique chair.

I sat down and waited. For a while she said nothing, just watched me quietly while I fidgeted. I remembered my first impression of her, back in Kings Hollow, when she'd reminded me of a spider lurking at the side of its web. Nothing had happened since to shake that image from my mind. There was something rotten about her, something cold and unnatural.

At last she said calmly, "Don't you have anything to say?"

I'd already decided my best course of action would be to act as meekly as I could and not let her guess my suspicions. I had no idea what excuse Adam might have offered up, so the less I said the better.

"I'm sorry," I muttered, lowering my gaze to my folded hands.

"I'm disappointed in you, Holly. Your father warned me you might be a bit of a handful, but I assured him we achieve excellent results with *all* our difficult students."

Anger welled at the thought of my father discussing me with Verena. She knew all about me, no doubt—about the dreadful accident I'd caused, the man I'd killed. Mum leaving, our lives falling apart.

Verena drummed coral-painted fingernails on her desk. "I've been far too lenient with you, Holly. I see that now."

I said nothing, certain I would only make things worse if I did.

"Pursuing a friendship I expressly banned," she said. "And sneaking offsite without permission. That, I'm afraid, is one of our most serious rules. What if there had been an emergency? How would I have known where you were? You could have put everyone at risk, as well as yourself. You've been supremely selfish, but that's what I've come to expect from you."

I could hold my tongue no longer. Springing to my feet, I gripped the edge of her desk. "You left us no choice! We're worried sick about Jess. You won't tell us where she is, you won't let us visit. *Why?* Is it something to do with Lydia?"

Instantly on her feet, she leaned across the desk, looking for all the world like she wanted to strike me. "I told you not to mention her."

I knew I should shut up, but the words kept coming. "Why? Do your worst. Expel me. See if I care! I don't even know why you want me here. It's obvious you hate me."

"Is that so?" she said through gritted teeth, nostrils flaring, her face just inches from mine.

At last, I thought, we're getting to the truth. I imagined Dad's angry reaction when he heard about my failure, and I realised it didn't matter. The veil was being torn aside, and I would find out where I stood, even if the answer was nowhere I wanted to be.

I clenched my fists, determined to meet her gaze. That was when I noticed something off. Verena had regained her poise and a tiny smile curved her lips. Her eyes gleamed as she took her seat.

"You'd like to be expelled, would you?" She opened a drawer to her left and withdrew a sheet of pale blue paper. "Well, there might be a problem with sending you home. This letter arrived this morning."

Unease crept through me. Dad often wrote on blue paper. I'd seen him do it. I tried to focus on the handwriting, but she pulled the letter back and waved it in the air.

"Is that from my father?" I asked.

"Indeed it is. He informs me that something has come up, requiring his attention, and requests that you stay with us throughout the half-term holidays."

"What's come up? Is he all right? Let me see that." I tried to snatch the letter, but, again, she drew it out of reach. However, I'd seen enough to tell that the sloping handwriting was his.

"He doesn't specify what the problem is. Sounds to me like you'd be in the way, dear. Maybe he's got a girlfriend? Your mother left you, didn't she?" She eyed me curiously, like I was an exhibit in a museum.

"I don't believe you," I said. *You're lying, like you are*

about Jess.

She nodded slowly, her lips pursed. "I do sympathise. It's understandable you prefer to think me a liar, rather than confront your own shortcomings. Truth is, I expect your father has become accustomed to a much more enjoyable and peaceful life, now that you're no longer around to spoil it. So, much as you'd like to be expelled, I rather feel I'd be letting Mr Champion down. I promised him a respectful, obedient daughter, you see. You won't see him again, until you have reformed."

I was so shocked and angry, all I could do was gape like a stranded fish. Did Dad really hate me that much?

Verena replaced the letter in the drawer, locked it and pocketed the key. "Yes, it must be such a worry for a father, having a problem daughter like you. Personally, I can think of few things as important as making one's parents proud. My whole life has been centred on making my own father proud. Sadly he's no longer around to appreciate my achievements."

I couldn't imagine her having a father, let alone missing him. I stared out the window at the falling rain.

"As for your punishment," Verena continued. "I'll need to give it some thought. For now, I'm inclined to feel this letter has done part of my work for me. In addition, I'd like an essay from you by the end of the week, on the subject of family duty. Very apt, I'd say. Three thousand words. You may go."

Fighting back tears, I fled from the office and ran outside into the drizzle. I crossed the courtyard, sliding on damp cobbles, and raced down the stone steps. Crashing waves roared in my ears as I ran along the beach in the direction of the boathouse. I burst inside and collapsed onto the upturned crate. Shoulders heaving, I covered my face with my hands.

Something moved. I looked up to find Adam staring at me.

He stood by the old rowing boat, a startled look in his eyes. Before I could speak, he shot across and sank onto the second crate, beside me.

"Holly, what is it?"

"It's my dad—he doesn't want me home, not even at half term. And Verena, she just doesn't care. I hate her. *I hate her.*" I turned away.

Adam waited. At last my breathing grew steady and I began to feel embarrassed about my outburst.

"What did she tell you?" he asked. "Did your dad ring the school?"

"She showed me a letter. She didn't let me read it, but I recognised Dad's handwriting."

"You surely don't believe her? She's lying."

"D'you think so?" I looked into his eyes, desperate to believe him.

"'Course she is. The letter might really be from your dad, but she's lying about what it says. Why else wouldn't she let you read it?" He stood up and paced the boathouse floor.

"What about you?" I asked, remembering that he'd also been summoned to Verena's office. "How did you get on?"

"Huh. Much as you'd expect. Verena put me on cleaning duty and gave me a shedload of extra homework … Oh, and here's a nice thing. She banned me from playing guitar. They've actually taken it from my room."

"Oh no!"

He shrugged. "Don't worry. None of it matters."

"What d'you mean?"

"I mean I'm out of here. Tonight."

CHAPTER 14

I stared at Adam. "You're leaving?"

"I'm going to look for Jess. Anything's better than waiting around here, getting nowhere." He sank down onto the crate and gazed at the leaking boathouse ceiling. Then, to my surprise, he rested his hand on my arm.

"It's been three days now," he said. "Jess is in danger, I can feel it. I've got to find her."

"What'll you do?" What I really wanted to say was *Don't leave me.*

He pulled his hand away, as though he'd only now noticed it was there. "I'll start with Verena's office. There might be some clue there."

"What, break in, you mean?"

Adam rolled his eyes. "No, I thought she'd invite me in for coffee and cake. Of course I mean break in."

"No need for sarcasm ... Sounds a good plan. She probably locks everything, but it's worth a try."

"If I draw a blank, I'll head for town. Lamledra, or wherever the nearest police station is."

"What'll you tell them? We still don't know what's happening here, let alone have any proof. And you know what Jeannie said. Verena's got this way with her. She can twist people round her little finger."

Adam frowned. "Got a better idea?"

"No. But one thing's for sure. I'm coming with you."

***

Slipping between the rocks, we made our way back along the beach. It was still raining, and the beach smelled of wet seaweed.

"So we're agreed, right?" Adam wiped the drizzle from his face. "Act normal today, and tonight we make our move."

"Okay."

He eyed my crumpled uniform and no-doubt straggly hair. "Oh, Holl, you do look a mess."

"Thanks. You're not much better." As I quickened my pace, Lydia's diary, which was squeezed into my skirt pocket, banged against my hip. "Oh no! I meant to show you something. A verse Lydia wrote."

"Show me later. Lessons start in five."

He was right, but every instinct told me the little rhyme might be important. "Have a quick look. You'll have all day to think about it."

Adam sighed. "Quickly, then."

We stepped out of view between two large rocks. I pulled out the journal and found the right page. He scanned the verse, lips pressed together in concentration.

149

"How weird is that?" he said. "I mean, she's got a great sense of rhyme. I wish mine was half as good, for my song lyrics. But the meaning's all over the place. *My heart will skip with the joy of beating time.* If your heart is beating time, it can't be skipping, can it? And *Where the dove met V Tresawle?* What on earth is that supposed to mean?" He slammed the diary shut and handed it back to me. "C'mon, last thing we need is to arouse suspicion before we leave."

We moved on, jogging along the sand.

"I've been puzzling over it all night," I told him breathlessly. "I can't work it out, but I do get a feeling from it. It's cheerful at first, then gets miserable. I think that's how Lydia felt. What do you think about the title? The V?"

"She means Violet, I suppose."

"Or *Verena*."

"Yeah, or it could be some kind of code. But Holly, let's discuss it later."

On the approach to the stone staircase, I glanced all around to check no one was in sight.

"You go ahead," said Adam, keeping his voice low. "I'll follow in a minute." As I hurried onto the steps, he grabbed my arm. "Wait. Are you sure about this? I mean, it'll be the end of things, as far as you and Acorn are concerned."

"Huh! As if I care. All I care about right now is finding Jess and getting home. If Verena was telling the truth, and Dad really doesn't want me, well, I'll have to worry about that when the time comes."

"All right. I'll knock for you at one. Everyone should be fast asleep by then." He reached forward and wiped a drip of rain from the end of my nose. "I hope we're doing the right thing, and someone will listen to us."

I had the same doubts, but now that the plan was made, I wanted more than anything to leave.

"Look," I told him. "Verena's keeping you from your sister. The police will have to take notice of that. And we've got the journal. It might be enough to make them re-open the case about Lydia. Did you try your uncle again? Has Verena rung him about Jess?"

"Huh, that's another thing."

"What?"

"I didn't want to worry you even more, but ... Old Craddock followed me to my room last night, marched me inside like I was some sort of criminal. After he'd left, I went to get my phone. It was gone."

"Are you sure?"

"'Course I'm sure. I left it plugged in—I told you. He stole it, I know he did."

***

The day passed slowly. I tried to stay calm, keeping my head down in lessons and pretending to study. All the while my mind was whirling with possibilities as I braced myself for the night ahead. Would we find anything in Verena's office, even if we managed to break in? Would the police listen to us? What would we do if they didn't?

I performed my kitchen duty as calmly as I could, and even managed to sneak a couple of bread rolls into my apron pocket when Mrs Craddock wasn't looking. As I cleared the dishes, I glimpsed Adam, talking to Peter. Adam was smiling, giving every appearance of being relaxed.

Avoiding him, I gazed at Peter, looking for signs of the cheerful boy I'd met that first day. He looked solemn, his eyes glassy and dull beneath neatly combed hair. Had he been working hard, trying to fit in, or was it something more sinister? I swept past, all the more convinced Adam and I had made the right decision.

As my eyes swivelled past Adam, he gave a slight wink. A warm feeling spread through me. Before the night was out, we would be gone from this crazy place, on our way to the town.

I spent a couple of hours in the common room, pretending to read while the other girls studied or played table tennis. As usual, they were quiet and serious, even when playing games. At nine, bursting with the effort of acting normally, I stood and gave a dramatic yawn.

"See you in the morning, girls," I said, but no one bothered to reply.

Keeping my steps slow, I made my way upstairs. I would have to wait until after Mrs Craddock brought my cocoa before getting my things together, in case her sharp eyes spotted something out of the ordinary. By the time she knocked briefly and let herself in, I lay propped up in bed, a book open in front of me.

As she plonked my cocoa down on the bedside table, the coat of arms on the side of the mug no longer seemed to mock me.

"Thanks," I said, wishing I could tell Mrs Craddock what to do with her *Glory in Obedience.*

She tucked a strand of hair behind one ear and smoothed her overall. I waited for her to go, pretending to be immersed in my book.

"Drink it up, then," she said.

"Uh, I'll drink it in a minute, thanks, Mrs Craddock."

"It'll go cold."

She hovered beside me, chin stuck out, watching me through narrowed eyes. I picked up the cocoa and took a tiny sip. It was sickly sweet, just as I remembered, and made my lips curl.

"Mmmm," I said, as convincingly as I could. "Lovely. Bit hot, though. I'll finish it later."

She smirked. "I'm not surprised you're in trouble again. If it was down to me, you wouldn't get any cocoa, not after sneaking about in the village like that. Flirting with a boy. A fellow student, what's more."

"I was not!" Heat crept up my neck.

"I saw you get back, remember? Don't add lying to your list of sins. A liar needs a long memory."

I'd meant I wasn't flirting, of course, not that I wasn't in the village, but there was no point in explaining. While I forced myself not to rise to the bait, she sighed theatrically and retreated towards the door.

"Make sure you finish that. You know how Miss Blake frowns upon waste."

I counted to twenty, listening as her footsteps faded. When I was certain she'd gone, I turned off my lamp and flew into action. Working by torchlight, I tossed my sturdiest clothes into my backpack, together with all the money I possessed. I slipped the little gemstone bracelet Jess had given me onto my wrist and felt a sharp pang. I hadn't known Jess for long, but before Acorn had made her ill, she was the warmest, kindest person I'd ever met. I remembered when she'd given me the bracelet, how her eyes had gleamed brighter than the stones. Was she in a room somewhere, alone, wondering why no one came for her? Could we even be sure she was still alive?

Blinking away tears, I went into the bathroom cubicle and tipped the rest of the cocoa down the sink. I combed my hair into a ponytail, brushed my teeth and gathered together some essentials.

As I came out of the bathroom, a noise startled me. A movement outside my door. Something else, too, like faint whispering. It might be Mrs Craddock, on her way back after the cocoa round. Sometimes one of the students helped her. I'd better take extra care.

My bear, Horace—my going-away present from my friends back home—seemed to watch me with a sorrowful expression. This was no time for being sentimental, and I knew I should leave him behind, but I couldn't. I stuffed him in my bag, right to the bottom, so Adam wouldn't see.

I was ready in twenty minutes, which left me more than two hours with nothing to do. I tried to doze, but was far too wound up to sleep. After a while, I got up, crept across the room and sat in darkness in the window seat.

The courtyard lay in shadow, the sea beyond an intense dark blue. That view was the only thing about this stuffy room I'd miss. Despite everything, I felt light and hopeful, like I was emerging from a long, black tunnel. Whatever the future held, in a few hours, I'd be out of here, looking for Jess. On the move. With Adam.

Unable to relax, I fetched my torch and opened Lydia's journal, turning to a random page.

Sometimes when I can't sleep I sit in the window seat and look out to sea. It's lovely and still in the dark. I wonder who's out there and what they're doing. Sometimes I watch the boat coming from the island. I see it when there's moonlight. It goes fast, and has a small light. When it gets to our shore, it goes out of my view. I always wonder what it's doing.

They told me no one lives on the island, so I could be mistaken. I suppose it could be different boats, coming from the sea behind the island, but it always looks like it comes from the island, so it might well be the same boat.

I paused. A boat coming from the island? Could that be right? Like Lydia, I'd been told no one lived there. All the same, if the island was privately-owned, the owner must visit it from time to time.

A memory nagged at me, but I couldn't quite pin it

down. I made a note to tell Adam about that section. It was worth mentioning anything unusual.

I turned a few more pages and managed to decipher a paragraph that was even harder to read than the rest.

Even Abedi won't listen, and I thought he was my friend. I suppose it's because he's leaving soon, before the end of term. He won't even tell me where he's going, only that he's got a good job. When I asked him what his new job was he looked all mysterious and told me he couldn't say. Maybe I did something to upset him.

That was interesting. Who was Abedi? Up until now, I'd found no mention of any boy. She spoke of him as a friend, not a boyfriend. All the same, it was another name Adam and I could give to the police.

The grandfather clock in the hallway sounded twelve o'clock. With an hour to go, I re-read Lydia's verse. It made no more sense than it had before, no surprise there. But I kept looking at the title: *V.*

V for Verena, or V for Violet? With a start, I realised that there was also a third V, one Adam and I hadn't considered. The Violet on the gravestone George Kellow had been examining. Could there be a connection?

I had the strangest feeling, like I was missing something obvious. Something to do with the way Lydia had written out the verse, so carefully spaced into a square, with some words more widely spaced than others, to preserve the shape. Was Adam right? Could it be in code?

With a groan, I tossed the book aside. All these Vs

were making my brain fizz. For all I knew it could even be a roman numeral, a number five.

I glanced at my watch. It was already half past twelve, and I was stiff and achy from sitting so long bunched up in the window seat. I got up and stretched, then stuffed Lydia's journal into my jeans pocket—it wouldn't help to leave *that* behind.

I went to the bathroom and clicked the door shut. By the light of the small spotlight above the mirror, I splashed my face with cold water and stared at my reflection. I looked pale, and there were dark circles beneath my eyes. Not surprising, as I'd barely had a good night's sleep since I got here.

With nothing better to do, I rooted about in the bathroom cupboard and found my cherry lipstick, the other present my friends from home had given me. As I put some on, something made me shudder. I had the feeling someone was peering over my shoulder, into my reflection. The feeling was so powerful, I could almost sense their breath against my neck, like a soft breeze.

No one was there, of course, but my throat tightened. I remembered the story about Violet Tresawle's ghost, and how frightened Jess had been. She even said she'd seen her. I told myself not to be daft. Lydia's journal was getting to me.

The sooner I got out of here, the better. Closing the bathroom door firmly behind me, I sat on the bed, backpack at the ready.

Come on, Adam. Hurry up.

I'd been certain he'd be early, eager to be off. I

waited, motionless, unsure if I was more excited or nervous. The stillness of the house was overwhelming, a deep silence, broken only by the occasional call of a fox or hoot of an owl.

The minute hand reached the hour and passed it. Adam was late.

Horrible doubts crept over me. Might he have changed his mind, decided to leave me behind?

No, I remembered his hand on my arm, the look in his eyes as we'd made plans. There was no way he'd leave me, not after we'd agreed. He wouldn't let me down.

As the seconds stretched into minutes, I no longer knew what to think. Perhaps something unexpected had caused a delay. Maybe he'd even got the wrong room.

I shook myself. Of course he'd know which room I was in. He'd fetched Jess from hers, more than once, and he knew mine was next door.

For the hundredth time, I glanced at my watch. It was eighteen minutes past one. I couldn't avoid my growing fear—that something had gone terribly wrong.

At last, fed up with waiting, I decided I might as well set off in search of him. I wouldn't know which room was his, but maybe I'd bump into him in the hallway, or hear movements inside one of the rooms. At least I'd be doing something instead of sitting around worrying.

Throwing my backpack over one shoulder, I crossed

to the door and turned the handle. The door was locked.

CHAPTER 15

I grasped the handle, praying I'd been mistaken, that the door had only jammed. I couldn't be locked in, not really, could I? They wouldn't dare.

I turned and pushed as hard as I could. Definitely locked.

Throwing down my backpack, I sank onto the bed. I rubbed my temples, trying to stay calm. If only we'd left straight away, when we had the chance.

Adam hadn't left me behind—of course he hadn't. He was locked in too, had to be. The more I thought about it, the more convinced I was.

A chill spread through me as another explanation crossed my mind—that something had happened to him, the way it had to Jess, and possibly to Peter. That I was now completely on my own, powerless to stop it happening to me.

I pulled down the window blind, switched on my bedside lamp and threw a shirt round the shade to make it dimmer. Then I paced the room, searching all round for some means of escape. The panelled walls and door were sturdy and impenetrable, the bars beyond the sash windows thick and solid. I was thoroughly sealed in.

Verena must have locked my door, or sent Mrs Craddock to do it. Most likely I'd been in the bathroom, and hadn't heard the key turn in the lock. Verena had decided on her punishment for us, Adam and me, and half-measures weren't her style.

I considered banging on the door, screaming to make someone come. But then what? I suspected it would get me nowhere. They might even think of worse ways to keep me under control.

My hands a little shaky, I stuffed my backpack into the wardrobe and lay down on the bed. My only shred of comfort was that someone would have to let me out for lessons, surely. First chance I got, I would go in search of Adam. When I found him, we would leave. Walk out and go to the authorities, tell them about Jess and persuade them to hunt for her. Acorn had no electric fences. No one could stop us.

As long as I could find him.

***

Hazy sunlight streaked across the morning sky. I sat on the bed, dressed in my uniform. Waiting. No one had come, and not so much as a footstep had sounded in the hallway. My panicky feeling had faded. Instead, I boiled with rage. How dare they do this to me?

As I came out of the bathroom with a glass of water, voices sounded in the corridor. The key turned, and Verena Blake stood in the doorway.

She was composed as usual, smartly-dressed in a salmon-pink suit, that annoying faint smile on her lips.

"Did you sleep well, Holly?"

"How dare you lock me in my room! What have you done with Adam?"

Her eyes glimmered. "That boy again."

I chewed my lip, furious with myself for giving so much away. Her confident air hinted she somehow suspected I'd planned to meet him. Now I'd gone and confirmed it.

"Are you hungry?" she asked. "I'll get Mrs Craddock to bring you something."

"I'll get my breakfast downstairs, like I always do. You can't mean—"

"Oh, but I do, Holly. Last night I came to the difficult decision that extreme measures are needed in your case. You won't leave this room until you've mended your ways."

"But my lessons! I need to do my lessons."

"We'll sort something out about your studies. For now, it's more important that you accept Acorn's ways, and learn the meaning of obedience. *Gloria in Oboedientia*. This is the lesson all Acorn students must learn. The easy way ... or the hard."

"You can't keep me locked up." I tried to stop my lip from quivering. "It's inhuman, and illegal too." I didn't know this last bit for sure, but it seemed a fair guess. My eyes flicked to the door as I weighed up my chances of pushing past, but Verena was already retreating from the room.

Pausing in the doorway, she turned back. "That scowl makes you ugly," she said. "Not the way an Acorn girl should look at all."

"You can't keep me here forever."

She raised her perfect brows. "I wouldn't try anything silly, if I were you. Mr Craddock is just along the corridor. I need only snap my fingers. Mr Craddock is always eager to please."

The door shut and the key scraped in the lock.

Until this moment, I'd been angry rather than seriously worried. Now it began to sink in. Crazy though it seemed, Verena had every intention of keeping me prisoner.

But why? What did she want of me? Obedience, that's what she said. However, her eyes told me something else, something unknown.

I crossed to the window and scanned the courtyard. Lessons hadn't started yet, and students stood in small groups, bathed in autumn sunshine. Faruzi and Marysia were in solemn conversation. Carole and Amy gazed out to sea, the breeze ruffling their neat hair. There was no sign of Adam. He was being held prisoner, the same as me. I was sure of it.

It was quite a way down, but if I shouted loudly enough, would they hear? Without thinking, I leaned towards the glass and opened my mouth—then stopped.

Who was I kidding? Even if I could attract their attention, there was next to no chance they'd be prepared to help.

What about Carole, though? She'd helped me once before, by covering kitchen duty for me when I pretended to be unwell. Then again, Carole was clearly devoted to Verena, and would never go against her wishes. For all I knew, they could be in league together.

There was movement in the hallway, and the key turned once more. Mrs Craddock stepped in with a tray. One look at her sour features told me there was no point in trying to reason with her. Without a word, she unloaded a bowl of cereal, a spoon and a foiled package onto my desk, then pulled back quickly and locked the room.

The minutes trickled by, turning to hours. The room was stifling, and my appetite had vanished. All the same, it was important to keep my strength up, so around lunchtime I unwrapped the foiled package. Inside I found two cheese sandwiches. I took one to the window seat and watched the courtyard while I forced it down.

As I took the last bite, something caught my eye. A movement below, just out of my direct sight. I leaned forward as far as I could, bashing my forehead against the window, and squinted for a better view. Someone was standing in the courtyard, but I could only see the person's arm. It was a woman's arm, dainty and slim, clad in a green sleeve.

I had a weird feeling, like I knew who was there, as though I recognised her, just from that arm. It couldn't be a student—they'd be in uniform—and green wasn't Verena's colour either, at least, I'd never seen her wear it.

Almost in a trance, I watched as the figure stepped into view. She was tall and willowy, with golden-brown hair wound into a coil at the back of her head. I felt tingling all along my spine.

It couldn't be. But it was. The woman was my mother.

She was talking to someone, her eyes narrowing the way they always did when she was upset.

I banged on the glass. "Mum! Mum! Up here."

She didn't look up. Verena followed her into view, calm and unruffled.

"Mum," I yelled, even louder.

Verena was steering her across the courtyard, past the well. I could no longer see her face, but she was nodding, a slow nod.

I stared about for something that would break the window, so my voice would carry further. I grabbed my Acorn mug, ran back to the window and smashed it against one of the panes. The glass shattered and fell to the sill, some of the shards bouncing off and down to the courtyard below.

"Mum!" I shouted through the gap.

It was too late. Both figures were gone.

***

I stared for a long time at the empty courtyard, praying Mum would somehow hear my thoughts and return. The fiery ball of the sun stained the western sky brilliant orange, casting long shadows across the courtyard. Pigeons fluttered across the cobbles, squabbling over bits of bread, and a large gull cut a swathe through them, strutting around the well. I pressed my face against the window frame and breathed in the fresh air streaming through the broken pane. I had to face facts. Mum wasn't coming back.

I threw myself on the bed, fighting back tears. Three whole months had passed since I'd last seen her. Her heart-shaped face was as gentle and lovely as ever, but she'd looked tired and gaunt. What was she doing at Acorn? And what had Verena told her, to make her go away?

Perhaps she'd only now found out about the Academy, and had come to see for herself where Dad had sent me. That's what I longed to believe. But her air of misery, her bowed shoulders, suggested this was no ordinary visit. Could it be something to do with that letter, the one Verena wouldn't let me see? Had something awful happened?

As I replayed the scene, letting my thoughts drift, the image of the courtyard kept coming back. Something was nagging me, in a far corner of my mind, something I couldn't quite grasp.

I'd sometimes watched the sunset, or the comings and goings below, looking for scenes I'd like to sketch. There was nothing unusual about that. All the same, I kept seeing the stone well, or to be exact, its little pitched roof. The pointed shadow, creeping across the square courtyard, describing a …

Describing a V shape.

V

An idea struck me. I jumped up and fetched Lydia's journal, together with some paper and a pen. I sat at my desk and opened the journal to the page with the verse.

Maybe the words in Lydia's verse didn't mean anything at all. Maybe they weren't supposed to. V didn't mean Verena, or Violet, or even the number five. It was the V itself, or rather the shape of it, that was important. I felt certain I was on to something.

What would happen if I drew a V through that square?

V

If by chance you read my script
With a wave I will say hi
Win or lose my heart will skip
With the joy of beating time
On the earth I spend my years
Water runs through wood and sea
Crying ever happy tears
Smothering where others be
One who misses other fame
One who spoils another call
Even shocking all who came
Where the dove met V Tresawle

I traced a V through the verse, noting down the letters. The first letter of the first line, the second letter of the second line, the third of the third, continuing down the verse, forming the left-hand side of the V.

I, i, n, h, e, r, e, i, s …

It seemed to make some sort of sense: *I in here is*. But as I continued through the verse, down to the bottom and then upwards for the right-hand side of the V, all I got was gobbledegook. I, i, n, h, e, r, e, i, s, i, n, e, m, g, n …

I sighed and pulled at my hair. That didn't mean anything. You could draw all sorts of V's through the square, and it would take hours.

I tried describing the V in another way: first and last letters of the first line. Second letter and second-to-last letters of the second line, down through the verse. I, t, i, h, n, k. No luck there, either.

Wait a minute, though. If you tinkered with the order, those letters did make sense: *I think.*

Maybe I was getting somewhere this time. With growing excitement, I gave it one more go. This time, I made the V by toing and froing through the verse:

Forwards through the first line, taking the first and last letters. *I, t.*

Backwards through the second line, taking the second letter from the end, then the second letter from the start: *h, i.*

Then forwards through the third line: the third letter, followed by the third letter from the end, *n, k.*

I continued through the lines, down through the verse. By the time I reached the last line, selecting the *e* and the *m* from the middle of it, I had traced a perfect V shape through the square of the verse.

Holding my breath, I looked down at what I'd written.

I t h i n k t h e y a r e p o i s o n i n g m e

CHAPTER 16

I sat motionless at my desk, staring into space while Lydia's message repeated itself in my mind. As my gaze dropped to the second cheese sandwich, a bitter taste filled my mouth.

I think they are poisoning me.

It couldn't be true, could it? Even though I'd begun to suspect the same thing, it was a crazy idea. Why would anyone poison the students of their own school?

Unless it was just the students who misbehaved. Maybe this was Verena's way of ensuring her high success rate with *difficult cases*.

That didn't add up, though. I saw no evidence in Lydia's diary of any bad behaviour, nothing deserving of such extreme punishment. And Jess ... Poor Jess. She hadn't done anything wrong either, not as far as I could see.

Unable to think of a good reason why Verena would poison Lydia, or any other student, I turned my attention to how.

The answer was so obvious, I almost slapped myself. I saw Mrs Craddock hovering over me, her eyes boring into mine. Her spiteful voice echoed in my mind. *Drink it all up ... Speciality of Acorn, that is, enriched with herbs and spices to tone the mind.*

How could I have been so blind?

It had to be the cocoa. There must be some drug in it, something which made the students behave the way they did. It was the only explanation for why I wasn't affected.

Did Adam leave his cocoa too? He'd never mentioned it. I couldn't remember him enjoying anything sweet, but that didn't rule it out.

I picked up the remaining sandwich and gave it a sniff. The smell was perfectly ordinary, cheese and tomato, with a whiff of onion. Drugs could be undetectable, though, couldn't they? I remembered the way our meals were all laid out for us in the dining hall, labelled with our names, and how waste was frowned upon. There were plenty of opportunities for anyone to poison us, if they wanted to.

Keep calm. It was surely the cocoa, otherwise I'd have been affected long before now. Nevertheless, I picked the sandwich up, wrapped it in the foil and stuffed it in my backpack. It might be valuable evidence, if I was wrong about the cocoa.

Too tired to think, I curled into a ball on my bed.

***

Voices in the corridor jolted me awake. It was gone six, and the light outside was already fading. As the footsteps grew louder, I recognised Carole's voice. She was talking to another student, Amy possibly, although

I couldn't be certain.

Carole's words were indistinct, although I thought she mentioned my name.

Still groggy, I stumbled across the room and banged on the door. A day cooped up on my own had made me desperate to talk to someone, anyone, to try to find out what they knew.

"Carole, is that you? Can you hear me?"

The voices stopped.

"Carole?"

There was a long pause, then she said, "Yes, Holly. What do you want?"

"You've got to help me. I'm locked in."

"I know. Miss Blake explained."

"Explained what?"

"You have been confined to your room, for your own good."

I shut my eyes briefly, my fist falling to my side. Her attitude came as no surprise.

"How is it for my own good, Carole? Can't you see how wrong this is? Think! My mum was here. Verena sent her away."

Another pause. "Would you like me to bring you your homework?"

"No, you idi—" I stopped myself just in time, and thumped the door instead, gritting my teeth. The girl *was* an idiot, but maybe it wasn't her fault.

"Miss Blake is right to be concerned," Carole said to her companion. Their footsteps faded along the hallway.

I paced to and fro, desperate to come up with a plan. Acorn students would never believe me about the drugs. They were blindly devoted to Verena, and wouldn't hear a word against her. I shuddered, wondering just how far they would go, if Verena asked them.

I scanned the room for anything which might help me escape, moving around, tapping the walls from top to bottom. Everything sounded as solid as it looked, even the ceiling, with its thick black beams.

As darkness fell, solitude enclosed me like a sheet of steel. Even the gulls had vanished, and I missed their cawing. There was an eerie calmness about the sea, as though it was gathering its forces.

My stomach rumbled. I'd eaten only that one sandwich all day, and daren't risk eating the other. All the same, I ought to eat something. I rooted through my backpack and found the bread rolls I'd stolen from the kitchen the day before. As I grabbed one, Lydia's message sounded once more in my mind. The thought of eating any of Acorn's food made me queasy.

The roar of a sudden downpour startled me. Outside, raindrops as big as marbles battered the windows and sliced through the gap in the broken pane. I ran over and put my face to the gap, let the icy drops run down my face. The salty air smelled like freedom, and made me long more than ever to get out of this dreadful place.

As I sat once more upon the bed, the key scraped in the lock. Mrs Craddock stood in the doorway, a tray in her hand. On it was only one thing: an Acorn mug, filled to the brim with steaming cocoa.

"Compliments of Miss Blake." With a sneer, she set it on my desk.

I gritted my teeth and said nothing. It wouldn't be wise to let her know what I suspected. I had to play along, let them think I was drinking the cocoa.

"Cat got your tongue?" she asked.

I forced myself to mutter a polite word of thanks.

As she retreated, her gaze flitted to the broken window pane. Rain still pelted through, gathering in a puddle on the window seat. Her mouth fell open and she uttered a little shriek, making the mole between her eyes rise up.

"You little vandal!" She stared at the gap as though she couldn't quite take it in. "Miss Blake will have to be told. Don't you realise how old these windows are?"

Something snapped inside me. "Just wait until I get out of here. This place will be closed down."

She shrugged. "Think what you like."

"You'll go to prison."

A smirk spread across her lips. "I doubt it."

I sized her up. She was shorter than me, but solidly built with powerful legs and arms. If I was quick enough, could I push past her?

As I braced myself to leap up and try, Mr Craddock's hulk filled the doorway behind her. He yawned, his face unshaven and doughy-looking.

"Everythin' all right, Faye?" he asked his wife.

His eyes locked with mine, and I knew I had no

chance.

Mrs Craddock turned to him. "Look what she's done, Ken. Look at the damage."

His gaze followed hers to the window, and they both stared, as though they could piece it back together by effort of will.

I sprang to my feet. "What do you expect? You're keeping me prisoner. Where's Jess, where's Adam? … *Where's Lydia?*"

Mrs Craddock exchanged a glance with her husband, then glared at me. "What do you know about her?"

"I know she's vanished." I was probably making things worse, but the words kept coming. "Is this what you did to her? Was she a prisoner too?"

Mrs Craddock's eyes bulged. "Drink your cocoa."

The three of us looked at the mug.

I sprang towards it, to knock it over, but they were too quick. Despite his size, Mr Craddock was light on his feet, and he pushed me so hard, I fell backwards onto the bed. As I tried to sit up, he bounded behind me and held my arms, twisting them painfully, his knee pressed into my back. His wife picked up the mug of cocoa and stepped towards me.

"Let me go!" I cried, powerless against Craddock's bear-grip.

"That's right," cooed Mrs Craddock. "You hold her tight, Ken, and I'll make sure she drinks her lovely cocoa. Speciality of Acorn, this is. All the finest ingredients."

As I fought and struggled, Mr Craddock's fingers ground into my arms, while his wife tried to prise open my mouth. Shafts of pain shot down my neck. I clamped my jaws together, aching from the effort. Then she changed tactics and pinched my nostrils tightly shut, so I couldn't breathe.

I tried to wrench my head away, but the Craddocks were too strong. Everything faded and began to go black. Mrs Craddock's fingers forced their way between my jaws and the hot cocoa dribbled in, almost choking me. It tasted disgusting, sweet and gooey, covering my throat in a gummy layer.

She let go of my nose. I coughed and spluttered, trying to spit out as much as I could. The Craddocks held me fast until every drop was gone, either down my throat or over my chin and shirt. Then, with a grunt, Craddock let me go and got to his feet.

"Don't even think about causing a fuss," said Mrs Craddock. "No one will hear you, and if they did, no one would help. Everyone has their instructions. Mr Craddock will be keeping an eye on things, and you can rest assured he'll come down hard on any further vandalism."

Her husband crossed to the window and collected together the pieces of glass which had fallen inside the room, and placed them on the tray. As they headed for the door, Craddock's voice reached me as if from far away.

"You were right, Faye, she wasn't drinking it. But you told Verena that days ago."

"Shhh, you oaf, she'll hear us."

"All right, keep your hair on. I'm just saying, what's Verena waiting for? We could've avoided all this hassle."

"For God's sake, shut up." She pulled him outside, switching the light off as she went. "Miss Blake will have her reasons, don't you worry."

The murmuring grew faint, interspersed with Mrs Craddock's shushing.

Trembling all over, I sat up and rubbed at the sticky patches on my face. I must go to the bathroom, make myself sick. Any second, the drug would begin its evil work. I would get ill or start to change, become like the others.

As I stood up, giddiness overcame me and I sank back to the bed. My head spun, the ceiling swivelling and glowing like a Catherine wheel. I tried to fight it, to keep my eyes open, but the pull was too strong. My eyelids drifted shut.

***

A clap of thunder startled me awake. The room lit with lightning. My head felt like it was stuffed with wool, and a dull pain throbbed at the back of my skull. For a moment, I was totally disorientated, convinced I'd had a nightmare, and was back home in my room in Kings Hollow.

Slowly I became aware of where I was. I stretched a hand towards my lamp, but knocked it to the floor. I fumbled for it and managed to switch it on.

How could I have let myself fall asleep like that? I should have gone to the bathroom straight away. Maybe there was some sort of sedative in the cocoa, alongside whatever other poison it contained. Now I had given it time to work. For the moment, I still felt like me. But if that changed, would I even realise?

My watch showed twenty past three. I'd slept for half the night. As I lay still, my eyelids grew heavy, and I felt myself drifting off once more. I wanted to give up, just lie there and go along with whatever they wanted.

Or … maybe I should just pretend to change, enough to persuade them to let me out of the room? A shred of hope glimmered, but soon died. It might take ages to convince them, giving them all the more time to treat me with their drugs—long enough for me to change for real. I remembered Adam's words: *You've got one of those faces. You can't hide things.* It was true. I'd never be able to pull it off.

I banged my head on the pillow and forced my eyes open. *Don't give in.* Jess and Adam were out there somewhere. They needed me.

I rolled into a sitting position, stood up and headed for the window, to get some air. After only a step, I fell back onto the bed, legs too shaky to hold me up. I'd barely eaten for over a day. No wonder I felt weak. If only I had some food, something which hadn't been prepared at Acorn.

There was nothing for it. I'd have to risk the bread

roll. Then I remembered. The noodles! I'd bought them at the village shop, along with some peanuts, the night Adam and I searched for Aunt Jeannie. I'd eaten the peanuts, but forgotten all about the noodles. They must be here, somewhere.

I heaved myself once more to my feet and took a few steps, stumbled to the wardrobe and rooted around on the shelf above the clothes rail.

The small packet was thrust to the back—dried noodles, with a flavour sachet, the type you make by adding boiling water. I ripped it open and broke the block, keeping half back for Adam. I placed my half in a plastic lunchbox and added some water from the bathroom.

I stirred the noodles with the spoon Mrs Craddock had brought with my cereal. They tasted like cardboard might taste, but to me, they could have been the finest gourmet meal.

With food inside me, which I knew for certain wasn't poisoned, I felt stronger, and my headache lessened. I had a quick shower in the bathroom cubicle and put on my jeans and hoodie. Then I sat on the bed and rocked to and fro, hands pressed to my temples. If I couldn't think of something soon, I'd never get out of here, not until I started to behave like Carole and the others. Or until I collapsed, as Jess had.

I stared desperately around the room. There *had* to be something I could do.

My gaze fell on the fireplace.

CHAPTER 17

THE fireplace was sealed off by a Japanese-style screen painted with hummingbirds and cherry blossom. It was such a familiar part of my room, I'd never really thought about it before.

I got to my feet and went across to look. The screen was made of iron, pressed in close to the marble mantelpiece. Struggling with the weight of it, I heaved it aside. Behind it, the fireplace itself was sealed off by a large board.

I tapped the board. It didn't sound too thick. Some sort of hardboard, held in place by nails spaced around the sides and top. I scanned the room for something I could use to prise it off.

I spotted my Acorn spoon, still on my desk. It was heavy and well-made. It might just do the trick.

Wind and rain were still shooting through the broken window pane. As I went to pull down the blind, I noticed a thin sliver of glass, still in the frame—one which Mr Craddock had missed. I teased it out and wrapped it in some sheets of paper. It might come in handy, I thought grimly, stuffing it inside my hoodie pocket.

By the light of my torch, I crouched in front of the chimney breast and got to work with the spoon and a nail file, sliding the file into a narrow gap at the bottom.

After lots of twisting, I made enough space to insert the spoon. Sweat plastered my hair to my forehead as I pushed and wriggled it further in. I paused a moment, my ear cocked towards the window. Hopefully, the wind and rain would mask any noise I made.

This could all be a waste of time, but I wouldn't know until I saw what was behind the board. The chimney space might be full of bricks or rubble, and that would be the end of that.

After around ten minutes, the spoon was far enough in to give me a little leverage. I gritted my teeth and rocked it back and forth, praying it wouldn't bend.

The nail gradually loosened, and at last popped out. One corner of the board was free. I leaned back on my heels and rubbed my sore hands. Then, squirming my fingers inside the gap, I worked on the other nails.

When the fifth nail snapped out, the board wobbled, releasing a puff of cold air. As I began on the next, something sounded in the corridor. Footsteps, getting louder. Someone coming to check on me? I tried to scrabble to my feet, but fear turned my legs to jelly. I stared at the door like a deer mesmerised by a lorry.

The footsteps faded. I breathed again, and continued with my work. At last, the final nails came free, and the chimney was revealed.

It was a horrible, damp space, smelling of mould and decay. The grate hadn't been cleaned properly before it was sealed, and contained a charred, half-burned log shaped like a pig's head. The chimney above it, however, seemed to be unblocked.

I leaned inside and peered upwards, my face chilled by the dead, icy air. A ledge covered more than half the space and, even with my torch, it was too dark beyond that to see anything. But there did seem to be enough room, just, to squeeze inside.

And then what?

How many chimneys were there altogether, and how did they connect? I tried to picture Tresawle House from outside, but my mind was blank. Then I remembered the drawing I'd made when I was supposed to be writing to Dad.

I crept to my wardrobe, fetched my sketchpad and rifled through the pages. Yes! There it was. The drawing clearly showed four pairs of chimneys spaced along the roofline, all topped with narrow chimney pots.

No chance of emerging onto the roof, obviously. But indoors, there were other fireplaces, including an enormous one in the lounge, which I'd yet to see lit. The chimney chutes must be linked in some way, mustn't they, inside the walls? Might it be feasible to climb up this chimney and find a way into another one, maybe scrabble down and emerge downstairs?

It was a crazy plan, but I was desperate. Taking a last look around my room, I crammed the half-pack of noodles I'd saved and Lydia's journal into my pockets. Then, acting fast before I changed my mind, I cleared away the debris by the fireplace, sat on the floor and wriggled backwards towards the grate. I dragged the hardboard and the screen back into place behind me, as close to the gap as I could. With any luck, no one would guess where I'd gone, or at least be puzzled enough to give me a head start.

As I poked my head through the gap, into the flue, the sound of rain outside vanished. The smell was sharp and pungent, thick with soot and ash. I shone the torch upwards. The tiny beam danced over the sooty walls. It would be a tight squeeze, but my plan might actually work.

I braced my elbows across the gap and hauled myself over the ledge, into the chimney. Pressing back against one side, I placed my knees against the other. Then, caterpillar-like, I propelled myself upwards.

Progress was slow. It was hard to hold onto my torch, so I stuffed it down my shirt and continued in pitch darkness. As I dug my fingernails into brittle, centuries-old layers of soot, chunks loosened and fell. I remembered something I'd read about a Victorian chimney sweep who'd suffocated in a fall of soot. He'd moved his knees too far and ended up stuck. I shuddered, thinking what a slow, agonising death it must have been.

My neck and shoulders ached. Soot spattered my face, and grimy moisture trickled into my eyes. I'd no idea how long I'd been climbing. There was no sign of the chimney ending, nor of other flues joining it. I had a horrible suspicion I was wrong, that the flues didn't join at all, that they were individual chutes leading up to solid, capped chimney pots. I was imprisoned in a dark vertical tunnel, with no escape except back to the cell I'd just left.

I paused a moment, terrified of going further. Then I pictured Adam, sick with worry about his sister, his face scrunched in misery. I had no other plan. I kept climbing.

I developed a rhythm as I climbed another few metres. Then, with a single movement, my shoulders jammed.

I tried to retreat, and my knees wedged. I gulped at the musty air.

I willed myself to slow my breathing and wait for my heart to stop pounding. Then, tensing my whole body, I twisted sideways and thrust down.

My knees jerked loose. A chunk of soot fell. I shut my eyes, queasy.

I retrieved my torch and shone it upwards. The chimney was bending out of view—but the gap was far too narrow for me to get through. There was no way out. I'd have to go back.

The taste of soot was bitter in my throat as I made my way down. I cursed silently, miserable about my failure, desperate to get out of the chimney. It was hard not to rush, and the chimney seemed to have tripled in length. As I paused for a brief rest, I heard a cry.

"Oh Ken! Where is she?" Mrs Craddock's voice was

muffled by the thick walls.

"She can't have," cried a second voice.

"Check the bathroom. Under the bed."

There were scurrying sounds, followed by a grunt from Craddock. "She's gone."

"Get after her!" cried his wife. "If we don't find her double quick, we'll have to let Miss Blake know. She'll skin us alive. It'll be our fault, or that's what she'll think. Hurry up! You're wasting time, you oaf."

Footsteps sounded, a door slammed. I held myself completely still, not daring to breathe, waiting to see if they returned.

I counted to twenty, heard no further sound. Then, as quickly as I dared, I wriggled down the remaining stretch of chimney and thrust my legs through the gap. I fell into the grate, soot and ash swirling round me, and kicked the screen out of the way.

I dragged myself to my feet, gasping. If the Craddocks had rushed out in panic, would they have bothered to lock my door?

Muttering a quick prayer, I crossed the room and grabbed the door handle.

Unlocked. Not only that, but the key was still there. I pulled it from the lock and fled into the hallway.

CHAPTER 18

I glanced left and right, giddy from the sensation of freedom. After the pitch-blackness of the chimney, my eyes quickly adapted to the more subtle darkness of the hall. I'd have to be quick. The Craddocks might not be the brightest pennies in the purse, but even they would surely work out what I'd tried to do, and soon. They could be after me any second.

I must find Adam and get out. There was only one snag: I had no idea where he was.

His bedroom was the obvious place to start, but I'd never actually been there. Worse still, for all I knew, they might have moved him somewhere else entirely.

With the storm outside wailing in my ears, I picked my way past the staircase and into the boys' corridor. Every step seemed to echo and creak. I didn't want to use my torch, but the hallway was so dark and shadowy, I'd have to.

The tiny beam darted left and right over the rows of doors. They all looked identical, and weren't even numbered. No light showed beneath any of them. I shone the torch along the carpet, searching for anything which might help, dredging my memory for a chance comment of Adam's which might give me a clue.

At the end of the row, the beam fell on a human form.

I gasped. Then, just in time, I realised it wasn't a person standing there. It was a life-sized suit of armour, just like the one we had in the girls' wing. Unnerved, I glanced back the way I'd come. I was totally exposed here, with nowhere to hide. If the Craddocks switched on the hall light, they'd easily find me. Maybe it would make more sense to get out while I could, come back for Adam later.

I turned—then hesitated. No, I couldn't leave him. Even if I managed to get help, it might be too late. Every delay gave the drugs more time to work.

I reached the end of the corridor. As I doubled back, my torchlight flashed over the bottom of the door nearest me, and something barely visible made me stop. I moved closer and shone the beam. Poking out from beneath the door was a tiny, dark shape. I knelt down for a closer look.

It was a flat teardrop of plastic. I'd seen Adam use it to play his guitar. A plectrum, he'd called it. Would any of the other boys be likely to own such a thing? No, he'd already told me how disappointed he was that none of them were interested in music. This was Adam's room. It had to be.

As quietly as I could, I gripped the handle and turned. Locked. I fished in my pocket for the key I'd retrieved from my own door. Praying it was a master key, I inserted it in the lock.

There was a click. Success! The door opened with a small squeak.

The room lay in shadow, lit only by dim lamplight from the courtyard below. I shone my torch into the darkness, towards the bed.

A figure jerked up and thrust itself against the wall.

"Who's there? Leave me alone!" The voice was thick and raspy, but recognisably Adam's.

"Shhhhh!" I hissed. "You'll wake everyone." I stepped inside the room, pulled the door shut behind me and darted over to his bed.

He peered into the gloom. "Holly?" Eyes wide, he snatched the torch from my hand and shone it all over me, finishing on my face. "Oh, Holly, what have they done to you?"

"Me? What d'you mean?" Then I remembered—I was covered from head to toe in soot.

"I'm okay, honest," I told him. "No time to explain. Come on, let's go."

He stood up, grasped my shoulders and turned me to face him. "Are you sure you're okay? Is that—soot?"

"Yes, hurry up!" I pulled away.

At least he was fully dressed, in jeans and a shirt, which would save us valuable time. But instead of springing into action, he sank back onto the bed. His face was gaunt, his hair dishevelled.

"What's wrong?" I asked.

"Not sure … I was looking for a way out. Fell asleep."

Had they given him a sedative? Or something worse? I'd have to tell Adam about Lydia's message, about the drugs, as soon as I could. But right this second, I didn't think it would help him to know that he might have been poisoned.

"Give me a minute," he said. "Don't feel so good."

I seized his arms. "Oh Adam, we don't have a minute! The Craddocks are after me. They're bound to check on you, too."

His head snapped up. "What? Why didn't you say?"

I helped him to his feet and we hurried towards the door.

"Wait," he said, stopping.

"What now?"

"You're a right mess. You'll leave marks everywhere. They'll be able to track us like in Hansel and Gretel."

Before I could answer, he grabbed a towel from the back of a chair and quickly rubbed me down. Frantic to get going, I wiped the worst of the soot from my hands and shuffled my feet on the rug. I'd need a thorough scrub, as soon as I got the chance, but it was better than nothing.

We staggered out into the hallway. As an afterthought, I stepped back and locked his door, pocketing the key once more. With any luck, the Craddocks would assume Adam was still imprisoned in his room.

We turned onto the dark staircase and crept down the stairs.

"Knew you'd think of something," Adam murmured. "Knew they must have locked you in as well. I put that plectrum there, so you'd know where I was. Did you see it?"

"Shhh!"

He sounded more awake, but there was an odd edge to his voice. Could it be another effect of the drugs?

We rounded the bottom of the staircase and made our way towards the front door. Not far from the lobby, outside Verena's office, footsteps sounded in the distance. A light went on in the lounge. I dragged Adam back around the corner. We ducked in close to the wall, on the far side of a bookcase.

Another lamp went on. Footsteps approached. Just in time, I turned off my torch, praying they hadn't spotted the beam.

The Craddocks lumbered past, not far from where we were hiding. They stopped by Verena's office, and I heard a light tapping noise.

"Miss Blake, are you in there?" Mrs Craddock said in an anxious, wheedling voice.

"I told you she wouldn't be in her office at this time of night." Ken sounded scornful.

"Well, that's where you're wrong, Mr Smartypants. She often works at night, especially when she's got something to take care of. Big day tomorrow, don't forget."

"What about her mobile?"

"We'll ring her if we have to." There was another knock, louder this time. "No, she's not here. She'll be over there, I expect. Which is good news for us. Bad signal. Gives us a chance to sort things out before she gets back."

"Right. So what do we do, Faye?"

She sighed. "Do I have to decide everything? The girl can't have got far. She'll have taken the road. Even *she* wouldn't be stupid enough to risk the cliff path in this storm. Get in the van and scout round. I'll check the grounds. Could be she's hiding out somewhere till it gets light."

The footsteps resumed. The main door banged. I stayed still for a moment, making sure they'd gone.

"Did that make any sense to you?" whispered Adam. "Where's Verena? Where's *over there*?"

"Dunno. She's not here, that's the main thing. How're you feeling?"

"Better. Bit groggy."

I grabbed his arm and propelled him towards the exit. "Come on then. Soon as the coast is clear, we'll take the road to Lamledra. Go to the police."

He came to a halt outside Verena's office. "No, wait."

"What for?"

He nodded towards the door. "We need to take a look inside."

CHAPTER 19

"WE haven't got time to look in her office," I cried. "We need to get out of here! If they catch us, we'll land straight back in our rooms. Then we won't be able to do anything."

Adam stopped, one hand on the wall. "It's just … Wait a minute."

I halted beside him. "What is it? Are you okay?" I licked my still sooty lips, glancing nervously ahead and behind, terrified Verena would materialise out of thin air. Something about this corridor bothered me, but I couldn't figure out what it was.

Adam lowered his voice to a whisper. "We need something, some idea what's going on. Otherwise, Verena will slip away from us, I know she will, and my last chance of finding Jess will go with her."

With every passing second, our chances of escape were fading. All the same, what he said made horrible sense.

"There's a code on the door," I said. "How will we get in?"

Adam paused for a moment, then turned back the way we'd come. "I've got an idea."

He sped along the corridor, into the lounge. Racing after him, I watched him stop by the awards cabinet.

"Hold your torch up for me," he said, peering through the glass. "Can't see a thing."

"But what——?"

"Shh. You'll see."

I shone the torch over the cabinet, waiting while he slid back one of the glass doors. Carefully, he stretched in his arm and removed something I'd noticed before—the bronze statuette of an African tribesman, complete with shield and spear. The little metal spear was sharp and lethal-looking.

"This'll do nicely." He wriggled it from the warrior's grasp, then replaced the statue in the cabinet. "C'mon. Now we need to get outside."

I didn't waste time asking questions. Almost running, we reached the lobby and exited the building. If anything, the storm was worse. Raindrops glowed like fireflies in the light of the streetlamp and bounced onto the glistening courtyard. I rubbed my cheeks and matted hair, glad of the chance to remove more of the soot and grime. The rain felt pure and cleansing, and I felt like I never wanted to be indoors again.

Adam peered at me. "Now you're all streaked."

"Oh!" I rubbed some more. "Any better?"

"Not much, if I'm honest. You look like a zebra." He leaned forward and wiped at something beneath my eye. "What the hell happened, anyway?"

"Tell you later," I said. "You won't believe me."

"When it comes to you, I'd believe anything."

Adam was starting to sound more like his old self, and the knot of tension in my chest eased a little. He set off briskly, keeping tight to the wall. I followed behind, scanning the courtyard for movement.

Adam stopped by Verena's office window, an old-fashioned sash one, just like those upstairs, except that there were no bars. He slipped the little metal spear beneath the framework of the outer panes.

"What if there's an alarm?" I asked.

"We'll soon know." He jiggled the spear beneath the centre, where the catch was, trying to find the right place. Then he grasped the ledge with both hands and pushed. The window creaked open.

I stood poised and ready to run if an alarm sounded. All was quiet.

"Hey, you should be a burglar when you grow up," I told him.

"Funny."

We both grinned, but I wasn't feeling hopeful. Verena didn't seem too bothered about security. To me, that suggested there'd be nothing to find.

The window wasn't particularly high, and with his long legs, Adam clambered in easily, pushing aside the thick velvet curtains. He turned to help me, and I wiggled through the gap. A familiar flowery scent hit me, the one which reminded me of funerals.

Adam closed the window and yanked the curtains back into place, plunging us into darkness.

"We'll have to use your torch," he said. "Search together. We can't switch on the light."

"Obviously. I'm not stupid."

The small beam cast jagged shadows, revealing the antique furniture and walls lined with gloomy oil paintings and tapestries. We hurried across to a filing cabinet.

"It's open," I said in a louder voice than intended. Taking care not to leave smudges, I slid out files with labels such as Uniforms, Rotas and Lesson Plans. I pushed the drawer shut and we skimmed the contents of those beneath. The files in there were much the same.

"Nothing." I was disappointed, but not surprised. If Verena was involved in criminal activity, she was hardly likely to leave proof lying around. I opened my mouth to say we were wasting our time. When I saw Adam's face, his jaws clenched in grim determination, I didn't have the heart.

"What about that corkboard?" I shone the torch on the wall by the door, where a large pin-board was covered in bits of paper. Adam nodded.

As we slipped across the room, a tap sounded at the window. I froze and held my breath, waiting to hear voices, or for someone to appear. Our eyes met, Adam's wide with alarm.

Several seconds passed. Silently, I switched off my torch. Hearing no more, I crossed to the window and twitched the curtain. No one was there. It was just the wind, pressing a tree branch against the pane.

"It's okay," I whispered. "But we'd better be quick. The Craddocks could arrive any time."

Together, we shone the torch over the corkboard and scanned sports schedules and notices about meetings.

"Boring," murmured Adam.

I pointed to a calendar on the left. "There's a date ringed. Tomorrow's date. Well, today's, technically."

Adam shrugged. "Could be a hair appointment, for all we know."

I wasn't so sure. A ringed date wasn't much to go on, but in my bones I felt that something a lot more ominous than a haircut was on the cards.

"Didn't one of the Craddocks say something about tomorrow being a big day?" I asked.

"Let's check Verena's desk." Adam's voice was dull, as though he didn't really expect to find anything.

The desk was neatly arranged, empty of ornaments except for a golden paperweight in the shape of a rearing cobra. We searched in vain for a desk diary, then had a quick look inside some neatly-stacked files.

Adam sighed and ran a hand through his hair. "Homework. What else? And the drawers are locked … Of course they are."

"We really need to go. I don't think there's anything here."

"Yeah, I know." His gaze fell on the phone, which had five or six numbers written on a sticker at the base, together with various initials. "What about those?"

I looked through them. "E.M. is Miss Mallett—her name's Emily. And F.F. is Mr Foreman. Their home numbers, I should think. Plus the part-time staff. I don't know who S.B. is, though, do you?"

He jabbed with his finger. "No, I don't. But I recognise the number. It's the one Verena gave me for the so-called hospital, the one that didn't exist."

"Oh! So she—"

"She only pretended to take it out of her notebook. It's a landline, so whoever it is, she must have known they wouldn't be at home."

"Devious," I said. "Just as you'd expect. I wonder who it is, though. Another part-timer perhaps, who's on holiday or something? It's a start, but it doesn't really help."

I pulled a piece of paper from beneath the cobra paperweight and shone the torch beam on it.

"Anything?" Adam asked.

"Not really. It's a menu. Days of the week with our meals filled in." I peered at it closely, looking for clues about possible drugs or poisons the meals might contain, but the plan seemed perfectly ordinary. Fish pie on Monday. Spaghetti Bolognese. Seafood risotto. I almost laughed. What did I expect? Arsenic stew?

Adam read it over my shoulder, then pulled it from my hand. "Wait. Let me see. I've seen this handwriting before. But where?" He was silent for a moment, then tapped the sheet. "I remember. It's the same as the writing in that letter."

"What letter?"

"The one Jeannie showed us, from Lydia's boyfriend. I'm sure it is."

I snatched the paper back. The bold, square writing

did look familiar. "Maybe. But what does that mean? That Lydia's so-called boyfriend—the one she's supposed to have gone off with—Tom?—is working here? Or ..." I wrinkled my brow.

Adam shook his head. "What it means is, the letter was forged. Lydia didn't run off with any Tom. There is no Tom. You were right. Once again."

"Guess I was." It gave me no pleasure. Why couldn't I be right about good things for a change?

I gazed from one side of the room to the other. Something was niggling me, something about the layout of the office. I'd felt it earlier, when we walked along the corridor outside the room.

"Bring the note with you," said Adam. "We can show it to the police. They can compare it with Lydia's letter."

"Okay." As I folded the paper, I realised what had been bothering me.

"Adam! This room's square."

"Really? Your observation skills are awesome."

"No, listen." Frowning, I crossed to the wall bordering the corridor. "It's this wall. It's longer outside than it is in here. From walking along the corridor, you'd expect an oblong room. But inside, it's *square*."

"Okaaay." Adam raised one eyebrow, clearly thinking I'd lost it.

I examined the room, squinting a little to compare it with the image I had of the hallway outside. I walked around Verena's desk and tapped the wall behind it.

"I reckon there's something on the other side. It sounds hollow. See for yourself."

I moved along the wall behind the desk, tapping as I went, wriggling between chair and wall. Adam joined me, shaking his head.

At the end of the wall I came to a small picture, one I'd noticed before: the portrait of an arrogant-eyed girl clutching a porcelain doll.

"I wonder …"

"Holly, I love your imagination, but …"

Ignoring him, I pushed the picture to one side. Beneath it was a small flap. Lifting that, I found a button.

"Ha!" I turned to Adam, feeling smug. He stared at me, mouth twisted to one side. As though he wanted to believe me, but didn't dare hope.

I pressed the button. With a low hum, a vertical slit appeared in the wall behind Verena's desk. Parting at the centre, the two sides slid away neatly, leaving a gap just big enough to squeeze through. Beyond it, there was darkness.

Adam's eyes widened. "Holly, you're a genius."

I flashed a quick grin. What had I found?

He came to stand beside me. One by one, we slipped through the gap.

CHAPTER 20

THE beam flickered as I shone my torch around the confined space. "The battery's almost gone. Damn." I noticed a spotlight, set in the ceiling. "We'll have to put that light on."

"Don't be daft," Adam said, pulling my arm back as I reached for the switch.

"Look, it's gone five. If we're not away by dawn, we've had it. How're we going to find anything if we can barely see?"

"Yeah, I suppose. What if we put the panels back in place? Then we could risk the light."

The idea of sealing ourselves in made me nervous, but I could see no other solution. "Okay."

Taking a side each, we grasped the edges of the sliding wall and tugged. The panels didn't budge.

"There'll be another control on this side," I said, wishing I felt as confident as I sounded.

My torch beam found another painting on the adjacent wall, this one showing Tresawle House. Behind it was another button. As I pressed it, the two sides of the wall slid together.

"I'll get the light," muttered Adam, fumbling for the

switch. The room lit up, blinding me after so much darkness.

Right in front of me was a face. I gasped and took a step backwards.

"Shh!" said Adam. "It's just a mirror."

Blinking, I gazed at my reflection in the mirror opposite me, attached to a small wardrobe.

"Phew … Oh no! Look at me." Despite Adam's efforts with the towel and my quick wash in the rain, there were sooty smudges all over my face and clothes.

"No wonder you screamed," Adam said, cocking an eyebrow.

Switching off my torch, I looked around the poky room.

"It's basically a big cupboard," I whispered. "Somewhere to store textbooks and essays, by the looks."

Shelves on both sides were crammed with boxes, and a filing cabinet stood next to the wardrobe. The only décor was the oil painting, plus a tiger-striped rug on the floor.

I crossed to the wardrobe and opened its mirrored door. Perfume wafted from a row of clothes on hangers. Boots and shoeboxes were neatly arranged on a metal frame below.

I rifled through the clothes, recognising a couple of Verena's smart suits, and the weatherproof jacket she'd worn on the trip to Tredethy.

"Leave it." Adam stood by the shelves, examining the boxes. "A wardrobe's a wardrobe."

"Ha, is it, though? She's got her own room upstairs. Why does she need clothes here too?"

"Fair point."

As I reached the end of the row, I gave a little cry. I pulled out a hanger and swished a purple dress through the air.

"Look at this."

"Very nice, but we don't have time for a fashion show. What's the big deal?"

"Don't you see? This dress is similar to the gown in the picture above the staircase. Violet Tresawle's gown."

"Right." He squinted at it, taking in the shimmering silk, the beaded bands of silver at the throat, waist and wrists. "And?"

"The morning Jess was taken ill, she said she'd seen the ghost of Violet Tresawle. I thought at the time it was a nightmare. Don't you see? It could have been Verena, wearing this."

Adam shook his head. "Not so long ago, I'd have said that was a mad idea. But you've proved me wrong several times. We need more, though." He turned his attention back to the boxes.

I replaced the dress in the wardrobe. Adam was right. We needed more, a lot more.

I moved on to the filing cabinet, which, as expected, was locked. One file lay open on top, however, as though Verena had left in a hurry.

As I began flicking through, my hackles rose. "No way!"

"Anything good?" Adam looked up.

"It's—it's about us. All of us. Clippings from newspapers. Listen to this one: *Top academy intervenes in case of Polish teen.* That must be about Marysia. And here's another, from a London paper. *Homeless youth arrested in burglary* … and, oh my, you're here too."

"Me? What's it say?" He stopped ripping the lid off the box in front of him and came to stand beside me.

"It's about you and Jess. Your parents, the air crash that killed them. Everything."

He hesitated. "Well, she had to find out from somewhere. There's nothing unusual in that. She contacted my great-uncle after reading the article, I suppose."

"I guess." My uneasiness was growing. Would there be something about me?

I turned the page, read a few lines. "Oh no." I thrust the folder under Adam's nose.

"*Woman convicted of mother's murder,*" he read out. "Murder? Who's that?"

"The date's twenty years ago. But look at the photo. Imagine a few lines on her face."

He stared for a moment. "It's Mrs Craddock."

"Different hair, but definitely her." I scanned the report. "It says she was her mother's carer. Mother was bedridden." I drew a breath. "She gave her an overdose."

Neither of us spoke. Acorn was being managed by a woman who'd poisoned her own mother. With the full knowledge of the principal.

"Does it mention her by name?" asked Adam.

"Um … Yeah. Faye Grose. Maiden name, I suppose." I flicked the page. "And here's her adorable husband. Ken Craddock, sent to prison for six years for fraud and theft."

"Why am I not surprised?" Adam turned back to the shelves. "And Lydia? Anything about her?"

"Not yet." As I reached the last page, a bitter taste filled my mouth. Staring up at me was the face which had haunted my nightmares. A face with more power over me than any other, and I'd never even met him. Bold, dark eyes. A strong mouth, curved at the edges.

"Holly? Come on. There's no time to read the whole thing. It's newspaper clippings. We can look it all up online."

My eyes welled. "It's about me. The road accident, the doctor I killed. Bryan Lake."

"Oh." His voice softened. "Sorry. She was bound to know, though. She knows all our secrets. Leave it."

I shook my head and blinked away the tears. This was no time to get upset. I slammed the folder shut and replaced it where I'd found it.

Adam gestured to the box he'd opened. "It's hopeless. This is all catering stuff. Sachets of sugar, cocoa, that kind of thing. No use at all."

I looked across, about to give up. Then I spotted the image on the box. A giant eye, with the map of the world in its pupil. "Hang on. I've seen that logo before."

We both stared at the creepy logo, beneath which

was written *Globe Industries.*

"Where?" he asked.

I frowned, struggling to remember. "It was after Jess was taken ill. Yes, that's it. It was on a box Faye Craddock was carrying. I bumped into her at the bottom of the stairs."

"Why are the boxes stored here, I wonder? Why not in the kitchen?" He wrinkled his nose.

I had more than a suspicion. These weren't ordinary catering supplies at all.

"Take some and let's go," I said.

"Huh?"

"Just do it!" I grabbed a handful and stuffed them into my jeans pocket.

"What aren't you telling me?" He stared at me, hands on hips.

I glanced aside, avoiding his gaze.

"Holly? Spit it out."

"Oh all right, I didn't want to go into it until we were safe. I worked out Lydia's poem. She said they're poisoning us."

A door slammed in the distance, making me jump.

"That's Ken's van," Adam said.

I froze. Adam dashed towards the picture with the hidden button. Halfway across the room, he stumbled and fell.

"Adam!" I ran to help.

"Tripped on something," he said. Instead of getting up, however, he crouched motionless, peering at the deep-piled rug.

"Adam! We've got to get out of here."

Ignoring me, he reached out and yanked at the rug. "It doesn't move."

"What doesn't? What're you on about?"

"This rug. It's stuck down." He groped about, then took a breath as his fingers closed around something. Slowly, he folded out a small metal hoop. "Holly, this isn't a rug at all. I think it's a trapdoor."

CHAPTER 21

I stared at the tiger-striped rug, at the metal ring embedded near one end. Another door slammed, nearer this time. Raised voices echoed in the hallway outside the office.

"They're coming," I whispered.

Adam gripped the metal ring and twisted. With a click, the hatch sprang loose. He folded it back. A stale smell whooshed out as we stared into the gloomy, oblong hole. Nothing was visible except the top of a metal ladder.

"Switch off the light," Adam mouthed.

I got to it just in time. As darkness enveloped us, a door buzzer beeped, alarmingly close, and a snake of light appeared beneath the false wall. I heard voices. The Craddocks were in Verena's office. Would they know about this store room?

I couldn't see Adam, but was dimly aware of his movements as he vanished into the gap. I dropped into a crouch and fumbled my way back to the trapdoor, straining to hear the Craddocks' conversation.

"I don't understand," Faye said, her voice muffled and whiny.

"Neither do I, but facts are facts. Leave a note for Verena. She'll know what to do."

"Oh God, she'll be fuming. But the boy's secure. You checked on him, right?"

"Yeah, told you," said her husband. "Room was locked."

"You didn't go in? You're a lumbering great idiot—oh! Oh no."

"Huh?"

"I left my key in the girl's door."

"You *what*? And you say I'm an idiot?"

As their argument escalated, I grasped the two sides of the ladder and clambered onto it. My hands slick on the cold metal, I ducked below floor level and pulled the trapdoor shut.

All sound vanished as a sheet of chilled air enclosed me. Adam reached for my hips, guiding me down onto solid ground.

Darkness pressed in on all sides and the musty smell intensified. We waited a moment in silence, to make sure we were alone.

"Put your torch on," Adam whispered.

I pulled it from my pocket. The beam flitted across knobbly, white-painted walls, a pile of stacked chairs and some objects covered with dust sheets. I lifted one of the sheets to see an old coffee table. Another revealed a standard lamp.

"It's a cellar," Adam said. "There's nothing here. Just junk."

"How on earth are we going to get out?" I tried to

whisper, but it came out like a wail.

I ran the beam once more over the low ceiling and walls.

"Stop," said Adam. "Back a bit." He put his hand on the torch and guided the light along the far wall. "Over there. A door leading off. See?"

The small, arched door had blended in so well, I hadn't spotted it. We crept across the basement and Adam turned the handle. It opened onto a narrow tunnel, cut into the rock.

"Wow!" I said. "How far d'you think it goes?" I shone my torch ahead, but the beam was now so faint, it barely helped at all.

"Dunno. These old houses often had underground tunnels. Houses by the sea, especially. They were used by smugglers. Or when people needed to escape in a hurry."

He stepped through. I followed reluctantly, wishing we'd stayed above ground and gone to the police instead. As I closed the door behind me, the sound clanged and echoed all around. There it was again. A hint of something flowery in the dead air.

"Can you smell something?" I said. "Like stale perfume?"

Adam sniffed. "No, not really."

"Well I can. I think Verena's been here."

"Maybe, but there's no going back now."

The tunnel snaked downwards, barely wide enough for us to walk side by side. Our arms bumped as we inched our way along, but Adam seemed no keener than me to break into single file.

The stone walls were damp, and water dripped from the ceiling onto my hair. To conserve the battery, I used the torch only intermittently. I peered ahead, straining my eyes, but all I could see was shadowy blackness.

Adam stopped abruptly. "Holly, what you said … about the poison. D'you think they've given us any?" His voice, though quiet, murmured all around me, echoing off the tunnel walls like a whispering ghost.

"Let's talk about it when we get out of here."

We set off again, shivering as the air grew icy cold. Up ahead, there wasn't so much as a trickle of light. How deep were we going? What if there wasn't an exit, or it was blocked?

My head ached and I longed to get out of this cramped, still place. As thunder rumbled faintly in the distance, something brushed my foot. I shone the torch down and caught sight of a small, dark shape, slinking into the shadows.

"Only a rat," said Adam. "Won't hurt us."

"Could be a good sign. Means there must be a way out."

"Rats can get through the smallest gap."

"Great," I said. "But if Verena uses the tunnel, there must be an exit."

"Why would she, though? I don't get it."

Neither did I, but I could still smell the hint of perfume. What's more, if she wasn't in her bedroom or her office, where was she?

After perhaps fifteen minutes, the downward slope became sharper, bumpy with stones. I stumbled and Adam gripped my arm. The walls grew uneven and were wetter, glistening with moisture. As I put out my hand to steady myself, my fingers sank into patches of velvety lichen.

"It smells fresher," Adam said. "Feels like it's opening out."

He was right. A draught swept my face and I tasted salt on my lips. The roar of the sea echoed in the distance, mingling with the sounds of the still raging storm. I shone my torch upwards. The roof of the tunnel had broadened into a craggy ceiling of rock. Underfoot, the ground grew sandy, wet and crunchy.

"Look there," I said. "The sand's scuffed. Looks like footprints."

Adam gestured to a pale half-moon shape ahead of us, low against the ground, through which dim light filtered. "That's our exit. Got to be."

At that moment, the torch beam flickered and died. With a curse, I stuffed it into my pocket and tried to focus. The first hint of dawn gave a little light to see by.

"It's a cave," I said.

The space was small, five or six metres across, with rocks and stones dotted about the sand. Overhead, tiny, bony stalactites pointed down at us from the ceiling. The mouth of the cave was so low and narrow, it would barely be visible from outside. Raindrops dripped from its top lip.

"It makes sense," said Adam. "Cornwall's famous for smugglers. The cave would've given them somewhere to store contraband. If they needed to, they could use the tunnel to take the goods safely into Tresawle House, or into that basement we found."

I crossed to the exit, sank to my knees and peered out. In the distance, waves crashed onto the shingle. A small, oblong building hulked nearby.

"We're on the beach," I said. "Hey, I think we're by the boathouse."

When no reply came, I looked back. Adam was sitting on a large rock, trying to catch his breath. His face was a sickly yellow in the growing light of dawn.

"You look awful," I told him. "Let's have a rest. No one's here."

Adam nodded and rocked to and fro. "I don't feel weird or anything, but I'm groggy. It's an effort to put one foot in front of the other."

A shudder ran through me. If we did change, would it be gradual? Would we suspect anything? Or would we simply fall asleep and wake up different? Become like Carole or Marysia, like the other students at Acorn?

Adam banged his fist on the rock, startling me. "What they've done to us makes me want to kill them."

"Yeah." He looked too weak to kill a fly. If only we had something to eat, that might help. Then I remembered.

"Noodles!" I said, fumbling in my pocket.

"Huh? Is that your new swear word?"

I retrieved the half packet I'd saved and ripped off the wrapper. "Eat these. They're perfectly safe."

I heaved myself up beside him, the rock damp and slimy against my jeans. Adam bit off a chunk and crunched for a while, not even complaining about the taste. I let him eat, content for a moment to enjoy the tangy sea air and listen to the roar of the waves and the storm. A flash of lightning lit the cave with electric blue light, illuminating rivulets of water cascading down the walls. Thunder rumbled around us, so loudly I flinched. Adam barely noticed, he was so intent on eating.

I peered into his face. "You've got a bit more colour."

He gave a faint smile. "Got a beer to wash it down with?"

"If only." My lips were dry and cracked, and I eyed the water on the cave walls. Would it be safe to drink? Or would it be salty, and make us feel even thirstier? I decided to hold out for as long as I could.

"What did they do to you, Holly?" Adam asked after the final mouthful. "Was it the same as me? I was all ready to go. When I tried to come for you, my door was locked."

"Yes. I felt awful. I didn't know if you'd been locked in too or … I didn't know what to think."

"I'd never have gone without you. You knew that, I hope. Not after we'd agreed."

I looked at the ground, avoiding his gaze. "No, no. I didn't think you would."

Briefly, I brought him up-to-date with what had happened to me in that room, from the Craddocks force-feeding me the cocoa to my escape attempt through the chimney.

"The chimney?" he cried. "Holly, you're one crazy girl, has anyone ever told you that?"

"Hey, it worked, didn't it? Not the way I planned, but it got me out. What I keep asking myself is *why*? Why would Verena want to poison us?"

"It's a control thing," Adam said. "These drugs, whatever they are, they're powerful. They influence our behaviour. We should have worked it out sooner. We saw Jess changing. And as you noticed, Peter changed, too."

"Yes, and we didn't change. Because we didn't drink the cocoa."

"Huh?" Adam frowned. "What d'you mean?"

"The cocoa. That's what the drug was in. I never liked it, not from the start."

There was a long pause.

"But I did," he said. "I've been drinking it all along."

"What?" I shook my head. "No, you can't have."

"I think I'd know, don't you? It was a bit on the sweet side, but I liked it well enough. The drugs must be in something else."

I couldn't speak for a moment, I was so surprised. Was I wrong then, to suspect the cocoa? Why else wouldn't I have been affected?

"What are we missing here?" I wondered, almost to

myself.

Adam made a face. "Don't ask me. I've gone over it heaps of times. Tried to find links between Acorn students. Like, Jess and I are orphans. Peter is, too— and so was Lydia. Could it be, we're all alone? No one cares what happens to us?"

I swallowed. "I'm not alone. My dad …"

Dad wasn't going to win a parenting prize any time soon, true, but things hadn't always been that way. A memory jumped into my head, of a time I'd fallen out of a tree in the park and gashed my leg. Dad carried me across the fields to his car, all breathless, racing to get me to casualty. However much he disliked me now, he wouldn't want to see me hurt.

Adam was watching closely. "Yeah, you've got your dad, and some of the others aren't orphans, either. I've noticed another thing, though. We all have things in our past, difficult things. Regrets, maybe."

Something about the way he said it made me think he wasn't only talking about the loss of his parents.

"Regrets? Regrets imply guilt," I said. "What aren't you telling me?"

He gazed into the distance. "I … got into a bit of trouble. After Mum and Dad died. Got in with some older lads."

"Oh?"

"Yeah. I was stupid. The first time we broke into an old warehouse and larked about for a bit, no harm done. But the second time, it was a woman's house. My so-called friends told me it was just for fun, then

215

one of them started stuffing things into a bag." He paused.

"Go on."

"I knew it was wrong. I slipped away while they were arguing about what to take. They thought the woman was out, but it turned out she was home, she'd called the police. Everyone except me got caught red-handed. One of them ended up in prison."

I didn't know what to say. "So that's how you knew. Back there."

"How to break into Verena's office? Yeah." He sighed. "Jess was furious with me. I felt awful too. Kept thinking how upset Mum would've been."

I tapped his knee. "Hey look, we've all done stupid things. I should know. At least you realised in time, that's the main thing. It's all part of it—life."

He nodded slowly. "Yeah."

"I don't think it's connected, anyway. True, most Acorn students have had problems, but what does that tell us? In most people's eyes, it only goes to prove what a great person Verena is. She's rescued no-hopers and the homeless. You could easily see her as a hero. Only we know what she's really like."

"You're right. C'mon, let's get out of here, figure out what to do next."

He unpeeled himself from the wet rock and put out a hand to help me up. We edged towards the dim glow of the cave entrance, ducked low beneath the rocky crag and stepped outside. Rain lashed our faces and seeped into our clothes. The sky enclosed us like a dark grey dome, broken only by a pallor in the east, where daylight struggled to break through. I took a deep breath of salty air, with its underlying aroma of decaying seaweed and tiny corpses.

I peered all around and rubbed my shivering arms. To my right, I could make out the outline of the boathouse, amid jagged rocks. Up ahead, huge waves thundered and slammed onto the shore. On the horizon, the island was a dark turtle shape, greenish-grey in the advancing dawn.

My earlier excitement at being free had faded. It was great to leave the school behind, but part of me had hoped the tunnel would lead us to Verena—and to Jess. As it was, although we had the little sachets and Lydia's journal to show to the police, we didn't have much else. And if I was wrong about the cocoa, might I be wrong about the sachets?

"Where can she be?" I muttered, thinking about Verena, my eyes roving the stormy sea. Finally it hit me. I grabbed Adam's arm and pointed. "I know where Verena is."

CHAPTER 22

THE wind howled as we stood watching the horizon. The island was barely visible, bathed in grey mist, but I could make out the wooded canopy shaped like a turtle's shell and the low, flat area to the left where its neck stretched parallel with the mainland.

"Why would Verena be on the island?" Adam slicked back his sodden hair. "It's a nature reserve."

"Hmm. So we've been told. But Lydia mentioned something in her journal about a boat crossing. And you heard Faye Craddock. Verena's *over there*."

Adam looked down, scuffed the sand with his foot. "I don't know."

"Don't you get it? She can come and go whenever she wants. She's got her own private route, via the tunnel and by boat. No one would see her. She's even got that wardrobe, to change clothes."

"But why? What's the point?"

"That's what we've got to find out."

Adam retraced his steps, leaned against the rock face beside the cave and gazed into space. After a moment he said, "Maybe you're right. I've seen a boat coming from that island, too." He indicated a stone quay further along the beach, not far from where we stood. "It could dock on the jetty there."

We gazed towards the island, perhaps a mile away, divided from us by a blustery expanse of ocean. The foamy white horses weren't so high now, but beyond them the sea looked like it was boiling. After my near-drowning as a child, it gave me goose bumps just to look at it.

I sighed. "Perhaps if we tell the police, they'll—"

"I can't see the police setting off to explore the island on our say-so." Adam wiped the water from his eyes. "Will this bloody storm ever stop? ... Yeah, I know that's the sensible thing to do. But what if they think we're trouble-makers? Verena will wriggle out of it, I know she will. We'll end up back at Acorn."

"Jess is missing, though. They can't ignore that."

"True. But Verena could make up some story, say Jess ran off on her own, the way Lydia did. Who d'you think the students will back? Us or her?"

We stood for a moment, undecided. It would certainly take some smooth talking on Verena's part to explain two missing girls. All the same, if anyone could do it, Verena could.

Adam glanced at me. "You look freezing."

"I wonder why." It wasn't the cold that was making me shiver, though. It was the thought of what I knew we had to do.

Adam scanned the cliffs behind us. "Okay, how about this." He pointed to a narrow path in the steep incline. "You head up that track. Climb onto the road."

I folded my arms. "I don't like the sound of this."

"I know you can do it," he said, misunderstanding me. "Jess told me you're like a mountain goat. Head for Lamledra. I'll meet you there, soon as I can. If I've not turned up by tonight, go to the police."

He turned and marched off along the beach. Taken aback, I stood and glared.

"Come on," he called. "You can help me get her in the water before you go."

"Huh?" My feet sank into wet ground as I went to catch up with him. "Get who in the water?" Then the penny dropped. "Surely you're not taking that wreck from the boathouse? You're crazy. It's ancient!"

He reached the boathouse door and paused to look at me. His face was pale, his dark hair plastered to his head. "I've got to try," he said. "I'll never forgive myself if—"

"You'll never make it. You'll drown. C'mon, Adam, let's think of another way."

"There's no time." He rummaged in his jeans pocket and pulled out a few notes. "Here's thirty pounds. Might be enough for a taxi."

I ignored his outstretched hand. "Don't be daft."

Silence fell for a moment, then I sighed, resigned to the fact that he wouldn't be dissuaded from his crazy plan. "All right, then, let's go." At his puzzled look, I added, "I'm not letting you go on your own. We'll go together."

"No! Absolutely not."

"I'm not afraid," I lied. I stared him down, ignoring my thudding heart and the weakness in my legs. I had a horrible feeling that if he went alone, I'd never see him again, Jess neither.

He glanced at the sea, then up at the turbulent sky. "Too dangerous. I don't want you on my conscience as well."

"For God's sake." I thrust him out of the way and opened the rickety door. "It's almost light. We'll be spotted if we don't get a move on."

Adam followed me inside. "I'm not going to win this one, am I?"

"Too right."

I eyed the old hulk. It was even more dilapidated than I remembered. Dirt and mould grimed the planks of wood forming the seats—one each end and a third across the middle. The outer paintwork was a grubby mottled blue, the paint cracked and peeling. The boat's name—*Louise*—was so faded I could barely read it.

"She's seen better days," said Adam.

"Kind of an understatement, don't you think?"

He examined the shadowy interior. "Can't see any holes, though."

Even I knew that water could seep through the tiniest gaps, but there was no point in saying so. "At least the oars are still here," I muttered.

"You *can* swim, right?"

"'Course I can," I said, rolling my eyes. No way would Adam let me come if I told him the truth.

I grabbed the nearest side, the wood cold and damp

to the touch. Adam squeezed in beside the wall and gripped the opposite edge. We braced ourselves to lift.

"Okay," said Adam. "On the count of three."

The boat was heavy, but shifted surprisingly quickly. Half-dragging and half-lifting, we heaved it towards the doorway and down the ramp, then bumped it through the wet sand towards the shore.

"How long since you last rowed?" I asked, remembering that his parents used to take him out in a boat.

"A while. Couple of years."

"Hmm. Practically yesterday."

"You don't forget. What about you?"

I hesitated. "I've done it before." I didn't tell him that was years ago, as a child, and I barely remembered it.

As we reached the shoreline, I tripped on a rock and stumbled, wincing as I bashed my shin. We dropped the boat at the water's edge. When I saw the waves hurtling towards us, I went clammy all over, and the memory of the time I almost drowned came back so clearly, it could have been yesterday. The choking pain in my lungs. The desperate scrabbling. The roar of the water, the barely-heard screams in the distance. Indescribable panic as water flooded my nose and burned my throat.

We'll never make it. It's suicide.

Adam's gaze met mine. "Are we sure about this?"

"Let's get on with it," I said, gritting my teeth. If he suspected how terrified I was, he'd insist on going

222

without me.

As he reached down to grab his side of the boat, he said in a low voice, "I've never met anyone like you, Holly."

He mumbled something else, too. Although I strained to hear, the wind gobbled up his words. I desperately wanted to ask him what he'd said, but there was no time. Adam sure knew how to pick his moment. I gripped the boat and we plunged into the sea.

Foam swirled all around as water filled my trainers and engulfed my legs. *Louise* twisted this way and that, bobbing about with a mind of her own, the sea slurping at her like the lips of a hungry baby.

"Get in," shouted Adam. "I'll push her further out, then jump in myself. Hold onto the oars."

"Okay."

As I scrambled over the side, a wave rocked the boat, almost throwing me out again. I teetered and struggled to steady myself, then staggered over to the central seat. Just in time, I grabbed the oars from the floor of the boat.

Over my shoulder, I watched Adam shove the boat forward, the water up to his thighs. Then, much more gracefully than I had, he levered himself over the side and stood up.

"Move over here." He indicated the seat behind him. "I'll do the rowing."

"No, let me. It'll warm me up." I didn't like to say, but he still looked exhausted.

He opened his mouth to object, but I stared him

down. "We can take turns."

With a sigh, he sank onto the wooden planks behind him. "Okay."

I wriggled the oars into position and glanced back at Adam. He was frowning.

"Holly, you row a boat facing the stern, not the bow. You don't know how to do it at all, do you?"

"I'm a bit rusty," I admitted. "But that means it's better for me to go first, doesn't it, while we're near the shore?"

He sighed, like he was too tired to argue. I stepped over the seat and positioned myself across from him.

I grabbed the oars. "How am I supposed to see where I'm going, if I have to row backwards?"

"I'll direct you."

While Adam called out instructions, I drew the oars through the water. The boat moved—but in a wiggly line. However hard I tried, one oar moved us forward, while the other stabbed aimlessly at the surf.

"Is water coming in?" I shouted to Adam, not daring to take my eyes off the oars and the sea.

"No. Just the spray. Smooth, firm strokes, Holl. Whatever you do, don't let us turn side on. We'll capsize, if you do."

"Great," I managed through chattering teeth.

As I got into my stride, the boat sliced through the ocean in the vague direction of the island, and the solid ground of the mainland disappeared into the distance. My muscles ached as I pushed them to the limit, eager to escape this death trap of a boat as quickly as I could.

"The island's not getting any closer!" I fought to make myself heard against the roar of the wind and the crashing of the boat through the waves.

"My turn. No arguments. We're over halfway."

He sounded shattered, but I was too by now, so I agreed to let him take my place. As I stood up to switch seats, an enormous plume of spray drenched me, followed by the biggest wave I'd ever seen. The boat lurched and tilted, and I flung my arms wide. There was nothing to grab. As my hand found the side of the boat, another wave crashed over us. I flew through the air and plummeted into the sea.

CHAPTER 23

"HOLLEEEE!" Adam's cry was distant as oily darkness submerged me. The freezing water smashed the breath from my lungs. I forced open my stinging eyes. All I could see was a swirling, foamy mass.

My rib cage felt like it would burst open. I whirled my arms, desperate for air, but couldn't tell up from down. I writhed and twisted, somersaulting through the icy spray. The seawater began to fade into blackness. The ringing in my ears diminished, until I heard only silence. Everything felt light and floaty, like I was drifting to sleep. The darkness rippled and sparked with tiny flashes of light.

Something hard jabbed me in the back. My face broke free of the water and sweet air filled my lungs.

"Grab hold!" Adam was perched on the side of the rocking boat, leaning forwards at a perilous angle as he stretched the oar towards me. I flailed madly but couldn't grasp it. Adam leaned out even further, sure to topple over. Glimpsing the oar only dimly through the foam, I scrabbled towards it. It slapped against my fingers but the current swept me out of reach. At last, I gripped the oar and held on tightly.

Adam gave an almighty tug and I scythed through

the water like a fish. Firm hands clutched me and pulled. I slid over the side of the boat and collapsed in a heap.

The waves were still hurtling around us. While I crawled onto the seat opposite him, Adam seized the oars. I sat shivering and spluttering while he rowed as though his life depended on it.

He yelled to make himself heard over the roaring surf. "Are you all right? Can you breathe?"

I nodded, my teeth chattering too much to speak.

"You lied," he said. "You can't swim."

I rubbed water from my eyes, too dazed to reply.

The island loomed over us, shadowy green. As hazardous rocks rose like fists from the sea, I scanned the shore, desperately searching for a place to land.

"There!" I shouted, glimpsing a gap. "Right a bit. Between those tall rocks. There's a beach."

Adam nodded, glancing over his shoulder to where I pointed. The boat veered towards a strip of pebbles and sand.

With waves swelling in all directions, Adam pulled an oar free and used it to manoeuvre us between the rocks. Near the shore, we leapt into the sea and dragged *Louise* the final few metres. She ground to a halt on gravelly sand, half in and half out of the water. Soaked and exhausted, we fell face down beside her.

I lay shivering, grateful to be alive. Adam laid a hand on my arm.

"You're definitely all right?"

"Freezing, thirsty, scared. Apart from that, fine." I

cleared my throat. "I'm sorry I lied about being able to swim."

"I'll teach you, when this is over." He heaved himself slowly to his hands and knees. "C'mon, we'd better hide the boat. Anything happens to her, we're stranded."

"As if I need reminding." I studied the scrubland at the foot of the cliff. "What about the trees at the back there?"

"Good plan."

We grabbed the boat and tugged. It was much harder-going than it had been on Acorn's beach. Rolls of seaweed slithered aside as we forced our way across the shore. A gull soared overhead, shrieking, surprising me so much I nearly fell over.

When we reached the trees, they looked nowhere near as dense as they had from the shoreline. We hauled the boat across the wiry grass and into a ridge behind a pine, where it was shielded by brambles.

"It'll have to do." Adam looked at me and frowned. "Um, I'd offer you my shirt, but it isn't much dryer …"

"Not necessary," I said, thrusting a palm at him. "I'll dry off."

Glancing about, I found a cord-like piece of seaweed and managed to tie a ponytail in my matted, sticky hair.

Adam watched, smiling. "Very chic. You'd make a great castaway."

"Funny."

"At least your sooty streaks have gone."

"Even drowning has its benefits."

"Half-drowning. You didn't actually drown." He stepped onto a rock and squinted up at the cliffs. "Right then, let's explore this island of yours. Can't see anyone around, but I guess we'd better keep our voices down."

I pointed in the opposite direction, towards the turtle's head. "It looks more wooded that way, less exposed. And I think I can see a path, snaking round to the top."

Adam followed my gaze. "Could be. We'll get a good view of the other side from up there. Okay, you win—again."

Cold and weary, we left the pebbly beach and struggled across slippery rocks gleaming with mussels and limpets. The overgrown track wound upwards between stony outcrops, with gorse, ferns and wild flowers on either side. As we got higher, woodland rose around us, mostly pines. We spoke only when necessary, walking side by side where the path allowed, or in single file where it narrowed or disappeared.

Jess had once called me a mountain goat, but my movements were far from agile now. Weak from lack of food and sleep, my legs ached and every step was an effort. My wet clothes clung to me as I dragged myself along, trying to warm up, or at least dry off.

Glancing back the way we'd come, I saw that Tresawle House was now visible, a pallid smear set back from the cliffs. If I could see Acorn, might someone at the Academy see us? With a pair of binoculars, they certainly would.

As if to taunt me, the storm gave a last gasp and a wintry sun crept out from behind the clouds. By the time we reached the top, we stood exposed beneath an expanse of clear blue sky.

We'd seen no buildings of any sort, no sign of human habitation, not so much as a sweet wrapper. Wildlife, however, was everywhere. Bees buzzed across the heather, rabbits ducked into bracken as we passed. Birds trilled warnings and black-backed gulls swooped at us from the cliffs, as though resenting our intrusion.

I began to wonder if the island was just as it was supposed to be. A private nature reserve.

Adam nodded towards a puddle, brimming from the night's rain. "D'you reckon that's safe to drink? I'm dying of thirst."

"So am I."

We cupped our hands and drank, too thirsty to care about germs. The water slid down my parched throat, cool and refreshing.

As I stood up, a movement in the bay below caught my eye. Two grey heads broke the surface, smooth skin glistening.

"Hey, look," I said, grabbing Adam's arm.

We watched the seals stretch their bodies and float on the water. For a second I wished Adam and I were here on a day trip, reunited with Jess. I'd longed to see this island, but never in my wildest dreams had I imagined visiting it in circumstances like these.

I shook my head sadly. "What an amazing place."

"Yeah. No people to spoil it."

We set off again, plunged into shadow by woodland. Fir trees lurked either side of us, like soldiers waiting for battle. The storm had ripped limbs from some of them, while one lay completely flat, its roots dangling like snakes. We crept along nervously, glancing in all directions for signs of people.

Adam pointed upwards, to the highest patch of land, the top of the turtle's shell. "That ridge. We should be able to see the other side from there."

"Looks a bit steep, even for me. But let's give it a try."

We climbed slowly, slipping on mud and stones. As we emerged onto the rocky ridge, a stunning panorama opened out. We could now see the island pretty much in its entirety. Hoping to spot something of interest, I peered all around.

The far side was barer, grassland dotted with heather and gorse. There were no buildings, no vehicles of any sort. I scanned the view a second time.

"There's nothing here. It's just an uninhabited island. I'm so sorry, Adam."

He shook his head. "Don't be daft. Not your fault."

My hunch about Verena's whereabouts had been wrong, and by the time we got back to the mainland, we'd have wasted precious hours. We'd risked our lives to get here, and it had all been in vain.

Adam walked a few steps, peering between the gorse. He stopped and raised a hand.

"What?" My gaze followed his down the hillside.

"Down there, by the sea. D'you think it could be a small quay? Somewhere you could moor a boat, anyway? Can't tell for sure from this angle. We certainly wouldn't see it from Acorn."

The partially concealed line of rock did look smooth and straight, possibly man-made.

"And look there!" Adam pointed halfway down the slope.

"What? I don't see anything."

"By those bushes with the berries."

In a dip beyond the trees, I spotted an odd semi-circle of grass.

CHAPTER 24

THE autumn sunshine had started to dry my clothes, but my feet were still damp inside soggy socks. I shivered as I surveyed the distant patch of grass, halfway down the hillside. It looked fairly ordinary—except for a curious grass lip, curving around in a semi-circle. Some kind of raised rim, dipping down on the far side, towards the sea.

Adam kept his voice low. "Looks way too neat to be natural. And the area around it is more landscaped."

"Could it be one of those observation shelters, for watching wildlife? Something built into the hillside?" Part of me couldn't help hoping it was.

"Let's go see. Keep your head down."

We slunk along, low to the ground. Darting between bushes, we zigzagged down the hillside, approaching the semi-circle from behind. The grass was sodden from the storm, slippery with mud, and it took all my concentration not to skid and fall.

We hid behind a clump of rhododendrons, perhaps a hundred metres away. As Adam had suspected, this area was more like a lawn, dotted with red-berried shrubs. He pointed past the semi-circle to a flat area, previously concealed behind bushes.

"That bit's tarmacked. Could be somewhere for helicopters to land."

"And look there," I said, pointing beyond it. "A boat!"

Moored among the rocks was a small white motorboat with blue trim, which bobbed gently in the water, a gull on its roof.

People came here, that much was certain. We broke cover and made a dash for a shrub near the semi-circle, the closest we could get without being exposed. From there, we could see that it was definitely man-made—some kind of grassed platform, opening out of the hillside towards the sea.

"We'll have to crawl onto it," said Adam. "Then we can peer over the ledge and see what's on the other side."

"Wait," I said, holding him back. "We'll be right out in the open." By now it was mid-morning, the sun bright in the sky.

"Sure, but we need to see what this thing is. We can't just walk down and around to the front."

"Okay. Guess we don't have much choice."

We sprinted towards the semi-circle. At the point where the grassed platform swept out of the hillside, we crouched onto hands and knees and edged gingerly onto it.

The surface felt sturdy beneath the grass. All the same, I crawled slowly, anxious in case it wouldn't take our weight. With every movement, I expected to go crashing down to whatever lay beneath.

I looked left and right, listening for signs of life, but the whole area was silent. We flattened ourselves near the edge, wriggled forwards and peered over the roofline.

Below us was the curving front of a building, perhaps eight metres wide and three high. A tarmac path led up to it, flanked by grass slopes. Apart from some narrow strips of wall, the façade was made entirely of glass, the door and window panels flowing seamlessly together to make one curved whole. The glass was tinted grey, making it impossible to see what was inside.

"Looks a bit hi-tech for a bird-hide," I whispered.

"We need to get closer," Adam said, his face tense. "We'll have to go down."

We snaked to the side, then scrambled down the sloping bank. I looked left and right, but there was still no sign of anyone. Pressing close to a small section of wall, we stopped near the first window, then edged back for a moment to get a quick view of the structure as a whole.

My eyes widened. "Wow!"

The bank of windows swept around in a smooth crescent, all smoky-grey glass apart from a darker ring at the centre, where the door was. It was subtly done, but the effect was dramatic—that of a giant glass eye, staring down the hillside towards the sea.

There was no doubt in my mind. This place was connected to Acorn Academy, to the sachets with the eye logo. It had to be.

We sneaked back up the slope and sat on the edge of the roof, peering down at the façade below.

"Could be bigger than it looks," Adam whispered. "Can't tell how far it goes into the hillside."

"Not very secret, though, is it? Any passing ship would see it."

Adam shrugged. "All they'd see is an odd structure, on private land. Nothing illegal in that. We need to get inside."

I nodded, my thoughts racing. From what I could see, the door had no handle, just a small keypad, tinted to blend in with the eye's iris. We'd have no chance of discovering the code, and even if we did, someone could be waiting for us on the other side.

"Maybe there's another way in," I suggested. "A back way somewhere."

"Shh." Adam put his hand over my mouth. Following his gaze down the slope, I saw one of the windows opening.

We watched in silence as the bottom ledge of the window levered out a few centimetres and stopped. I half expected to hear someone call our names, but nothing happened, no one appeared.

Adam turned to me, smiling at our good fortune. A whisper of doubt stole through me, but I brushed it aside. The people who came here, whoever they were, would have little need to worry about intruders in such an isolated place. Besides, with all that glass, it must get quite hot and stuffy inside. No wonder someone had opened the window.

We made our way once again down the slopes and fell to our knees. The open window was the third one in. Adam slithered like a lizard beneath the first, then the second. Concealed by the strip of wall running under the windows, he paused below the open one, bunching up so I could join him. I waited beside him, crouched right down, listening for sounds from inside.

The room was totally silent, but that didn't mean no one was there. Whoever had opened the window might be alone, quietly working—or sitting just inside, watching the view.

With careful movements, Adam gripped the bottom ledge. There was a soft scraping as he levered the window out a few centimetres more. The room remained silent, no one came running to see who was outside. He tugged again. The window locked into place perhaps two feet from the ledge. We waited, listening hard. Then, with the utmost stealth, we poked our heads up through the gap.

No one. I saw a small office, with a couple of desks and some filing cabinets. It was modern and smart, with pale lilac walls, computers and a huge spiky cactus in one corner, like a caveman's club. On the far side was a door, shut. Whoever had opened the window must have left the room that way.

I ducked down again, out of sight, but Adam was already pushing himself further inside, wriggling through the gap.

I glanced about wildly, still anxious that this could

be a trap. Maybe I should stay outside, just in case. But then, almost against my will, I found myself following him. I'd seen too many horror movies not to know that splitting up never ended well.

I landed with a thump on the wooden floorboards, almost losing my balance. Realising I'd been too tense to breathe, I sucked in some air. Adam flashed me another smile, but I couldn't return it. My skin prickled at the thought of how easy it had been. Maybe too easy.

I tiptoed over to a bookshelf and scanned the books. They seemed perfectly ordinary, mostly on natural history or related subjects—exactly the kind of books I'd expect to find at a nature reserve. The only unusual thing in the room was an antique toy theatre sitting on a filing cabinet, showing some kind of palace ball, with masked puppet dancers wearing harlequin gowns and costumes. It was creepy, especially the puppet representing death, with his grinning skeleton mask and scythe. Not exactly suspicious, though.

My gaze fell on a folder on a desk. In the top corner was the logo of the eye, the tiny map of the world clear in its pupil. Beneath, in flowery italics, was printed the name *Globe Industries.*

Silently, I pointed it out to Adam. He nodded. While he checked the filing cabinet for unlocked drawers, I examined the folder in more detail.

It contained a report, hand-written in a dense, spidery script, peppered with scientific names and graphs. It made no sense to me at all. I shut it and left it as I'd found it.

We crept to the door, opened it a fraction and glanced through. Dimly-lit corridors snaked out of view to left and right. We turned right and followed the curving path into the hillside. The place was deathly quiet. Not so much as a bird call reached us from outside.

After a few paces I stopped and wrinkled my nose. "Perfume," I whispered, tasting it on my lips. Something floral, with an underlying chemical smell.

A flickering fluorescent strip lit the way as we crept along. I moved quietly, like a cat, with frequent glances over my shoulder. With every step, the flowery smell intensified.

As we approached an open door to the left, a shuffling noise came from within. I froze, then flattened myself against the corridor wall. Adam followed suit.

I glanced behind at him and he shrugged. If we wanted to check out the entire building, we needed to get past the door. Should we take the risk?

I shifted my weight from one foot to the other, and my trainer gave a tiny squeak. I tensed, certain I'd given us away.

No further sounds came from within the room. Inching towards the doorway, I peered around the edge.

The room looked like a laboratory, with wooden workbenches, computer screens and large shelving units crammed with bottles and jars. Nearby, a man stood bent over something, his back to us. Behind him other men worked in silence at computers. Dressed in dark suits, they seemed solemn, absorbed in their work. The man nearest us appeared more casual, dressed in a grey polo neck sweater over black trousers.

He straightened up and stretched, shaking back a mass of shaggy grey hair. My stomach flipped as he turned a little towards us, but he didn't see us. Beyond him I glimpsed a microscope and small trays. I nodded quickly to Adam. We slipped past the door and raced on down the corridor.

The further in we went, the more uneasy I became. I remembered the time I'd got lost in the Hall of Mirrors, as a child, when I'd thrown myself at a mirror in my desperation to get out. We passed another door, plain white. Hearing no sound coming from inside, I gripped the handle and cautiously tried it. Locked. Then, on the right, we came to another room, one with a small window at eye level.

Heads together, we scanned the interior. It was small and cell-like, simply furnished with a narrow bed, bedside table and desk. No people.

I flinched as a noise sounded in the distance: *thud-thud-thud*, like some kind of machinery. I glanced nervously along the corridor, which snaked out of sight in the direction of the noise.

Adam moved on to the next room, and peered through the little window.

He froze. With a gasp, he stood back, his mouth open. Darting to join him, I gazed through the glass.

The room was similar to the previous one, except for one crucial difference.

A girl sat at the desk, bent over some papers. She wore a plain red dress with a white cardigan. Near her hand lay a teacup and a small plate.

Her face was turned away from us, but the glossy dark hair was unmistakable.

CHAPTER 25

ADAM sank against the wall, blinking, as though fighting for control of his emotions. As one, we turned back to the window in the door. The girl sat at a desk to the left, sideways on to us. She was writing, working from an open book at her elbow. Curly hair, hanging loose, hid most of her face, but we hadn't been mistaken. It was Jess.

Adam went to tap on the window and I put out a hand. "No!" I whispered. "She might cry out."

Without any real hope of success, I gripped the door handle and turned. To my surprise, the door gave. Adam and I shared a glance. Slowly and quietly, not daring to breathe, I pushed the door open further. Jess must have heard us by now, but she didn't look up. Silently, we sneaked into the room.

"Jessie!" Adam cried.

Jess turned her head. An icy chill ran through me as I saw how pale she looked, with bloodless lips and sickly skin, her eyes ringed with blue shadows. Seeing Adam, she made a small sound, like a moan, and the pen she held slipped from her grasp.

Adam put a finger to his lips. Jess stared, as though

unable to move or speak. She looked stunned for a moment. Then it was as if a veil drew across her face, draining the life from her eyes.

Adam embraced her, squeezing tightly, his face buried in her hair. Jess remained motionless in the chair, her arms limp.

"Let's get you out of here," Adam said.

He urged Jess to her feet, half-lifting her from the chair. She submitted like a rag doll, hardly seeming to notice. I checked the corridor. It was still empty, but surely our luck would run out soon.

When Jess was standing, Adam hugged her for a brief moment.

"Come with us, Jess," I murmured. "Quick as you can."

Adam gripped her round the waist and they shuffled towards the door. At the threshold, her face clouded and she stopped.

"No." She tried to draw away.

"Jess, come on," hissed Adam.

"I like it here."

Adam shot me a desperate look. Jess hadn't spoken loudly, but wasn't making any effort to be quiet, either. Stepping forward, I took her free hand. It was hot to the touch, almost burning, and beads of sweat stood out on her forehead. Together we tried to coax her through the doorway. Jess shook her dark curls, refusing to budge.

"We're taking you home," I said, then bit my lip, regretting my words. Neither Jess nor Adam had a home any longer.

"Have to stay here!" Jess stood firm. "They made me well. If I leave, I'll get ill again. They t-told me."

"They're lying," Adam said.

Jess pulled away from us, eyes narrowing. "No."

With every wasted second, our chances of getting caught multiplied. I looked all round, ears alert for sounds. "Jess, we don't know what they're doing, but it's not for your good. You remember me, don't you? I'm your friend."

Jess frowned. Her lips parted as she tried to say my name, but all that came out was a soft *hoh*.

"Holly," I finished for her.

Blinking rapidly, Jess glanced from me to Adam, then back to me again. "You're my … my …" Her eyes brimmed, and a tear rolled down her cheek.

"Yes! We're friends, good friends." I pulled up my sleeve, exposing my bracelet of amethysts and blue beads.

"Look. You made this for me." I forced myself to speak softly, as though Jess were a frightened fawn, and would bolt at the first sign of danger.

Jess stared at the bracelet. "I made …?" The trace of a smile lit her face. "It's pretty."

While she was distracted, Adam propelled her through the doorway and into the corridor. I followed swiftly and pulled the door shut behind me. Sandwiched between us, Jess took a few halting steps. Then, gaining momentum, we hurried towards the exit, back the way we'd come.

Although still reluctant, Jess walked with us along the snaking corridors. The biggest danger would be getting past the room we'd seen, the one with the men in it, but there was no sign of it yet. I realised I was gripping Jess's hand so tightly, I must be crushing her fingers. I relaxed my grip, hoping and praying we could keep her quiet long enough to escape.

The corridors all looked the same, and seemed to go on forever. "This doesn't seem right," whispered Adam, his face misted with sweat. "D'you think we've gone the wrong way?"

"It does seem further than before," I said.

Then, with no warning, Jess dug in her heels. Eyes rolling upwards, she shook her head from side to side and began to moan.

"No … no!"

I tried to clamp my free hand over her mouth, but Jess writhed and twisted, determined to pull away. Footsteps sounded, out of sight beyond a bend.

Someone called out, "Jessica? Is that you?" The voice was gravelly, deep and authoritative.

"Help!" cried Jess. "They're taking me away."

Adam swore. "Oh, Jess, what have you done?"

I glanced about wildly. Might we get out another way, if we turned back? Or would we be sealing ourselves further inside the hillside?

Too late. A man came into view, one I recognised from the laboratory. He saw us and stopped, his mouth dropping open in an almost comical way. His shaggy mane of hair, together with sideburns and a beard, gave him the look of a grey wolf.

"Well, well!" He folded his arms. "Uninvited guests." Glancing back over his shoulder he added, "It's all right. I'll handle this."

"Saul," called Jess, struggling in my grip. "Help me!" My palms were slippery, making it almost impossible to hold on.

"What d'you think you're doing?" The stranger stood watching us, blocking our escape.

My mouth went dry as he strode towards us. He was solidly-built, beefy and muscular. With sudden strength, Jess pulled free of my grasp and reached for his outstretched hand. Clinging to her other arm, Adam tried to pull her back.

"They made me!" she whimpered.

I stood frozen, my legs refusing to move. I couldn't believe what Jess was doing, though I knew it wasn't her fault.

Greywolf took her hand and patted it. "There, there, sweetheart. Everything's fine. Let's get you back to your room, eh?"

"Leave her alone!" yelled Adam.

The man gave a lop-sided grin. "It's not how it looks, y'know."

Adam tightened his grip on Jess's arm. "Jess is my sister, and I'm not going anywhere without her."

"Hmm, yes, that's understandable. I can explain, if you'll give me the chance."

"Explain what? What have you done to her?"

"I'll tell you everything you want to know, I

promise. But we need to get Jessica back to her room." His eyes were blue, as pale as a cloud.

When we made no move, his voice grew wheedling. "The dear girl will panic, if we don't. She could hurt herself. You're free to leave, any time you wish. But please, give me this chance."

Jess gazed into space, a faraway look on her face. Adam looked at me, then at Greywolf.

"Any more distress and she could have a seizure," the man added, his tone more urgent. "Not nice, I assure you."

Adam let out a sigh, clearly unsure how to react.

"Tell us, then," he said at last.

I stood to one side while Greywolf—or Saul, as Jess had called him—threw his arm around her shoulders and walked her back towards her room. Adam and I followed close behind. I shook my head at Adam, convinced the man was lying, yet equally at a loss to know what to do.

Jess scurried into the room and threw herself on the bed. She drew her legs up in front of her and watched Saul as a dog might watch a master.

"What's wrong with her?" Adam asked, a catch in his voice. "Why is she here?"

Saul lowered himself into the chair by the desk, calm and unhurried. He gestured to another chair against the wall, but I remained on my feet, near the door. Adam sat beside Jess on the bed and reached for her hand. She let him take it, but without any interest, her fingers resting limply in his.

I looked to Saul. He strung out the moment, his face tense as he gazed at his well-manicured nails, then up at the ceiling.

"Do forgive me," he said at last. "I haven't even offered you a drink. Cup of tea? Lemonade, perhaps?" He raised an eyebrow.

Adam shook his head. I ignored the offer, my stomach churning. Why wasn't Saul more curious about how we got here, and who we were? Come to that, why wasn't he angry with us for breaking in?

In the distance the thumping noise started up again, the *thud-thud-thud* we'd heard earlier, which came from the depths of the building.

"It's only the generator," Saul explained with the glimmer of a smile, although neither of us had asked. He steepled his fingers beneath his chin. "Well, Adam, I'm afraid your sister … I'm afraid Jess has a rare delusional illness."

He waited a moment for his words to sink in. From the way Jess had behaved, what he said came as no surprise. What shocked me more was his use of Adam's name. We hadn't mentioned it, had we? Had Jess told him?

Saul went on, "Jessica requires round the clock care. The good news is, she's in the best possible place. Here at Globe, we're at the cutting edge of research into these kinds of illnesses."

I finally found my voice. "You're saying you're her doctor?"

He gave a benign smile. "Her doctor and her

friend."

That didn't sound like something a doctor would say. I frowned at him, folded my arms. "How did she get here? Is Verena—"

"Holly!" warned Adam.

I wished I could learn to think before I spoke.

Saul sighed, drumming a light beat on his thighs. For a while I thought he wasn't going to answer, then he said, "Jessica has been very fortunate. Miss Blake was able to identify the signs and get her straight here into capable hands. Affording her the very best chance of recovery."

I looked at my feet, playing for time. *Globe Industries* might well be a private hospital of some sort. We'd seen nothing to suggest it wasn't. However, if Saul was involved with Verena Blake, we obviously couldn't trust him.

When I looked up, he was watching me closely, one pallid eye half shut.

"Truth is," he said, "Miss Blake saved Jessica's life."

"Huh!" I blurted out. "She's been keeping Adam and me prisoner. That's what she's really like."

Adam groaned and shook his head. Next to him, Jess's face was blank, her gaze glued to Saul.

Saul tugged at his beard. "I wouldn't know anything about that."

"It's true!" I said, unrepentant.

"She must have had her reasons." He wriggled in the chair. "You can trust Verena Blake one hundred percent. A sterling individual, she is. Smart, too." He gave a quick grin, showing sharp little teeth.

I scowled at him. Did he seriously rate her so highly, or had she fooled him too, brought him under her spell?

Saul got slowly to his feet. "It's natural to be concerned. Who wouldn't be? Adam, it's your right to do so, but you won't help Jessica by taking her from this place. You can see how confused she is. Even your being here is enough to tip her over the edge, and we've worked so hard to build up her confidence, to gain her trust."

I chewed my lip. Every word Saul spoke struck an off chord with me. I felt more certain than ever that we couldn't believe anything he said. We needed to get away, and fast.

Adam sighed and squeezed Jess's limp hand. "She doesn't even know me. Not properly, not the way she should."

"Yes, yes," Saul said with an understanding nod. He towered over Jess, grinning broadly. "Well, young lady. We'd better let you catch up with your studies." He peered over his shoulder at the exercise book on her desk. "Kings and Queens of England, eh? Charles the First, Henry the Eighth and all that? Food for thought, eh?" He turned to Adam. "Come along, now. Let's continue our discussion in the lounge, give the girl some peace."

I didn't think we should leave her, but Adam let go of her hand and stood up. Surely he didn't believe Saul's explanation? Finding her like this must have shocked him, thrown him into some kind of stupor. Or maybe he was going along with things for a minute, to buy us more time.

As we shuffled from the room, I tried to catch his eye, but Saul stood between us, his large bulk blocking my view.

I glanced back at Jess and forced a smile. Huddled against the wall, she eyed me warily. Saul pulled the door shut and steered Adam and me along the corridor.

"That's the spirit. How about that tea? The lounge is this way." His voice held a soothing sing-song quality. "We'll have a chat about getting you back to the mainland. Nice cup of tea while we work things out … or we've got cola, lemonade."

My mind whirled. If we could only get out of here, at least we knew where Jess was. We could hide in the woods, form some rescue plan. Or leave the island and go straight to the authorities. Kick up a fuss, force them to investigate.

In order for that to work, I mustn't blurt out anything more about Verena. I must let Saul think we'd swallowed his story and were prepared to do things his way. I had an idea.

"Uh, feel a bit faint," I said, fanning myself. "Can we go outside? There's not much air in here."

At last, Adam snapped out of his daze. Picking up my cue, he stopped and turned. "Yeah, good idea. I'll take you out for some air, Holl."

"Nonsense," Saul said smoothly. "The lounge is just here." He kicked open a door, arms held wide to steer us through. "A glass of water, that'll see her right."

"Holly doesn't want anything to drink," Adam said, turning back from the door. "Neither do I. Come on, Holl."

In fact, I would have killed for a glass of water, but by now I felt more wary than ever.

"The young lady can speak for herself," Saul said as he swept us inside. "A little refreshment before you leave. Believe me, the best thing you can do right now is return to Tresawle House. Let Verena handle this."

"You've got to be joking!" I cried. "I'm never going to let that woman near me again."

"Now that's where you're wrong," said a familiar voice.

Inside the room, Verena Blake looked up and smiled.

CHAPTER 26

THE room could have been lifted straight from Tresawle House. Tapestries and paintings hung on wooden panelling, above a rich red carpet like a pool of blood. A chandelier glimmered, catching the light from a glowing open fire. Although totally lifelike, the logs must surely have been fake, since we'd seen neither smoke nor chimney above ground.

Verena sat in a winged armchair, holding a floral cup and saucer. She looked relaxed and elegant in a grey suit, the scorpion brooch pinned to her lapel. The smile curving her lips suggested she'd been waiting for us, biding her time, like a cat stalking a mouse.

At the sound of her voice, Adam and I tried to back out of the room. Saul thrust us further inside, then stood in the doorway, blocking it with his bulk.

"My dears, there's no need to be afraid. Have a little drink with us before you go." He gestured to an ornate wooden table set against a wall, laid out with various bottles and glasses.

I glared. *No way are we drinking anything with you.*

Saul grinned and spread his hands. "Then, when you're refreshed, Verena will take you back where you belong."

Verena waved a hand. "Saul, there's no point in keeping up this charade. I told you there was no way they'd return of their own accord. We'll do it here. It makes no difference."

"All right, Vree. Have it your way."

Before we could react, Saul whipped something from his pocket. Black and chunky, with a square end, it looked fake, but I had no doubt it was a real gun. He pointed it at us, baring his sharp teeth.

"Aren't you a bit old for toys?" Adam's eyes flashed with anger.

Saul smiled and cocked his head. "Don't you like my Taser? Don't worry. They're rarely fatal. The little beast will give you a nasty electric shock, though, which is quite horrible and rather painful, so they say. I very much hope I won't need to use it. It goes against all I stand for."

Footsteps sounded in the corridor and a man in a guard's uniform towered over Saul's shoulder. He was young, under twenty I guessed, powerfully-built with close-cropped hair.

"I've found the boat, sir," he said. "We've smashed it up, like you said."

Oh no, poor *Louise.* The old boat might not have been much, but she had got us here.

Saul nodded towards a pistol at the man's waist. "Now that's what I call a real weapon, kids. Glock 27, .40 calibre. That one *would* kill you, so … on your best behaviour now, that's the ticket." He winked at the young guard. "Good work, Abedi. Go and man the entrance now, if you wouldn't mind. Tell Kris to stand guard outside this room."

"Yes, sir!" The guard turned and left.

"A great asset, young Abedi," Saul said to Verena. "You were right, Vree. As usual."

He grinned round at Adam and me. "You'd never believe it, but four years ago, Abedi was a child soldier in a dark corner of Africa. Now look at him. Smart, good prospects. Making his way in the world."

With a jolt, I remembered Lydia had mentioned a friend called Abedi in her journal. He'd left Acorn to take a job. So this was where he'd ended up.

"Out of the frying pan into the fire," I said. "That's what I'd call it."

Verena tutted. "Ever the insolent one, Holly." Her face changed as she and Saul shared a secretive glance. "I've been very patient, but the waiting is almost over. Today's the day, eh?"

Adam was staring at the wall furthest from us, at a row of CCTV screens. One showed the eye-shaped glass entrance to the building, outside which Abedi already stood, gazing towards the trees. The other screens displayed locations across the island, including the shoreline where we'd landed and the stone jetty with the white speedboat. As I watched, the images faded into views of the complex, including Jess's room, where she lay asleep beneath her bedcovers, only her hair visible.

"They reeled us in," Adam murmured to me. "They

knew we were here all along."

Verena leaned forward and placed her cup and saucer carefully on the table. "Did you really think you could break into our little hideaway as easily as that? I must say, I admire your pluck in getting here in that old rust-bucket of a boat. You were lucky not to drown—depending on how you look at it. But yes, you're right. We've been following your progress ever since you arrived. We've had such fun, haven't we, Saul?"

Saul waved his Taser. "Oh yes, indeedy. Watching you climb in the window was my favourite part. Better than telly, any day."

I edged closer to Adam. "What is this place?"

"I've already told you," said Verena. "It's a nature reserve."

"Stop winding us up," demanded Adam. Then he shrugged and added, "You might as well tell us. We're clearly not going anywhere."

"Yes, that's certainly true." Verena fell silent. I looked past her to the painting taking pride of place above the fireplace. Another portrait of Violet Tresawle, this time wearing a gown of pale grey, the same shade as Verena's suit. In this painting, Violet appeared just as stern as in the portrait on Acorn's staircase, but she was older, with a sad look in her eyes.

"Verena?" prompted Saul. "What are you waiting for?"

She batted her eyelashes. "I've waited a long time for this. I wish to savour the moment."

"Okay, sis, I wasn't fishing for an argument. There's no rush."

Sis? Verena and Saul were brother and sister?

She stood up and held out an arm. "Come with me."

When neither of us moved she added, "Well, do you want to know what we do here or not?"

Adam looked at me. I gave a slight shrug. If we left this room, we could at least stall for time. What's more, I was desperate to find out what was going on—not that I really believed she'd tell us.

Saul backed out of the way as we followed Verena into the corridor. He shadowed us, brandishing his Taser theatrically, as though he'd seen too many Westerns. My legs were unsteady beneath me. Adam grabbed my hand and squeezed, as if to say *Don't worry. We'll get out of here.*

Verena halted as we passed a second guard. "Kris, keep your weapon trained on them at all times."

The man nodded and turned to follow. He was young like Abedi, with golden-brown hair the same shade as my mother's, though his face contained none of her gentleness. Tears welled in my eyes. Where were my parents when I needed them? Would I ever see them again? Would Wilk pine for me, and wonder why I didn't come home?

"Put any thoughts of escape from your mind," Verena continued. "Jessica is now locked in—thanks to you—and Abedi and his colleagues are under orders to shoot, if they have to. Furthermore, as you heard from Abedi, your little boat wreck has been, well, wrecked, you might say. Smashed to smithereens. The command to shoot includes all three of you, by the way. I'd advise you to remember that. If she tries to escape, Jess will be shot, too."

"You're bluffing!" Adam cried.

"I never bluff," said Verena. "Truth is, she's becoming rather tiresome."

Adam's jaws twitched as he ground his teeth. We continued along the curving corridor, further into the building than we'd been before. Glancing over my shoulder, I saw the guard named Kris bringing up the rear, gun in hand.

"So you and Saul are brother and sister," I said to Verena. "That figures."

Adam snorted. "I get it. He's S.B. Saul Blake. That hospital phone number she gave me, the one she lied about."

"Rather clever of me, I thought," said Verena. "Saul's mainland residence, as it happens. Somewhere I knew to be empty at the time." She walked on for a moment, a smirk on her face. "Now, here's another little puzzle for you, my dears. I'll bet you can't tell me who our great-grandmother was."

I pictured myself on the stairs at Acorn, gazing at the portrait of Violet Tresawle. I thought of the painting in the room we'd just left. Something I'd begun to suspect for a while clicked into place.

CHAPTER 27

"YOUR great-grandmother was Violet Tresawle," I said.

Verena stopped walking and scowled. "Ever the know-it-all, Holly. It's a shame how you waste your intelligence. But you're right. The great family of Tresawle may be traced back to the times of William the Conqueror. Tresawle House itself is over three hundred years old. One of our ancestors was a friend of Queen Anne herself, and served at her court."

She waited, as though expecting a compliment. When none came, she strode along the corridor, heels clacking. "Poor Violet suffered a great deal, watching her father gamble away the family's wealth and land. You must have heard the story. All Acorn students are familiar with it. What's not so well-known is that, after the estate was sold, Violet went to live on the continent. There, she carved out a new life for herself."

I dragged my feet, playing for time, but with two weapons trained on us—Saul's Taser and the guard's gun—our options were limited, to say the least.

"What sort of life?" asked Adam.

Verena said, "Well, she married our great-grandfather, Frederick Blake. She had a child, Deverel, to continue the line, despite the fact there was no longer any house or fortune to inherit … or name to continue."

"Hmm," said Adam. "And that poor child was unlucky enough to have you and Saul for descendants."

Verena ignored him. "Violet swore that, one day, Acorn would be ours again. She raised our grandfather Deverel to do everything in his power to achieve this."

She stopped by an arched door and entered a code into a keypad. The door clicked open and she stepped through. We waited outside, Adam still gripping my hand.

Saul poked me in the back with his Taser. "Step lively, young lady. Verena's giving you the opportunity of a lifetime. We're rather proud of what you're about to see."

As I shuffled over the threshold, a wave of muggy air washed over me, smelling faintly of flowers. I heard soft sounds, little rustlings. Saul and the guard followed and shut the door.

We found ourselves in a muggy enclosure. Lining the white-washed walls, set into them at intervals, were large glass cabinets, which reminded me of the reptile house at the zoo.

Verena came to a stop by the first cabinet. Close up, I saw that it was cube-shaped, the size of a small greenhouse.

The scene inside was the picture of paradise—a slice of man-made rainforest. Mist swirled in the air and formed droplets on glossy-leaved plants and lush ferns. A soft breeze rustled delicate tendrils. Exotic flowers swayed beside a small pond covered in water lilies, fed by a mini waterfall.

Verena indicated a willowy shrub, just inside the window. "See there, halfway up that bush? The spider's web?"

Fascinated despite myself, I peered where she pointed. At first I couldn't see anything. Then I noticed a tangled mass of greyish threads, woven between V-shaped twigs. It looked like a lacy handkerchief which had been ripped to shreds. Gazing beyond, I saw similar webs hanging in the branches.

"What about it?" I frowned, reluctant to show any interest.

"That, my dears, is the web of *Anelosimus octavius*, a 'tangle web' spider from Costa Rica."

A spider hurtled towards us along the bough. Its torso was bulbous, silvery-white with a dark stripe, looking far too large for its long legs.

Thanks to my mum, who'd brought me up to relax around insects, I must have looked far less afraid than Verena hoped. Adam, however, showed more than enough fear for both of us. Sweat stood out on his forehead and his grip on my fingers was painful.

Verena chuckled. "What's this? A big lad like Adam, frightened of a little spider? Well! Who'd have thought it?" She tapped a screen next to the cabinet. "You can get a better view from the close-up camera."

Adam winced and shrank back, while I stood

mesmerised. The Costa Rican spider, magnified to the size of a grapefruit, scurried towards me on its spindly legs. Its wide mouth curved up at the edges. Its beady eyes glistened as it examined us.

"Interesting," Adam croaked, raking a hand through his hair.

"Now come and look at this one," Verena said.

The next glass container housed similar tropical foliage, but very different webs hung between the branches. I scanned the scene, half-expecting to see hundreds of stampeding legs, but I couldn't see a single spider.

"This vivarium was also home to the *Anelosimus* spider." Verena pointed to the nearest tangle of threads. "Note the *was*. As you can see, this is no ordinary web."

She was right. Compared with the previous web, it was much more solid and symmetrical, with a sheet over the top, stretched like a trampoline.

"This is the web of a spider infected by a parasitic wasp named *Zatypota*. The wasp injects the hapless spider with an egg. The larva hatches in the spider's abdomen, and feeds on her fluids. When it's ready to emerge, it hijacks the spider's brain."

The relish in her voice made me queasy. Her eyes glowed, their usual dullness gone.

"I'll bet you didn't know there were real-life zombies, did you?" she asked. "Well, this spider becomes a kind of zombie slave. Under the influence of the wasp larva, she builds a completely different web, covering it with a protective sheet. She spins a platform and opens a space below, where the larva may suspend its cocoon."

She studied our faces for a reaction. I tried to keep my face blank. Adam's eyes were wide with terror, and he looked so pale, I worried he'd pass out.

"The wasp larva thanks its generous host by killing her and crawling out of her body. It sucks the carcass dry and tosses her aside. The creature is now free to take up residence in its tailor-made abode."

I stared into the lacy handkerchief web. Sure enough, in the densest part, I could make out a tiny mummy-like oblong, suspended beneath a little stage.

Saul's breath brushed my neck as his gravelly voice boomed in my ear. "Fascinating, eh? And there are many, many examples of these creatures in nature. Here at Globe, we boast the finest collection of living parasites and host species on earth, all displayed in their natural habitats. Scientists visit us from across the world."

He paced the room, flinging his arms out left and right. "Here we have flies which eat the brains of ants, and pop out of their heads! There, barnacles which invade crabs' bodies and turn them into nannies for their young … Check out this zombiefied caterpillar, which plants itself in soil, so a fungus can grow out of its brain." He stopped and tapped a window. "And this, a personal favourite. A parasitic hairworm, which forces the grasshopper it lives inside to commit suicide by drowning." He shook his head in wonder. "Nasty."

Adam and I broke into single file as we followed. The humidity was stifling. Moisture trickled down my neck as I stared into the cabinets, both horrified and fascinated. Many of the creatures weren't visible to the naked eye, and could only be seen on the screens. Their habitats varied, including underwater environments for fish and crustaceans, and grassy scrub for flies, ants, snails or grasshoppers. Some were underground burrows, where worms writhed and beetles scurried.

"See kids?" said Saul with a broad grin. "Our own little nature reserve. What did we tell you?"

I said nothing. I couldn't deny I was impressed, as well as revolted, but there had to be more to Globe than this. Did they really intend to tell us?

At the end of the central walkway, Verena opened a door and strode through. Still waving his weapon, Saul pushed Adam and me after her. Adam trotted quickly ahead, clearly anxious to put some distance between us and the creatures on display.

We found ourselves in the laboratory, the one we'd seen earlier, only this time accessed via a different door. As I considered making a run for the opposite door, the guard marched across and stood blocking the way. His dead eyes rested on me, his hand never leaving his gun.

More screens dominated the walls in here, displaying single objects. Some were oval or wormlike, others shaped like stars or cylinders. I stared at the nearest one, which showed a melon shape with a slash in it, like a horrible red mouth. I gasped as the red slash twisted.

Saul smiled. "Oh yes, it's alive, alive-o. Greatly magnified, of course. The images on that wall are close-ups of our tiniest creatures, many of them single-celled. This one's the Lancet liver fluke. Ugly brute, isn't he?"

"Not as ugly as you," I said.

Saul laughed. "I dare say you're right, dear. But this clever little fellow lives inside ants and persuades them to crawl up onto blades of grass. Why? Because that's where the ant will be eaten by grazing sheep. Once inside the sheep, the fluke is able to complete its life cycle." He gave a satisfied sigh. "Kids, you've seen only a fraction of our living collection. We also house thousands of preserved specimens."

He walked over to a group of glass-fronted cabinets. Inside, gruesome shapes floated in jars. Ribbons, tiny hearts, eyeballs, worms, patches of fur. Others resembled grey beans—I dreaded to think what they really were.

Verena said, "Parasites are some of the oldest and most misunderstood organisms on the planet. Gruesome or macabre to some, exciting to others—but everyone must admire their success. Many have only one cell, yet manage to complete a life cycle involving separate hosts. They do so by changing the host's behaviour."

"All very interesting," said Adam, his voice hoarse. "What's it got to do with us?"

Don't ask, Adam, don't ask.

"Patience, my dears." Verena leaned against a desk. "You need to understand something important—that human progress always incurs a sacrifice. Look at smallpox. Smallpox vaccination was a tremendous leap in the fight against global disease, right?"

Adam shrugged. "I guess."

"Well, let me tell you how it came about. You see, Edward Jenner developed his vaccine by taking cowpox pus—similar to the deadly smallpox, although milder—and rubbing it into scratches on a healthy, eight-year-old boy. Later, this boy was inoculated with smallpox itself."

Saul crossed to Verena and heaved himself onto the desk. "You can imagine the consequences if things had gone wrong. However, as Jenner predicted, the experiments were a success. Thing is, his method would be considered wholly unethical by today's bleeding hearts. Yet in its day, it was a milestone of modern medicine." He grinned. "No pain, no gain."

"Exactly," agreed Verena, sharing his smile.

"So that's the sort of thing you've been working on here?" I asked. "Cures for diseases? Because you care so much for the human race?"

"I see what you mean about her, Vree," said Saul with a chuckle. "Sarky little madam, isn't she?"

Verena smiled. "She certainly is. In fact, *Globe Industries* was set up by our grandfather, Deverel. By a happy stroke of fate, a legal mistake was made in the sale of the estate, which meant that the island—this island—remained in our family. Tresawle House, meantime, had been bought by a trust and turned into a hospital. A psychiatric hospital."

This rang a bell. I remembered being told about it, on my first day at Acorn.

Adam folded his arms and glared. "So what?"

Verena paused to smooth back her hair. "We are all part of the animal kingdom, are we not? And, like other species, we play host to a range of microscopic life. Human cells are actually outnumbered in our bodies by non-human ones! A microbe may determine whether you'll be fat or thin. Another can affect how reckless you are, and can actually increase your chances of being involved in a car accident."

Saul laughed. "Haha, you could say, I'm less of an *I,* more of a *We.* Our cohabiters are a mixed bag, of course. Bacteria, fungi, viruses. Many of them essential for our health. What interested Grandfather Deverel were the parasites. How organisms such as those on display here might affect human beings."

Verena smiled. "In his notebooks, Grandfather wrote how odd it was, that people consider themselves separate, somehow immune from the effects of other organisms. Human vanity knows no bounds."

"His work made him rather rich, eh, Vree?" Saul licked his lips. "You'd be surprised how many people there are—politicians, drugs companies, despots— eager for Globe's research and products."

Verena nodded. "Grandfather Deverel bought out the hospital in no time. Returning Tresawle House to its rightful owners—our family. Which was not only the dearest wish of his mama, but also the ideal place to continue his research."

Adam clenched his fists. "The hospital patients. He used them. Those poor people."

"No, no, no," said Verena, shaking her head. "He *helped* them. He gave hope to the abandoned. Schizophrenics. Drug addicts. People whose disorders made them a burden. He took in homeless teenagers and other unfortunates. Over time, he developed new parasites. Parasites able to influence the mind so subtly, they make the average behavioural drug look as effective as a sweetie."

"Show them the Invertex," said Saul with a wink.

Verena crossed to a shelf of boxes similar to those we'd seen back at Acorn, all bearing the *Globe Industries* logo. She withdrew a sachet from one, tore off the top and emptied the powder into a saucer.

She held it out towards us. Adam and I stepped back.

"For Heaven's sake." Verena poked it with a rose-painted fingernail. "It won't bite."

I wasn't so sure about that, but I leaned forward and peered into the saucer. The powder looked like grey salt, laced with tiny strands of a mould-like substance.

Verena said, "This powder is seeded with a genetically-engineered parasite, *Linneola placator*. Our trademark product, along with all the nutrients it needs to thrive. It's as easy to use as a sugar cube. That's the beauty of it, you see?"

Saul nodded to a screen taking pride of place on the wall. It showed a roundish object, a metre high, mottled green apart from a small red oval inside. The oval contained yellowish oblongs, like decaying teeth.

"There's *Linneola* close-up," he said fondly. "A type of protozoan—single-celled animal to you—which hitch-hikes through the body by pretending to be part of our immune system. *I'm a good guy*, it says, *I help you fight infection*." He thumped the desk. "See how clever it is? Like a Trojan Horse. It infiltrates the central nervous system, and finally the brain, where it's free to do its work."

"You're monsters!" I cried. "Using us to test your drugs. It's disgusting."

"Not drugs," said Verena. "Haven't you listened to a word we've said? *Parasites*. Very clever parasites, designed by even cleverer people."

The four of us were silent. Everything seemed unreal, as though Verena and her brother were spinning their own web around Adam and me.

After a while, Adam asked quietly, "What about Jess?"

Saul shrugged. "It's a dreadful shame. Every so often we get a reactor."

"And the same thing happened to Lydia?" I asked.

"What does she know about Lydia?" said Saul, turning to Verena.

Verena waved a hand. "Oh, I think our duo have been doing a bit of detective work. But yes, like Lydia, poor girl. In her case, it didn't happen right away. Things seemed fine—but her organs gradually weakened. By the time we realised, it was too late to save her."

I took a breath. "You're evil. Lydia never did anyone any harm."

Verena hesitated. "You're missing the point. A child may appear obedient, it's true, but who can know the allegiance of the heart?" Catching Saul's frown, she added, "Oh, Saul, it doesn't matter what we tell them. Very shortly, they'll have forgotten our secrets, or if they remember, they'll no longer care."

"Huh," said Adam. "Threaten us all you like, but it hasn't worked on us so far, has it?"

A sly glance passed between Verena and her brother. "Shall we tell them?" Verena asked.

"Have it your way," he said with a shrug.

She crossed to a cabinet, opened a drawer and reached inside. Then she whipped around. In her hand was a Taser, identical to Saul's.

"Let's make ourselves comfortable, shall we?" she said.

She pointed it at me and fired. I felt a blow, somewhere around my chest. I was dimly aware of Adam rushing forward, of Saul's arm moving, of Adam collapsing.

I tried to cry out, but my mouth went slack, my tongue thick and useless. Shock radiated throughout my body, and I crumpled to the floor.

CHAPTER 28

THE next few moments were a blur. My muscles twitched as rough hands grabbed me and hauled me to my feet. Drifting in and out of awareness, I felt myself being pulled along the corridor. I tried to turn my head, to look for Adam, but he was nowhere to be seen.

***

I opened my eyes, wincing against the harsh light. The air smelled unpleasant, of chemicals. Looking down, I found myself half-sitting up in a narrow bed, fully clothed beneath a rose-coloured counterpane. A rope held my legs in place and my arms were pinned to my side, wrists tied to the metal frame.

Looking up, my eyes met those of a porcelain doll, sealed in a glass box on the wall. She was the only ornament in a room like a hospital ward, with four beds, two on each side, along with bleeping monitors and other apparatus. Adam lay diagonally across from me, in the furthest bed, his face white, blue hollows beneath his closed eyes. He was restrained by ropes, same as me. He'd also been gagged, his lips clamped around a white bandage.

"Adam?" I called.

No response.

"Adam, wake up." The words came out thick and slurred. My eyes drifted shut.

The door opened and Verena swished through, wearing a white coat over her suit. Smiling, she dragged a chair over and sat beside me.

"Holly. Glad you're awake. How are you feeling, dear?"

My body felt heavy and sore, like it wasn't my own. My head ached and my mind was groggy and sluggish.

"Never better," I told her.

"You may feel a little weak. We've taken the precaution of giving you a sedative, the same one we gave you back at Acorn. My goodness, you and Adam must be fit and healthy, to have fought it sufficiently to escape your rooms. Adam, especially, who was more than happy to drink it, so I hear. I was truly impressed. We've given you a stronger dose this time. It'll keep you docile while we get to the real business of the day."

She leaned across me, her face so close I could see the downy hair on her cheek.

"Before we start," she said. "I want to ask you a question."

I heard a moan. Adam was coming round, stirring in the bed. He looked across at me, his gaze confused.

Verena slapped me. My cheek stung, but I managed not to cry out. Instead, I scowled at her, determined not to show any weakness.

"Pay attention," she said. "I repeat, I want to ask you something. My question is: Have you ever lost someone you truly loved?"

Her words were so unexpected, I didn't know how to react.

"Give me an answer," she demanded.

The answer that sprang to mind was a resounding *yes*. My mum. My dad. I'd lost both of them, in different ways. Unwilling to play Verena's games, I kept my mouth shut.

She said, "Okay, you're not feeling talkative. That's understandable. I do have a reason for asking. You see, it's intrigued me, working with young people as I do. Most Acorn students have encountered loss in their young lives. Adam and Jess, in particular, whose parents died in an air crash. You'd think it would be too much to bear, wouldn't you? And yet, in my experience, it isn't the youngest who suffer the most. I've seen children pick themselves up after the most appalling disaster and get on with their lives. Children are resilient, geared up for the continuation of the species, not for dwelling on the past. It's when you're older that loss cuts the keenest. I can tell you this for a fact."

There was something odd about the way she was looking at me, her eyes filled with an emotion I'd never seen before. Sorrow, perhaps, or hurt. Or maybe blame, as though things were all my fault. But how could that be? What could I possibly have done?

A muffled gurgling came from Adam's throat.

Verena rounded on him. "Stop making that disgusting noise, Adam, or I shall have to give you another sedative. And I want you to hear this. You realise you've teamed up with a murderess?"

Verena turned back, her gaze more intense than ever. Then she laughed, a jarring, unnatural sound.

"Is the penny beginning to drop? Do you even remember his name?"

All at once, I understood what she was talking about.

"Bryan Lake," I said.

She nodded slowly. "So, you do remember."

As if I could ever forget. I could see his face, too, his horrified, bulging eyes, the twisted red mouth as his car was about to crash. Dr Lake, on his way to attend an emergency. Dr Lake, the man I'd killed.

She uncrossed her arms and gazed down at her knees, smoothed the flaps of the white coat.

"Yes, I remember his name," I told her.

Verena pushed back her chair, making it squeak. She strolled to a table in the corner. On it stood a small aquarium containing a pink liquid. As I watched, I detected a tiny movement in the liquid, a rippling. I craned for a better look, but Verena's body obscured my view. Whatever was there, I knew it would be something gruesome—something meant for Adam and me.

Verena turned back. "The man killed in that accident was our father. Saul's and mine. The brightest star in our firmament. Funny, smart, incredibly intelligent. He would be enjoying early retirement by now—if your careless behaviour hadn't caused his premature death."

"It can't be." I blinked and shook my head.

"He had slipped into a coma by the time we reached the hospital. I sat with him while the life support machines were switched off. His hand went limp in mine as his life drained away."

"No! He was Bryan Lake. From the Midlands."

A smile twitched her lips. "One of his clever little aliases. He was always playing tricks like that. His name was Ryan Blake. You see, our organization has many tendrils. Medical practices and the like provide excellent camouflage for activities undertaken at Globe."

The room spun and rippled as I tried to process what she'd told me. Bryan Lake … the man I'd cried over, so many times. He'd been one of them? He couldn't be.

Tears slid down my cheek. Instinctively, I went to brush them away, but my hands were held fast by the ropes. Verena peered at me, her eyes cold and hateful.

"It was an accident," I cried. "You want me to feel sorry? I'll shout it as loud as you like … Because I really am. I'm *sorry!*"

Verena looked away. She was silent for so long, I wondered if she could be having doubts. Whether there might be a softer side to her, something I could play on, to make her change her mind. But as she turned back, the set of her mouth remained cruel and determined.

"Your sorrow is pointless," she said.

Didn't I know it. "You're right. But for months, he was the first thing I thought about when I woke up. My life was a mess. You think I got up and carried on? You think it didn't matter to me, because he was a stranger? That I could shrug it off, because I'm young? It's not true." I wrenched my hands until the ropes burned, but the knots remained as tight as ever.

Verena returned to the aquarium and sprinkled in the contents of a small vial. She picked up a whisk-like object and stirred the liquid, as though mixing a batter. A cloud of steam hissed from the tank.

I twisted and wriggled, every movement painful. My feet felt numb, hemmed in place by the covers. Across from me, Adam was also thrashing, fighting the sedative, but I didn't rate his chances any higher than mine.

All I could do was keep her talking, keep her mind away from whatever was inside that aquarium.

"So this is all about getting back at me? You contacted my father, persuaded him to send me to Acorn?"

She nodded, without looking round. "Don't flatter yourself. He didn't need much persuading. He was glad enough to get shot of you. And I had a little something up my sleeve, just in case." She smiled at me over her shoulder. "We have another handy product, you see, not a parasite, but a drug similar to alcohol, which induces a sense of well-being and trust. A little dose in a glass of wine—or water … To make a person more pliable."

I gritted my teeth, remembering the afternoon she'd visited us in Kings Hollow. Dad's weird attitude towards Verena, his vague behaviour afterwards.

"You drugged my dad?"

Verena chuckled. "Handy little product, Fidenex. Useful for life's irritations. Snooping police officers. Visits from fussing mothers. Not that I really need it. I'm quite capable of charming people all by myself."

I remembered being locked in my room at Acorn, seeing Mum outside, unable to make her hear. Smashing the window—but too late.

"You're hateful," I said. "You think you have the right …" My words tailed off as I remembered something else from that day. The shard of glass from my window frame.

I'd wrapped it in layers of paper and put it in my hoodie pocket. My right pocket, if I remembered correctly. I'd fallen in the sea since then, of course, and more besides. All the same, might it still be there?

Verena selected a book from a shelf and began to make notes, stopping occasionally to take the temperature of the liquid in the aquarium or sprinkle in another vial. As slyly as I could, I slid my hips as far as they'd go to the right, pushing my body towards my wrist. My movements concealed by the counterpane, I caught hold of my hoodie and squirmed my fingertips inside the pocket.

The pocket was deep, and at first I couldn't find

anything. I struggled further and something sharp pricked my finger. The shard of glass was there.

Verena glanced towards me. I stopped moving and shut my eyes, praying I hadn't given myself away. After a moment, I opened them to find she'd returned to her task.

My wrist chafing against the rope, I struggled to get a grip on the shard. I managed to trap it between thumb and finger, then wriggled it out of the pocket and bent it back towards the rope.

The next time Verena looked round, I moaned and struggled in an exaggerated way, using the counterpane to camouflage what I was doing. When she went back to her notebook, I gripped the shard firmly, forcing my wrist as far as it would go towards the rope, then even further, until it felt ready to snap.

I managed to saw a little at the rope, bracing it against the metal of the frame.

Verena looked at her watch and sighed. "Where is that brother of mine? He'd be late for his own funeral." She crossed to a grille near the door, pressed a button and spoke. "Saul, hurry up, would you? We're all ready in here."

Saul's gravelly voice came out of the grille. "Okay, be right there. One minute."

As soon as Verena's back was turned, I sawed again. My wrist ached, and I stabbed my palm several times. Who was I kidding? I'd never get free in time.

Back at the table, Verena selected another instrument from a rack, something like a large pair of tweezers with looped handles.

My voice came out high and thin. "These parasites. They were in the cocoa, right? That's why they didn't affect me, because I didn't drink it."

She pursed her lips. "You thought you were so clever, didn't you? I admit, for a while, you had me foxed. Of all the students we've had at Acorn, there wasn't one who didn't fall instantly in love with our special cocoa. I soon realised you weren't drinking it, of course. It would have been a simple matter to ensure you were infected with *Linneola* another way."

That had crossed my mind, too. "So why didn't you?"

Verena gazed off into the distance, almost as though she wasn't sure herself. I seized the moment to saw some more at the rope.

"It's all about the game," she said. "By the time I realised how you were evading us, I'd got to know you better, and you were every bit as annoying and self-centred as I thought you'd be. I decided it would be amusing to let you think you had the upper hand, until I was ready to crush you. I wanted to make you suffer, the way you did me."

"Okay. You want to punish me. I get that. But why don't you let Adam go? He's done nothing wrong."

Adam made a gurgling sound, as though telling me to shut up. There was no way she'd listen, anyway. He already knew too much. All the same, I had to try.

Verena watched him struggle, as though he were a lab rat. "An interesting case, your boyfriend. You see, as a child, he nearly died of bacterial meningitis."

Adam stopped wriggling and scowled. This was news to me, although I vaguely recalled Jess telling me Adam had been ill when he was little.

"So?"

"So, indeed. After such an infection, the body is often left weaker. But in terms of our parasites, we've noticed the opposite—that childhood diseases give increased resistance. Making Adam an ideal test subject. If we can overcome his resistance, we can overcome anyone's."

While her gaze rested on Adam, I sliced again. This time the rope gave a little—not much, but something, at least. My hand was wet and sticky from cuts, pain shooting up my arm. If any red blobs appeared, I prayed they'd blend in with the rose pattern of the counterpane.

The door clicked open and Saul strolled in. Humming, he sauntered to the bed opposite me and sprawled across it. He folded one foot over the other and swivelled his gaze between the three of us.

"Everything all right?"

"Nice of you to join us." Verena glanced pointedly towards a clock on the wall. "Do you want to do the honours, or shall I?"

Saul raised his hands, palms outwards. "No, no, feel free."

"What are you planning?" I asked, a tremble in my voice.

Verena smirked. "Today, we are proud to unveil

Dagares macchia. A fantastic new product, our best yet. Immensely powerful, much stronger than *Linneola*. Faster-acting, affording us almost immediate and complete control. Best of all, it's been engineered to enjoy a lifespan of many years. In practice, we expect it will die only on the death of its human host."

She looked towards the aquarium. My stomach knotted as I noticed two shapes in the liquid, sucking at the glass. They were wormlike, the size and shape of a small finger.

"Those things?" I cried. "You're putting them inside *us?* You can't!"

Verena pulled on a pair of latex gloves and grabbed her tweezers. Turning sideways, allowing me to enjoy the view, she poked the tweezers inside the liquid and tugged at one of the creatures. With a small plop, it came loose from the glass. She held it up so I could see.

The small shape curved on the end of the tweezers, bending into a *C*, then into an *S*. It was pale grey, with a fat round head and a sharply tapering body.

Saul got to his feet and stood at the end of my bed. "That's the initial host," he explained. "A type of worm we've developed at Globe."

Verena advanced across the room, her arm outstretched. The creature's mouth was opening and closing, as though it struggled to breathe.

"Our tiny parasites have grown fat on the worm's juices," said Saul, "and they have trained it to lock onto human flesh. Once it bites, the parasite is transferred to the human host. Makes its way immediately to the brain, from anywhere in the body. Neat, huh?"

Verena said, "There's still work to do. We hope to be able to offer *Dagares* in a simple, powdered form, like our other products. However, if all runs smoothly today, that will come in due course. As an added bonus, we have *two* candidates to test it on."

"Two for the price of one!" chortled Saul.

Verena looked from Adam to me, then back to Adam. "In moments, *Dagares* will be safely lodged in your brains. After a one-off, irreversible dose, you will be pleasant, biddable and obedient, as all good students should be. A credit to our school. After that, as they say, the world is our oyster." She waved the creature in a slow arc through the air. "Right then, who's first?"

CHAPTER 29

VERENA'S eyes bored into mine. Dizzy with fear, I couldn't move. Seeing no chance of escape, part of me wanted to stop fighting. Shut my eyes and block her out, along with the creature wriggling in the tweezers.

She licked her lips, cheeks flushed, and shifted her gaze from me to Adam.

"Adam first. I want Holly to see how it feels, to be unable to help someone she loves."

She stepped towards Adam, the pale-bodied worm leading the way. Adam writhed and twisted, gurgling through the gag. His eyes were round and petrified, his hair slick with sweat. I searched my mind for something I could do, anything I could say to postpone the inevitable.

"You won't punish me that way," I said. "I don't care about Adam at all. I don't even like him." I knew it was feeble, but I couldn't think of anything else.

She didn't even slow her steps. "You can't fool me. I've seen the way you look at him."

"That's rubbish! I've got a boyfriend back home. His name's, um, Joe. I only used Adam."

"You did?" Verena's eyebrows arched. "What for,

pray tell?"

"I wanted to … I thought …"

She waited, then shook her head and smiled.

"You're a useless liar, Holly. However, if you insist, we'll do it the other way around. It makes no difference to me. Now I think about it, I'd prefer you to be the first. In case anything goes wrong."

She switched direction and headed for me. I pressed against the ropes, trying to drag myself away from the abomination she held in her hand.

From the end of my bed, Saul watched intently. Unlike Verena, he looked uncomfortable, his face pale, sweat standing out on his upper lip. For a mad moment, I wanted to cry, to beg him to talk her out of it, but I knew there was no point. Even if he weakened, Verena certainly wouldn't.

In three steps, she stood beside me. The worm wriggled, twisting this way and that.

"We'll fight you!" I yelled. "We'll tell the police."

Verena smiled. "Our creations thrive in an environment of calm. They dampen negative feelings like rebellion, doubt and anger. It's a shame you're too stupid to appreciate this triumph, in a world where people die every day in senseless wars."

"Don't pretend this is all for our benefit. The people in charge—the people with the money to buy your horrible things—they're the ones who'll be using the rest of us, to do what *they* want."

"Our world will be a much better place, I promise you. Our citizens will live in peace. *Glo*ry in

*Obe*dience, you see? Get it? G-L-O-B-E? We're proud of that."

There was a tap at the door. Verena glanced at Saul and sighed.

Saul cleared his throat and called towards the door. "What is it? Can't it wait? We're busy."

When no answer came, he strode to the door and stepped into the corridor. Heart pounding, I listened while he spoke to someone in hushed tones. I couldn't make out any words, but thought I recognised Abedi's voice.

Forcing my hand to move, I sawed some more at the rope, but I was still stuck fast.

Saul stepped back into the room. "The white-footed ants are escaping. Some idiot didn't shut the door properly. I've gotta go."

"What, now?" asked Verena with a scowl. "These *Dagares* won't survive for long, you know that."

"You carry on. I've got to sort this out. If the ants get inside the other enclosures, they'll cause no end of trouble."

"But you don't want to miss this, surely?"

He stuck out his chin. "It's a necessary part of the research, as far as I'm concerned, but I don't revel in it the way you do."

As he scuttled away, Verena muttered under her breath. "Always trying to grab the moral high ground, my little brother is. He's just squeamish." She beamed at me. "Ready then, Holly?"

She advanced towards my left side, the opposite side

from where I was sawing at the rope. The worm filled my vision and my mind, as though it was the only thing that existed in the world.

"Get away from me!" I cried.

My sleeve had already been pulled up. Verena held my shoulder with one hand while she positioned the worm over the crook of my bare arm. Her voice was soft and cooing. "There's nothing to fear. It'll be like slipping into a warm pool. All you'll feel is a welcome sense of calm, a willingness to please. Now, won't that be nice? No more worries. No more pointless fighting."

She moved the worm slowly towards me. It raised its head, as though searching for the best place to latch onto me. Beneath the cover on the other side, I gave the rope another frantic slice. The piece of glass, already slippery, slid from my grasp to the floor.

Verena said, "In approximately three minutes, you'll do anything I ask. Push someone off a cliff. Plunge a knife into Adam's heart. You'll do it willingly, and if I ask you to forget what you've done, you'll do that too. You will be devoted to me, like all Acorn students."

I tried to turn away, but the worm mesmerised me, and I could only stare. I half-hoped the thing might kill me. Death would surely be preferable to what she planned. Better than staying alive, yet not as the person I knew myself to be.

The worm stopped wriggling. As it neared my flesh, its mouth opened in a wide circle, revealing a ring of tiny yellow teeth.

My body went rigid. The creature was poised to attack, its mouth gaping, sensing prey. Verena closed the gap. It grazed my skin. I gave my other wrist a last, desperate wrench.

The rope snapped.

As Verena paused, startled, I grabbed hold of the bedspread, pulled it up and flung it over her head. I drew back my arm, clenched my fist and gave her an almighty shove. Verena tottered and fell, landing on the floor next to Adam's bed.

In seconds, she began to rise, pushing aside the bedspread. I looked all round for the shard of glass. Streaked with blood, it lay on the floor nearby. I stretched out my free arm, but no way could I reach it. I gazed at the crook of my other arm, expecting to find the worm embedded in my skin. The creature wasn't there.

Verena grabbed the side bar of Adam's bed and hauled herself to her knees. As she stumbled to her feet, Adam dragged his legs free of his ropes and kicked out. Verena fell backwards, landing with a thud.

I expected her to get up or call for help. Instead she gave a blood-curdling wail. Her eyes darted and blinked, then rolled upwards in her head. She began to shudder and writhe, waving her arms. The breath rattled in her throat as she tried to mouth something. Her neck snapped to and fro. Then, with a groan, she flopped onto her side and lay motionless.

Outside, footsteps echoed in the corridor. Adam stared from Verena to me, his eyes wide above the gag.

"Saul's coming!" I fumbled with my damaged hand at the knots still binding the other.

Moving furiously, Adam tugged at the ropes binding his wrists. One of his arms twisted free. He yanked the gag from his mouth, leaving it dangling like a collar about his neck.

The footsteps clattered to a halt. The door burst open. But it wasn't Saul Blake who stood there.

It was George Kellow, the Viking.

Kellow stared round, taking in the scene. Then he darted to the table and grabbed a tool from the rack. A slim, deadly-looking knife. His hair flew wildly about his weather-beaten face as he sprinted towards me. I cowered, reaching feebly for my pillow, the only protection I could think of.

I shut my eyes, almost too exhausted to care. Then, sensing movement near my trapped wrist, I opened them. Instead of trying to stab me, the Viking was sawing at the rope.

In seconds, my arm was free. With his help, I wriggled loose of the rope securing my legs. Stunned into silence, I watched as he rushed over to Adam and cut through the last of his knots, too.

The sound of more footsteps reached us from the corridor. Kellow tossed the knife aside and it skittered out of sight beneath the nearest bed. As he straightened up, Saul swept into the room.

Saul gasped as his gaze fell on the twitching body of his sister.

"Verena!" He raced over and knelt beside her.

Her skin was mottled, her eyes bulging and glassy, the whites stained pink. Clamped to her neck, below one ear, I spotted the worm containing the *Dagares* parasite, its body now thin and still.

"You look after Verena," Kellow told Saul. "I'll lock these two in the cells." Grabbing Adam roughly by the shoulders, he jerked him to his feet.

Saul hardly seemed to hear. Kellow beckoned to me, his gaze sliding towards the exit. I shuffled to his side. He pushed us outside the room and shut the door, then charged ahead of us along the curving corridor. Adam and I hurried after him.

"But you're—you're—" Breathless, I stopped for a second and leaned against the wall. My world had flipped upside-down. I'd never trusted the Viking. Could he really be on our side?

Kellow frowned over his shoulder. "Hurry up! Follow me."

A heart-rending cry reached us from the room we'd just left. Verena. Adam and I staggered after Kellow. My legs numb, I struggled to catch him up.

"The ants Saul mentioned," I said. "Was it you who let them out?"

He nodded. "It was all I could think of. Had to cause a distraction somehow. There are plenty of guards, though. Armed. They'll be after us as soon as Saul raises the alarm."

"But how come—"

"Talk later," Adam cut in. "We've got to find Jess."

With a nod, George veered to the left and swept

through an arched doorway. "This way."

Running and stumbling, Adam and I chased him through the complex. I had no idea if we were in a part of the building we already knew, or somewhere else altogether. The corridors all looked alike, curving and white, with occasional doors.

"We won't have long," said George. "Saul will wonder how you got free. And there are cameras everywhere."

He stopped in front of a vaguely familiar door. Through the small window, Jess was sitting on the bed, gazing into space, her hands folded neatly in her lap.

George pulled a key from his pocket and inserted it in the lock. "She's got to come willingly. It's our best bet, if we're challenged."

The three of us slipped inside the room. Jess looked up, her eyes large and watery, lip quivering. "Where's Saul?"

Adam took her hands in his. "Jess, listen carefully. You need to come with us."

She shook her head. "N-no. Must stay."

"Come with us, Jessie," Adam urged. "It's an order. Saul said so."

George placed a hand on her shoulder. "Adam's right. Saul said you're to come."

Jess ran her tongue over dry, cracked lips. "Where is he?"

"He's busy right now," said George. "But he said you're to do as we say. You know how important it is to obey. He told you that, right?"

"Yes!" Jess brightened. "Glory in Obedience."

"That's right, Jess." I crossed the room to help.

As Adam tried to raise her to her feet, she let out a piteous moan, and pushed him away. "No, no, no! Leave me alone." A tear rolled down her cheek.

Adam looked to me in despair. We had no choice. We'd have to force her.

As I reached for her hand, an unexpected sound filled the air. A quiet melody. To my surprise, Adam was singing to her—a soft lullaby, something you'd sing to a child.

The effect was startling, almost miraculous. Jess stopped crying and stared. Slowly, as though in a trance, she let Adam pull her to her feet.

George went first, glancing up and down the corridor, then darting a few steps and beckoning. Adam and I hustled Jess out of the door. She seemed hesitant, her movements sluggish.

"Looks like he's leading us further inside the complex," Adam whispered to me. "Are we sure we can trust him?"

"What choice do we have?"

Up ahead, he had stopped in front of another room, and was fumbling a key into a lock. Without waiting for us, he disappeared inside.

"What's he doing?" Adam hissed.

"Maybe it leads to another exit."

We raced after him. Reaching the doorway, I looked inside the room—and froze, unable to take in what I was seeing.

CHAPTER 30

THE room was simply furnished, as Jess's had been, a cell-like bedroom with a desk and chairs. Over by the narrow bed, George Kellow was swooping a small, fair-haired girl into his arms. She lolled against him, her face pale, eyes shut.

My mouth dropped open. "Oh my—"

Adam gasped. "I don't believe it. Is it Lydia?"

Somewhere in the building, an alarm sounded, ear-piercingly loud.

"They're on to us," muttered George.

Carrying the girl, he charged out of the room and set off again through the rabbit warren-like building. I grabbed Jess's hand and pulled her after me.

"They told us Lydia was dead," I cried, catching up with George.

The girl lay limply in his arms, her long hair trailing. She was so slight, she barely slowed him down.

As we rounded the corner, we saw five or six men in suits, not far ahead. They stood in a group, their faces solemn.

"There they are!" called one, a large, bald man. "Quick, get the guards."

George did an about-turn, and we raced back the way we'd come.

"Down here," he cried, ducking into a tunnel. "There's a fire exit."

"Who are those men?" I asked.

"Scientists, clients. Bad ones."

The tunnel was cramped and stale-smelling, so small that we had to separate into single file. Adam stood back, ushering us ahead. Still holding Jess's hand, I pulled her in after me, trying to flash her a smile. She looked bewildered, but Adam's music must have triggered something deep inside her, and she came willingly enough.

I fought back claustrophobia as Jess and Adam blocked off the space behind me. The Viking and the girl filled the way ahead. After a few more paces, George stopped at a low, barred door. He placed the girl on her feet while he scraped back a bolt. Dressed in a long white nightshirt, she leaned against the tunnel wall. For a split-second, her eyes met mine. They were large and haunted, and I glimpsed the girl she must have been, a shy girl sitting at a table, writing poetry, or gazing out to sea.

The door wouldn't budge. Cursing, George gave it a kick, then another. It yielded with a crack. Lifting the girl once more in his arms, he barged through and rushed ahead into dim daylight.

Fresh, pure air filled my lungs as I emerged onto a grassy slope. Jess came next, still clinging to my hand. Then Adam, who turned and slammed the door behind him.

It was hard to be sure in the fading light, but we appeared to be on the hillside, not far from where we'd arrived. A hundred metres or so to the left, I could make out the eye-like crescent by which we'd entered the building, what seemed like a lifetime ago.

George set the girl once more on her feet. "Can you walk, Lyddie? Remember the game I told you about?"

The girl nodded. In the distance, someone shouted.

Abedi and Kris emerged from a clump of gorse bushes to our right. They were heading directly for us, both reaching for their guns. Behind us, another guard pushed open the door we'd just come through.

"Run!" yelled George.

There was no need to tell us. We started down the bank, George dragging Lydia by the hand. Stumbling at first, she started to pick up speed. Jess moved faster too, as though the fresh air had begun to free her mind from Saul's brainwashing influence.

A gunshot ripped past my ear, smashing bark from a tree in front of me.

"Duck into the woods," George cried, gulping for air. "Go through the thickest part, throw 'em off the trail. If we get split up, head for the speedboat." He pointed to the bottom of the hill. "Moored down there."

Adam nodded. "Seen it."

Jess hesitated, looking back towards the approaching guards. Adam and I dragged her behind a stand of pines, out of view. George and Lydia disappeared ahead, following a track between two fallen trees.

Plunging through the undergrowth, I gasped as brambles tore at my clothes and slapped my face. My injured hand throbbed. With darkness falling fast, it was almost impossible to find any path.

Emerging from the trees, we found ourselves on a high, narrow ledge, overlooking the jetty. Jess skidded to a halt and stared down at the shadowed rocks below.

"Come on, Jess!" Adam cried.

"No! I'll fall."

"We've got you," I told her.

Gripping her tightly between us, we stumbled down over the rocks. We slipped on seaweed and picked our way across carpets of spiky shellfish. As we reached the jetty, Jess tripped and cried out, falling onto hands and knees.

Shouts rang out not far behind, but I couldn't see anyone in the gloom.

Adam and I helped Jess up. She hobbled a few steps more. "I—I can't go on."

"Yes, you can," said Adam. "You've got to. We're nearly there."

The speedboat bobbed on the water, pale in the vanishing light. It was moored close to the jetty, facing inland. George and Lydia were already on board. As we neared the boat, George leaned across and thrust out his hand to Jess.

"Get the mooring rope," he yelled past her to Adam.

Jess and I climbed on board, while Adam flipped

the rope up and over the post. He leapt across after me, reeling the rope in beside him.

George knelt near the control panel and ran his hands over the ledges. Lydia stood quietly beside him, leaning against the side of the boat.

"Where the hell's the key?" George muttered.

Scanning the shoreline, I watched in horror as Abedi's silhouette appeared from behind a rock, followed by Kris's.

George's hands moved desperately over the controls. "It was here before," he moaned.

"There—on the boat!" cried Kris to Abedi. "Shoot them!"

"Shoot?" asked Abedi. "Mr Blake said to bring them back alive, if we could. He said to shoot them as a last resort."

"What d'you think this is? Kellow's with them. He's a traitor." Kris raised his gun and shouted. "Stay where you are. One movement, we shoot you all."

On board, George grabbed something with a triumphant cry, and rammed it into the slot.

As two more guards emerged between the bushes, Kris pointed his gun towards us through the windscreen.

"We've got to stop them," he told Abedi.

Abedi hesitated, then raised his gun with a trembling arm. Both weapons were now trained on us.

I stood mesmerised.

"Duck!" yelled George, pushing Lydia to the floor.

I threw myself down, while Adam grabbed Jess and

followed suit. A roar filled the air as the engine sprang to life.

An almighty crack rang out. The windscreen burst and George was thrown backwards. He slammed onto the floor beside me, a bright red mark at his temple.

CHAPTER 31

GEORGE lay on the bottom of the boat, his eyes shut, blood spreading over his face. The boat idled amid crashing waves, going nowhere. Adam made a dash for the controls. Beyond him, on shore, Abedi and Kris stood as if frozen. Abedi's mouth fell open and he lowered his gun, its muzzle wavering in his hand. I crawled towards George.

"They've killed him!" I cried to Adam. "Oh God, what do we do?"

George's eyes flickered open and a rattling came from his throat.

"Th-throttle," he managed.

As Kris raised his arm and aimed again, Adam grabbed a lever and pushed. With a horrible lurch, the boat jolted and sprang almost out of the water—towards the rocks.

"Other way!" George tried to lift his hand, but it fell back to his side.

Adam yanked the throttle in the opposite direction. This time the boat shuddered into reverse and pulled away from the jetty. There was another crack of gunfire. Spray leapt nearby as a bullet seared the sea.

With one hand on the wheel, Adam rammed the lever forward and changed course again. The boat churned the water as it sped away into the ocean.

The guards stared after us, firing.

I looked down at George. There was an alarming amount of blood, the red stain growing by the second. With fumbling hands, I dragged my hoodie over my head and pressed it against the wound, something I recalled from long distant First Aid lessons.

"George, stay awake!" My voice sounded shrill and panicky. Should I try to move him, put him in the recovery position? His head was turned at an angle, and I worried I'd only make things worse.

Lydia sat hunched against the side of the boat, barely moving. Jess climbed onto a seat and sat quietly watching. Wearing only the flimsy red dress she'd worn when we'd found her, she barely seemed to notice the howling wind blasting through the shattered windscreen.

The speedboat crashed through the waves. Behind us, Turtle Island faded into the growing darkness, while lamps twinkled on the mainland ahead.

George opened his eyes a sliver and said something, but I couldn't hear him above the engine's roar. I leaned over and put my ear close to his mouth.

"North-West," he murmured, struggling to form the words. "Tre-dethy."

"What?" shouted Adam.

"North-West," I repeated, pressing as hard as I dared on George's wound, hoping to God I was helping.

"How do I?" Adam scanned the instrument panel. "Okay, I've got it. There's a compass."

George groaned. Blood covered half his face, and the other half was pale and misted with sweat. He fell silent for a moment and I leaned over to check he was still breathing. His gasps were unsteady and shallow. I grabbed his hand and squeezed. He was clammy to the touch. As Adam glanced over his shoulder, the look on his face told me he feared the worst.

I shut my eyes briefly. We had only just discovered George was our friend, someone who could help us expose *Globe Industries*. Now it looked as though we'd lost him.

The coast grew large on the horizon. His steering less erratic now, Adam slowed the boat a fraction so we could look out for the wide river and rows of cottages marking Tredethy Village.

"There!" I pointed. "Go left."

Adam swung the boat and powered full throttle towards the mainland. Shadowy rocks loomed, and Adam veered wildly as one of them scraped the boat with a sickening screech.

The jetty hurtled towards us and I felt certain we'd crash right into it. Just in time, the boat slowed, coasting the last few metres.

"Tie her to the post while I try to keep her steady," yelled Adam.

As he took the speed right down, I grabbed the rope and stood ready at the side of the boat. When the jetty was close enough, I leapt across the gap onto solid ground. I crouched and tugged the boat as close as it would come. Adam killed the engine while I wound the rope tightly round a stone post.

On shore, someone had heard us. A man with a walking stick, heading uphill, stopped and looked over his shoulder. I raised my hand and cried out, and he hobbled back towards us.

"Quick!" I shouted. "Call an ambulance. A man's been shot."

***

At the hospital, George was rushed away on a stretcher, doctors and nurses giving instructions either side of him. Adam, Jess and I were sucked into a whirlwind of interviews and examinations, firstly by medical staff, then, after our wounds had been tended, by people from the police and social services.

No one seemed to know what to make of our story, and judging from the state of us, I could hardly blame them. Adam and I were weak and rambling, our clothes filthy and torn. Jess and Lydia were even more wretched, covered in cuts, and Jess's ankle was swollen. When anyone spoke to them, they were vague and incoherent, making no sense.

Finally, with night drawing in, the nurses lent us clean clothes and squeezed us into different wards, firmly informing the police we were to be left alone until morning.

No way could I sleep, I thought, as my mind whirled with the aftershock of all that had happened. As soon as I lay down, however, unconsciousness rolled over me like a fog.

CHAPTER 32

"A couple of visitors for you," said the nurse to the figure stretched in the bed. She seemed hesitant, unsure if she should let us into the ward or not.

"Go easy on him," she instructed Adam and me. "He's got the luck of the devil, but he needs rest." She left us alone, although I had the feeling she wouldn't be going far.

The small room was bright but stuffy, sunshine blazing through a shut window. George's face beneath the bandages looked gaunt, and he appeared to have aged ten years. When he saw us at his bedside, he broke into a tired smile.

"How are you doing?" he asked. "How're Jess and Lydia?"

I was still trying to process things, coming to grips with the fact that Lydia was alive.

Adam frowned. "We don't know yet. They're still being assessed."

"Verena said Lydia was dead," I told him, shaking my head.

George shrugged. "She wanted you to think that. To hurt you even more."

We lapsed into silence.

"I thought they'd killed you," I said.

Adam plonked a carton of grapes on the bed, which he'd just bought from the hospital shop.

"Yeah," said George. "Bullet grazed me. Lots of blood, but no real damage, so they think. They thought my skull might be fractured, but … tough old scallywag, me. A hair's breadth further in, well, they'd be booking the undertaker."

"Will you have a scar?" I asked him.

He smiled. "Hope so. Reckon it'd be a big hit with the ladies, a nice scar."

"I'll feel better once they've arrested them all," said Adam. "Once they're in gaol, where they belong."

George nodded. "Right. Police have put me through the wringer. I backed up your story, of course. Gave them quite a shock, I reckon."

I pictured the bewildered looks on the faces of the police officers who'd questioned us. "Huh. They didn't believe us, did they?"

"Well, they do now," said Adam. "We were a mess, Holl. I don't think I'd have believed us, either. Must have looked like we were drunk or drugged up or something."

Adam grinned at me, his eyes shining. The clothes he'd borrowed from the hospital hung loose on him, but he'd washed his glossy dark hair, and smelled of lemony soap.

"They've got one of those sachets to test," I told George. "The ones containing the *Linneola*. I crammed a load in our pockets before we left Verena's office. Most of them got lost in the sea, but one survived."

George nodded. "Hmm … Guess it won't matter if the boxes at the Academy mysteriously vanish, then." At my puzzled look he added, "The Craddocks are still there, remember. Covering tracks, I expect."

Questions clamoured at my mind, but I had no idea where to begin. "So … you were spying on them, is that it?"

"Kinda." George frowned and licked his lips. "I could murder a pint. Have to wait till they let me out, I suppose."

"Well?" said Adam, hands on hips.

"Okay, hold on." He wriggled in the bed, pushing himself up against the pillows. "Well, in answer to your question, I took the job as handyman in hopes of finding out what they were up to. Managed to piece together a fair bit."

"Why didn't you tell us?" demanded Adam.

"How could I? I'd worked hard to make them trust me. Couldn't risk word getting out, about who I really was. The day after I brought you back from Tredethy, they sent me to work on the island. Had me sorting out problems with the generator, servicing the boat, that kind of thing."

Adam plucked a few grapes from the bunch and handed a couple to me.

"Hey, keep your thieving paws off!" George popped a grape into his mouth and chewed. "I almost had the full picture, and was trying to think of the best way to expose them and get Lydia and Jess out of there. Then you two arrived."

The nurse poked her head around the door. "That's enough, kids. You're supposed to be resting, too, remember?"

I put on my best pleading expression, one I'd seen Wilk use at home to get treats. "Just a couple more minutes. Please?"

She glanced at George and he nodded.

"Okay," she said. "Two minutes, and no more."

I took another grape from the fast-vanishing bunch. "What I don't understand is ... are you some kind of undercover policeman or something?"

George laughed, his eyes crinkling at the sides. "No, no. I really am a handyman. But I'm related to someone you know. Lydia."

"No way," said Adam.

"Way," he said. "One of her ancestors went to live in Canada, and I'm a descendant on that side. I didn't have anything to do with my Brit relatives, but when Lydia's mother died and they were trying to find someone to look after her, that Aunt Jeannie of hers tracked me down via social media. I hate all that with a passion, but a neighbour saw something, put us in touch."

Adam frowned. "Jeannie never mentioned that."

He sighed. "No, no wonder. I said I couldn't help. Always been a loner. Not cut out for all that family malarkey. Wish I'd tried, of course. When I found out Lydia had vanished ..."

Adam jabbed a finger at him. "You should have trusted us. You could have told us who you were, the night you took us back to Acorn."

"Yeah, I guess. How was I to know you were in Tredethy looking for Jeannie? Two young lovebirds roaming the village—"

Adam's cheeks went scarlet.

George continued, "I thought it best—safest—to keep a low profile."

Something slipped into place. "It was you who sent me that note, the first night at Acorn, wasn't it? *Ask about Lydia?*"

He nodded. "I wanted to warn you, without scaring you to death. I wanted to put you on your guard."

"Why me?"

"I overheard Verena talking to the Craddocks about you, before you arrived. She obviously didn't like you, but sounded thrilled you were coming. I wondered why. Couldn't warn you straight out. I didn't know enough and I could've been wrong. When I saw you, I thought you looked smart. Someone capable of giving Verena a taste of her own medicine. And that you've certainly done."

I couldn't return his smile. "That horrible *Dagares* worm was clasped to her neck," I said, thinking back to my last glimpse of Verena on the laboratory floor. "D'you think the parasite transferred? What will happen to her?"

"Don't waste your sympathy," said Adam. "Whatever she's going through, it could have been us, and she'd never have spared us a thought."

Adam was right. Verena deserved all she got. I could only hope she recovered sufficiently to be brought to justice.

As we got up to leave, the nurse bustled back into the room.

"We're coming!" said Adam.

Ignoring him, she turned to me. "Holly, there's someone to see you."

Curious, I followed the nurse along the corridor into a small waiting area. A tall man in a tweed jacket and glasses stood perusing the noticeboard.

"Dad! Oh, Dad."

When he turned, Dad's face lit up, as though he was seeing me for the first time. I sped towards him and stopped, unsure. His eyes held mine, looking watery, then he spread his arms and I stepped into them. He hugged me for the first time in ages, tighter than I ever remembered. We stood like that for a moment, neither of us speaking.

"I'm sorry," he said at last, his voice muffled by my shoulder. "I've been a rubbish dad. I should have known …"

I broke away, brushing a tear from my face. "Verena used something on you, one of her horrible products. She slipped it in your wineglass."

"What? No, before that. You know, after what happened. I couldn't cope."

I hugged him again. "We'll sort it out, Dad. We'll make things better." I looked up and saw how pale he looked, how stiffly he held himself. "Oh, Dad, what's wrong?"

He moved aside and lowered himself into a chair. "Don't get alarmed. I had a heart attack, not long after you left. I wrote to tell you … it's why it's taken me so long to get here."

"Oh no!" So that was what that letter had said. "Verena lied to me, Dad. Told me you didn't want me home. Are you all right?" I plonked myself down next to him.

He gave a faint smile. "I feel like I've been run over by a bulldozer. But I'm lucky to be alive, I know that. They put things in my heart. Stents, to keep the arteries open. I'm doing well, as long as I take it easy. The best thing is … Now don't jump to conclusions, the way you usually do."

He was staring past me. When he didn't go on, I turned and looked along the corridor. A slim figure was headed in our direction carrying an overloaded tray. I blinked a few times, unable to believe she was there— or rather, that they were here together.

I leapt up. "Mum!"

She hurried towards me as fast as she could without spilling anything.

"Your mother's come back from France to help out," explained Dad.

Setting her tray of drinks and snacks onto a table, Mum hugged me, enveloping me in the fresh smell of primroses. "Holly, this is dreadful. What you must have been through."

"It's all right, Mum, don't cry."

We sat sipping our drinks, going over what had happened. Mum handed round some snacks, but I felt too traumatised to do more than nibble at a cheese biscuit. Every so often one of the people who'd interviewed me swished past, but no one seemed able or willing to stop and update us with developments at Acorn.

"Is Wilk here, too?" I asked, longing to hold his wriggling, furry body.

"He's fine," Dad said. "He's with a neighbour."

Mum's lip quivered. "I thought something was off about that Blake woman, when I tried to visit you at the school. The way she seemed so eager to get rid of me."

"Oh, Mum, I saw you from the window, but I couldn't make you hear."

"You did? Maybe I sensed you. I knew something was wrong."

"What did she tell you? Why did you leave?"

"It was the oddest thing. I was determined to check you were okay, since Dad hadn't heard anything, but Verena told me visits had to be pre-arranged. I'd have to come back at the weekend, she said. Once I got home to Kings Hollow, I couldn't understand why I hadn't insisted." Mum's voice was riddled with guilt.

"Did she give you anything?" I asked. "A drink?"

Mum looked startled. "A cup of tea in her office, that's all."

"That explains it, then. She drugged you, like she

did Dad. Gave you something to make you trust her and go along with what she said."

Dad sipped his tea. There was something different about him, something important. As I noticed a glance pass between him and Mum, I worked out what it was. He didn't have that boiling, angry look, which made him seem always on the verge of an explosion. There was a sorrow about him, but also a stillness. It was as though, despite everything, the tension had somehow drained out of him.

He cleared his throat. "Your mother's been amazing."

I held my breath. Hearing Dad say something as warm and open as that was unheard-of. It was like he'd been body-snatched and turned into someone else. His illness must have had a strange effect on him, or maybe it was to do with what had happened to me, I couldn't tell.

I turned to Mum and blurted out, "So are you together again or what? Are you home for good?"

There was an awkward silence.

"One step at a time," Mum said. "Dad's taken early retirement, so he shouldn't be so stressed." She picked up the packet of cheese biscuits I'd opened and thrust it into my hand. "Eat up. You're as thin as a whippet."

I laughed. "Oh, Mum."

At that moment I spotted PC Findlay, one of the officers who'd first interviewed me. Mid-twenties, perhaps, with an open, freckled face, she'd gained my trust straight away. Accompanied by a colleague, she was striding along the corridor towards us.

"Any news?" asked Dad.

PC Findlay nodded. "Saul Blake's been arrested."

"What about Verena?" I asked.

"She's in a bad way, apparently. Raving and drooling one minute, then meek as a lamb the next. They're bringing her to the mainland. And we've got the Craddocks," she added. "They're telling us all we need to know about Verena Blake."

Mum patted her chest, letting out a breath. "That's such a relief. So we can leave?"

PC Findlay exchanged a glance with her colleague. "I don't see why not, so long as the hospital agrees. We'll be in touch—there'll be lots more questions, I'm afraid. But for now, you're free to go."

***

As I waited on my bed to be discharged, Adam appeared by my side. He was grinning, his eyes shining.

"I've had an update on Jess and Lydia," he told me. "Looks like both of them were heavily sedated. Now they're away from that place, they're making good progress. It'll take time, but the doctors think they'll be okay."

Happiness welled inside me. "Oh Adam, that's great news. You know, I reckon Saul and Verena didn't actually want them to get better. Once those horrible treatments went wrong, they had to keep Jess and Lydia prisoner, to prevent them telling people what was going on over there."

Adam nodded. "Exactly. Well, they're on the mend now. What's more, the Viking—George—has said we can stay at his cottage for a bit, once they're out of hospital." He eyed me. "You'll come and visit, won't you?"

"Of course I will! You try and stop me." We shared a long smile.

Mum and Dad came through the ward doors and stepped over to my bed.

"You're officially released," said Dad, waving some papers in the air.

Mum drew me into her arms. "Come on, Holly. Time to go home."

THE END

ACKNOWLEDGEMENTS

Warning: Contains Spoilers!

A huge thank you to everyone who has followed the adventures of Holly, Jess and Adam. Like most writers, I am a reader first, one who has always longed to be able to create stories for others to enjoy, and I am grateful to every reader who takes the time to read my work.

The Mystery of Acorn Academy was a lot of fun to write, and those of you unfamiliar with the biology (as I certainly was when I began this story) might be interested to know that the section on parasites is very much rooted in fact. Yes, there are such things as zombiefied caterpillars and suicidal grasshoppers! In fact all the gruesome creatures referred to by Saul and Verena exist—apart from *Linneola* and *Dagares*, of course, but in the future, who knows? Although such things fascinate me, I'm no scientist, and I apologise for any errors, in this or any other aspect of my book. They are all my own.

I am indebted to many people, all of whom have made this novel so much better than it would otherwise have been. Firstly, a huge thank you to Richard Hardie and everyone at the fabulous Authors Reach. At the risk of making him blush, Richard is a wonderful author, as well as a publisher, and he is a great support to us all. Many thanks also to Maureen Vincent-Northam and Francesca Tyer for their sharp eyes and super editing and proofreading skills. I take my hat off to Gina Dickerson of RoseWolf Design for her amazing design and formatting abilities. How she was able to produce such a lovely cover from my half-baked suggestions is beyond me!

I am most grateful to Steve H and Fiona T for their help with the Latin, and to Di T, Caleb M and Adrianne, to whom I am indebted in many different ways. Thanks as ever are also due to my good friend Rog, for his sterling work on my website, as well as his constant inspiration.

This novel has been a long time in the making, and has been helped considerably by several colleagues and friends, many of whom are fellow members of Scribophile. Thanks are due to too many to name, but I must mention some of the fantastic critiquers and beta-readers who helped with this particular story. Jessica G and Suzanne S not only gave me their own valuable feedback, but also involved their delightful and insightful children. Leslie R, Carole M, John C, Belinda M, Brenda B, Michelle B, Michelle C, Ros C, Chris D, Elizabeth F, Roger S and Maiya H gave freely of their time, skills and friendship. Thank you so much, all of you. If I have forgotten anyone, I do apologise. I owe you a drink.

Thanks are due to family and friends who continue to encourage, inspire and cheer me on. You know who you are! Thanks especially to husband Mark, for digging me out of many a plot hole, and contemplating some pretty weird 'what-ifs'. This story is the first in a planned series of mystery adventures set in Cornwall, the county where I was born and have spent most of my life. My aim is to produce the kind of tale I loved as a child, stories which grab you and take you out of the everyday into an exciting, different place. I hope you will join me there.

ABOUT THE AUTHOR

Teresa Bassett is an author living in Cornwall, UK, in a house she helped to build. A graduate of the University of Bath, she worked for several years as a languages teacher and translator, meanwhile contributing features and interviews to a variety of magazines. She spent eleven years with educational charity The Eden Project, where she learned all kinds of wonderful things about plants and people.

In 2013 the manuscript for her debut mystery adventure *The Time Crystals* reached the final five Young Adult titles in the Amazon Breakthrough Novel Award, going on to win international contest The Next Novelist. In 2020 she was awarded first prize in Crowvus's Ghost Story competition. *The Mystery of Acorn Academy* is Teresa's second published novel, one of a series of planned mystery adventures set in Cornwall.

You can find Teresa at:
Facebook
https://treeandleafblog.com

For Teresa's latest author news, including special
offers, please sign up to her newsletter here:
www.teresabassett.co.uk

If you have enjoyed this book, I would be very grateful
if you would consider leaving a rating or online review.
They are so important these days! Thank you.

ALSO BY THE AUTHOR

The Time Crystals

Winner of The Next Novelist 2013

Shortlisted Amazon Breakthrough Novel Award 2013
(final five in Young Adult)

'a thrilling time travel page-turner ... What ensues is a series of hair-raising, edge-of-your-seat events culminating in a delightful story that packs a powerful values punch relevant to both young and not-so-young adults'— Publishers Weekly

Reviews

***** What a fantastic book! A real page turner with great plot twists and a sparky heroine who is brave and loyal, despite the difficulties in her personal life

***** It's got everything a young reader could hope for

***** Oodles of excitement and jeopardy

***** A fantastic debut

***** It's an exciting, gripping book for all ages

***** Mysterious and captivating

Authors Reach Ltd. is a thriving publisher producing books for Adults as well as Young Adults. Our genres include Fantasy, Adventure, Thrillers, Paranormal, Horror, History and Romance. Take a look and let the magic begin!

www.authorsreach.co.uk

Printed in Great Britain
by Amazon